I0775841

Dark Water Sacrifice

Also by Zach Lamb

The Suicide Killer

Mourning Glory

Dark Water Sacrifice

Zach Lamb

This is a work of fiction. All names, places, and characters are products of the author's imagination or are used fictitiously. Any resemblance to real people, places, or events is entirely coincidental.

Copyright © 2021 by Zach Lamb

Cover Illustration © 2023 by Eva Mout

Graphic Design by Fabled Beast Design

Author Photo by Darlin Images

All rights reserved.

No part of this book may be reproduced in any form or by any electronic or mechanical means, including information storage and retrieval systems, without written permission from the author, except for the use of brief quotations in a book review.

Paperback ISBN 979-8-9871527-2-0

Hardcover ISBN 979-8-9871527-3-7

For Greenlee. I only wish I could better show you the depths of your father's love.

Chapter One

Something malevolent hid beneath the churning black water. The entire Blackwell family knew to be cautious of the large lake that sat on the back of their property. His son blamed him and left town the same way he left them on that bank. It was as much his son's fault as anybody else's. He shouldn't have taken his eyes off her.

The water looked alive as it splashed and gurgled toward the falls. It wasn't his fault. Everything happened fast. One second she was asking him what kind of fish she saw, and the next, he was running down the bank trying to find her in the inky black water.

He woke with these images every morning and went to be with them every night like a lover he was ashamed of being seen with. She knew not to get too close to the water.

But she loved the water.

Any chance the little girl had she'd spend in the swimming pool behind the house. She was only six, but a strong swimmer. Every day after working on the family farm, Phil Blackwell sat and watched his granddaughter jump off the diving board and swim laps around the pool. He'd rest with a well-deserved ice-cold beer in his hand and laugh as Grace Ann played. She told him stories while she swam. Each resting point for her was another chapter in her book. Grace Ann loved to tell her Grandpa stories. They were all about monsters and bad guys. Except her stories always had a happy ending. Evil never triumphed over good like it did, sometimes, in her daddy's books.

At random intervals, she'd stop and act out her stories as she told them. She'd swim up to Phil and tell him to 'freeze,' or to 'put your hands up or I'll shoot,' and like any good-Grandpa-bad-guy would do, he put his hands high above his head. A devious smile crossed her young face as she pulled the trigger of her water gun, soaking Phil. As she swam off giggling, he'd jump up from his squeaking lawn chair and act like he was about to jump in after her. She kicked harder and splashed Phil, drenching him even more. When she reached the other side of the pool, she started a new chapter of her story about her great escape from the big chair monster. Phil laughed and fell back into his chair. The worn woven straps pulled against each other and sounded like a dry rotted knot being pulled taut. Each time he plopped down he told himself one day he'd end up on his ass if he didn't replace the old chair.

He looked out over 'God's country' as he called it, known as the 4B Ranch to everybody in town, and exclaim he was the luckiest man in the whole state because he had his farm and his family with him instead of scattered across the country by the four winds, like many of his friends from town.

Scarsville, pronounced Scarsvul, by Phil and most locals, was a one-traffic light town in rural Georgia. Most of the children in Scarsville dreamed of a better life away from the small town that swallowed up their parents' lives. They couldn't wait to graduate high school and load up their cars and leave. Some found the shock of big city life and others the shock of big city jobs and bills. More than a few found their way back home after flunking out of college because they partied too much, or because city living didn't end up being the great escape they thought it'd be. But not Phil's boys. They stayed home and had no aspirations of leaving their hometown. His youngest son, Brian, was like his father. He woke before the sun came up, worked all day and came home for dinner. Sometimes he'd have a date in town with one of the girls he graduated with, but it mostly consisted of dinner at Mama's Diner, or whatever they were calling it now days, followed by a few rounds at Sharky's Pool Hall.

Phil's oldest son, Adam, stayed home, but not because he didn't want to leave town. He was a writer and said he could live anywhere. It didn't matter to him. Adam married his high school sweetheart, and it mattered to her where they lived. Mandy went to college an hour away from home, but she wouldn't stay in the dorms. She didn't want any part of the city. She made the drive back and forth until she finished her degree in Early Childhood Education. It took her five years and two cars, but she graduated and stayed at home to teach at the county school with no plans of going back to the city for more than a visit. Phil was as proud of her as if she were one of his own children.

Adam woke up well after the crack of dawn, and stumbled out into the bright sunlight with his hands shading his eyes from the sun overhead and exclaim, 'bright light, bright light.' It was a movie reference, but Phil never knew which one. He'd track Phil down and ask him if there was anything he needed to do before he started writing. Adam wasn't like Brian. Brian woke up and knew what to do, but Adam had to be told what to do.

The farm life never agreed with him. His head was always somewhere else, lost in whatever new story he was writing. He had a few tastes of success with short stories and a well-received first novel. It was the first novel he published, but the second one he'd written. He hid his first novel in an old wooden box their mother bought in the antique store in the town square. Adam told him he never wanted to publish the book, or for anybody else ever to read it. He called it his trunk novel, but Phil didn't know why he'd want to write something and hold on to it. Phil asked if it was because he didn't think it was any good. A strange expression crept across Adam's face and he said it felt too real, almost prophetic. Adam looked sad, but Phil didn't push him to explain any further. He knew his son didn't like anybody to push him to talk about something he didn't want to discuss.

After Adam worked half the day with a break to eat and do a little writing, he spent time with the family and headed upstairs to his old room to write until the early hours of the next day. These unsolidified schedules didn't bother anybody. It made Phil happy to have his family together under the same roof.

But that was all before Grace Ann died.

The guilt made him see things. The first time he saw Grace Ann after her death, she was looking through the living room window. Phil sat passed out in front of the TV where he'd been watching the news through drunken eyes, swimming in cheap whiskey. He fell asleep as the talking heads argued about the horrible state of the country and its leaders. A loud static burst from the TV woke him. The sudden change to white noise, and the volume, startled him. He jumped to his feet and tripped over the recliner footrest. The world went sideways as he fell and landed hard on his left hip. Sharp pain ran through his leg and halfway up his back. Gritting his teeth, he lay on the floor trying to decide if he broke his hip, or if he could walk it off.

Snowy static raced across the screen. He didn't know TVs still did that. It had been years since he remembered seeing it happen. Black and white hyphenated lines jumped around the screen. It was like staring at one of those 3D pictures that were popular when the boys were young. He always had trouble seeing the image in the frame. No matter how long he stared, he ended up with strained and crossed eyes.

Then he saw her. Not in the snow on the TV, but through the window when he looked past the lines on the screen. The porch light reflected golden highlights off her brown hair. She giggled and moved one of her hands to her mouth. The laughter sounded like Grace, but it was farther away than where she stood. It had a hollow, echoey quality to it, like she was standing at the bottom of a well. Phil smiled at the little girl. She always laughed when Phil hurt himself, mainly because he used potty-words, and her mother told her ladies did not use that type of language.

He lifted an arm out to her, hoping she'd come in and help him up off the floor. Grace put both of her hands back on the windowsill. A blue flash ripped through her green eyes. Phil noticed the spark, but continued to smile. It was awfully good to see her again, even if it was a trick of his sloshed brain. Her eyes were two blue burning orbs. They reminded him of the stars he and Grace Ann saw through her telescope on clear nights.

A chill ran through his aching body, and his mind cleared. She can't be here. The hair on his arms stood on end. What he saw terrified him, but he needed to get outside and talk to her. She'd come home from wherever she'd been. If he got her to stay, maybe her parents would come back home too. He put both hands flat on the floor and pushed himself up. It'd been a while since he'd done any pushups, but he managed to get himself to the coffee table and fight the rest of the way up. His hip ached, and new pain sensations flowed down his leg. The hip didn't break, but he'd hurt like hell in the morning. Head spinning, he stumbled around the living room. Grace continued her sweetly haunted cave giggle.

Phil tripped his way to the door but stopped short of opening it to steady himself. It didn't work. There was no way to tell if it was still the whiskey or excitement that caused his hands to tremble as he grasped the knob and pulled the door open. Grace turned from the window and stared at him as he stepped outside.

Her hair no longer shined like before. It was dull and matted. It didn't reflect the porch light anymore. Now it seemed to absorb all the surrounding light, making everything around her faded and washed out. She wore the navy-blue dress she had on the last time he saw her. She loved that dress. Every time she wore it, she'd ask Phil to sit and watch as she twirled, making the pleated ends spin like a pinwheel. The water-drenched dress was darker, and pale blue light escaped through rips in the pleats. A large puddle of water had formed at her feet and spread out across the wooden porch. The edges of the puddle reached out like jagged fingers toward Phil's feet and caused him to take a step back. This couldn't be real. Grace Ann had been dead for two years. He must have hit his head when he fell. The best thing for him to do would be to go inside and lay down. But you shouldn't to go to sleep if you had a concussion, right?

He took a step toward the door, and she pointed her small finger at Phil. The shredded ends of her fingernail split down the middle and ran to the blackened cuticle.

"It's your fault."

"I-I'm sorry, Gracie. I only wanted you to enjoy yourself."

The light in the house extinguished, enveloping the living room in darkness. The change caught Phil off guard and when he turned to look, the little girl ran down the stairs into the damp grass. Missing her left shoe didn't seem to bother or slow her down. Phil ran into the front yard after her. She slipped through the barbed wire fence and continued into the pasture. Phil tried to shake the fuzz from his head. Did she run through the barbed wire? He hadn't seen her duck under the sharp barbs. He ran to the pasture, but it was a slow and meandering course. His head swam with the liquor he drank earlier.

He made it to the gate and yelled, "Grace Ann, come back ... please," and doubled over.

The gate held him as he caught his breath until he could stand up straight. The horizon glowed blue. All his years living here, he had never seen the sky glow like that. It was too late to be sunset. His eyes traced the winding trail of the radiant blue. It wasn't coming from the sky. It was coming from the lake. He opened the gate and walked toward the glowing water. That's where she was headed. Back to her new home.

<hr>

Phil woke up in his bed. The alarm clock on the nightstand read 2:02. The sun was out, so it had to be in the afternoon. He couldn't remember the last time he had slept this late. If he ever had. He also couldn't remember ever going to sleep. That wasn't as big of a surprise. There were many nights Phil didn't remember going to bed, but even on those nights, he still woke with the sun. What he did remember was Grace Ann standing at his window and blaming him for what happened to her. He should probably call somebody, but what would he say? They wouldn't believe him anyway, especially not Adam. He'd try to have him committed, but he wouldn't care enough to do that. He wouldn't even answer the phone.

Still sleepy, Phil walked down the stairs and outside. Clouds covered the sun, but did nothing for the heat. He sat down in his rocking chair, waiting for Grace Ann to return as much as trying to figure out what had happened to him the night before.

It didn't feel like it, but he must have sat in the same spot for hours because Brian returned from the fields after working all day. The sun was setting behind the lake. Brian looked pissed. Phil didn't blame him. He had left Brian to do all the work while he slept until after lunch and sat in this chair for the rest of the day. Brian walked up the steps with heavy feet.

"Hey, son. I wanted to say—"

"Save it. I don't want to hear what you have to say. I found you passed out in the middle of the pasture. I had to carry your drunk ass back to the house and get you in bed."

"I'm sorry you had to do that. You shouldn't have to see me like this, and I shouldn't've left you with all the work to do yourself."

"Hell, Daddy, I'm not mad about that. I'm used to doing most of this myself," Brian said, pointing a finger toward the barn. "What I'm pissed about is you left the damn gate open when you decided to go for a walk last night."

Phil hung his head to his chest.

"I spent the whole morning tracking down the cows that got out."

Phil looked up at his son. Brian loomed over him like a domineering father disciplining his unruly child. Maybe that's how Phil was acting.

"Did they all get out?"

Brian turned and spit a wad of chew off the side of the porch. Black juice ran down his face, but it didn't seem to bother him.

"No, but the ones that did made it three miles down the highway to the Martin's house. Mr. Martin called this morning and said they were at his house and had made Mrs. Martin's begonias their breakfast."

Phil smirked a little.

"It's not funny. Now, I have to go back over there and replace them all while that old woman stands over me yelling how I'm doing it wrong."

"I'm sorry. I don't know what happened."

"Looks like you fell off the Waterwheel again. I'm going to town," Brian said and went inside.

Phil stayed on the porch long after Brian left. Sometime after two in the morning, Phil decided he hadn't seen Grace Ann. It had all been a drunken hallucination, and there was no need to tell anybody about it and look like a fool. He continued to rationalize everything until he saw her again.

———

Two weeks later, Grace Ann was playing in the pile of shavings behind the barn. The wind blew the tarp, protecting the thin slices of pine from the elements. It waved in the wind like a large blue sail. Grace Ann stood at the top of the pile in her dirty blue dress. Her hair and dress were not blowing in the wind like the tarp. The dark brown strands of hair lay flat against her head and rested on her shoulders and didn't reflect the sunlight. The strength of the wind it would take to lift the tarp and keep it in the air should have sent her rolling down the other side of the pile.

She looked down the opposing hill of pine chips. Phil's breath caught in his throat as he waited for her to sit and slide down to the bottom of the hill the way she used to. She probably couldn't get hurt, but the thought bothered him all the same. Before her death, he'd be in the barn shoveling horse manure from the stalls, and she'd yell from the top of her castle, "watch me, Grandpa," and slide down the hill narrowly escaping the terrible dragon and nearly giving Phil a heart attack in the process. He'd yell for her to be careful because he was no longer the young prince who could swoop in and save her. The little girl would giggle and call him "the old king," and climb back to the top and do it all over.

Grace Ann turned her head to face Phil. Her movements were fluid. She didn't have to look around to find him. She knew he was staring out from his second-story window, watching her the whole time. He jumped back from the breath-fogged glass and hid behind the curtains. He gathered his courage and peered around the heavy navy-blue fabric. Grace Ann continued looking at him. She raised her hand and pointed at him. Her mouth moved, but he couldn't tell what she was saying. He strained his eyes and tried to read her hypothermic lips.

Phil put his hands on the frosted glass to wipe it clean. The sharp cold on the palm of his hand didn't bother him until he saw the trail of blood on the pane. He froze at the sight of Grace Ann through the thin yellow tint of his smeared blood. He tried to remove his hand, but it stayed frozen to the glass. His heart sped and felt like it was about to explode out of his ears. The skin stretched and pulled his hand back to the window. He searched his room for anything to separate him from the glass. There was nothing within reach of his free hand. He stretched across his body and slipped his left hand into his right pocket. Fumbling around, he lifted his thigh for better access until he found the skeleton handle.

The blade flipped open with a metallic click.

The tip of the knife screeched across the pane between his hand and the glass. He pulled back and screamed, not from the pain, but from the thought of leaving a filet of his hand on the window. The echo subsided as he looked at the ceiling. He gritted his teeth to prepare for surgery. The blade slid toward his hand, but he lost his nerve at the last second and hit the glass with the butt of the handle.

The glass shattered and a blast of humid Georgia air burst through the missing pane. It pushed him back as he fought his way back to the sill. He pushed his face close to the window, being careful not to touch the other frosted panes.

Her soft voice floated on the acrid breeze. "It's all your fault. We will be together soon, and it will all be over."

Phil fell back from the window and his right hand sliced across his arm, drawing blood from the attached glass. He jumped up, ran to the restroom, and turned on the hot water. A sharp, piercing pain shot up his arm as he held his hand under the faucet. It was like extreme cold on an exposed nerve. He twitched and writhed, trying to keep his hand under the water. The glass fell away, and he became lightheaded. The room grew dim, but he pushed forward before he passed out. He went to the window, but it was no longer frosted, and Grace Ann was gone.

That night, he didn't sleep. He sat on the edge of his bed, staring out the part of his window not covered by the lined alfalfa bag. He lifted the bottle of Waterwheel bourbon, stilled down the road in Maplebrook, to his lips. It went down smooth like the label advertised. He'd have to let them know the next time he went to the distillery. The bottle slid from his hand to the floor.

"She's gone," he whispered to no one. "And it's all my fault. No. No. It's not. I wasn't the only one there. I wasn't the only one who was supposed to be watching her. He can't blame me. Who? Whose fault is it?" he screamed at the wall.

The bottle rolled to the middle of the room and stopped. It caught Phil's attention, and he went to kick it. But it moved before he touched it. Barely rocking at first, then it spun slowly and picked up speed. It reminded him of the time he walked into his living room where his sons were having a party. All the teenagers scattered and left the coke bottle spinning in the center of the room. When it stopped, he picked it up and opened it carefully so it wouldn't spew and took a long pull. He exclaimed his satisfaction with a long, embellished ahhh, and walked out the door, leaving the stunned teenagers gaping at him.

Now he shuffled his feet toward the empty bottle, and it lifted off the ground. Phil jumped back, but the bottle didn't pursue. Blue light twinkled in the absence of liquor. It had to be Grace Ann, but she wasn't in the room. He stroked his two-day stubble like a wayward beard. The light grew brighter until the entire room filled with cobalt blue light. Phil shielded his eyes, and the light dimmed. The bottle stopped spinning, leaving the long neck pointed at him. It pulsed with a frosty blue glow.

"What? What the hell is going on?" he said and took a step to his left.

This time the bottle followed his movements.

"No, it wasn't just me."

The bottle glowed brighter.

"I couldn't help it. She was too fast. I wasn't the only one there."

Heated anger flowed through Phil and paced the floor. The glowing bottle continued to point at him.

"What about your father, huh? Did you ever think about him? Why don't you go and wave your bottle at him? He's the one who ran away. I stayed."

Suspended in air, the bottle swayed back and forth. The long neck bobbed from side to side like it disagreed with his argument. Phil put his hands up and backed away. The bottle revolved around the room and made a large circle around Phil. It swooped in close and reversed course. Phil turned, trying to follow its movements, but could not register where it was through the blue haze of light. The bourbon he drank while emptying the bottle didn't help either. He stopped turning and tried to focus. The bottle stopped its trajectory and flew toward Phil. The bottle crashed into his head. There was a loud thump like somebody testing cantaloupes, and everything went black.

<hr>

When Phil came to, he kept his eyes shut tight. His head throbbed, and he felt like he was being jostled around in the back of a truck speeding down a dirt road. Slowly, he opened his eyes and realized he was walking toward the pasture. He tried to stop his legs from moving, but he was no longer in control of his body. Icy terror flooded his body.

When he tried to raise his arm, it bounced limply at his side.

Phil approached the barbed wire fence. His useless arm shot up and indiscriminately grabbed the wire. The barb sank into his palm and sent jolts of pain the length of his arm. He tried to yell out, but his paralyzed voice only cracked. His arm pulled away from the fence, dragging the barb through his calloused flesh and ripped out of the web between his fingers.

Again, he tried to scream, and nothing happened. Blood poured from the ditch plowed through his hand and his head swam. He fought to not pass out again. If he did, he knew he wouldn't ever wake up.

His clumsy leg stepped through the fence, and his head ducked under the middle wire, barely clearing it. The other leg caught on the fence, and he stumbled forward, bending at the waist. Tears ran down his red face as his body bounced through the pasture. He walked along the bank of the calm black lake.

Something turned his head toward the water. There was movement too big for any fish he had seen before. The creatures were blacker than the water they swam in. A shimmering blue streak ran down their wet leathery backs. Phil wanted to continue to watch the animals, but his body had other plans. His head turned again, and he marched through the waist high grass to the waterfall at the north end of the lake.

On elastic legs, he climbed the hill to the top of the cliff. Water cascaded over the falls and splashed into a churning pit. The black fish were in the pit too. They slipped and slithered over each other in a tight knot of flesh. Phil forced a whimper from his haunted lips and searched his periphery for any sign of help. Sweat stung his eyes. Tears of relief joined tears of guilt and terror. He found his voice as he toed the edge of the cliff and spread his arms.

"No. I'll do anything you want. Don't make me do this, please. I'll help you get them all here if you let me live," he choked out.

From the pit, a low growl rose until it reached a gravelly laugh. The wind whipped around Phil, and his body stepped off the cliff. He hit the water and was in control of his body. He surfaced and fought the current trying to pull him under the water pouring down from the falls. There was no bank to use to climb out of the pit. It was like a cylinder had been dug into the earth and the craggy walls had worn smooth over the years.

Creatures swam between his legs as he fought to keep his head above water. He panicked and tried to swim away, but they pulled him down, flooding his mouth with oily black water. He forced himself back to the top, and the fish pulled him back down. Pain flared from his ankle as one of the fish clamped down on it, sinking its razor-sharp teeth to the bone. Phil tried to scream, but the fish shook him back and forth and pulled him under water. Phil reached down to grab his foot and hit exposed bone, sending bolts of pain through his body. Before the last bit of life drained from Phil's body, a shrill voice echoed through the pit.

"Only when you're dead, will you bring him home."

Chapter Two

dam Blackwell rolled to the edge of his side of the bed and sat up. He kneaded his temples to ease the throbbing pain in his head. Underwear hung from the headboard, and the low-cut black shirt he loved for her to wear on date night had knocked over the lamp on the nightstand. Charlotte was curled up naked in the comforter. He looked down at his own nakedness and stretched, letting all the hazy memories from the night before fade with the morning light. He grabbed a pair of shorts from the back of the chair in the corner of the room and slid them on. Before he left the room, he grabbed his empty glass and shook his head at her half-full glass. The saying goes, some people looked at a glass as half-empty, while others saw it as half-full, but the truth was that it depended on what was in the glass in the first place. He picked up her glass and slammed back the last of her cranberry and vodka. Sometimes it was empty.

He sat the glasses beside the sink and stared out the window. The pane was dirty. The entire apartment could use a deep cleanse. It was the weekend before the final week of school, and Adam had noticed Charlotte had marked her calendar to clean their apartment from top to bottom the Wednesday after she sent her graduating fifth graders home for the summer. She wasn't any better at keeping the place clean than he was, but she was better at cleaning it every couple of months. He had two more weekdays until school was out. When she finished her days packing up after the children left, she'd be home with him all day, every day. He wouldn't be able to get any writing done, or at least not as much as he needed to get done. There weren't any hard deadlines he had to meet to keep her out of his hair. Maybe he'd make one up.

Adam looked forward to her being around more, even though she'd cut into his writing time. The trick would be to keep himself on track without upsetting her. After dating her for the past year and a half, he finally figured out a schedule that allowed him to spend time with her and also have time to write. Before Chicago, his morning ritual was to wake, wander aimlessly from the bedroom to the kitchen and back before deciding to make a cup of hot tea. He'd finally sit and stare at his computer screen, daring it to flinch before he started writing for the day. Now, he slept in until lunch, made a cup of coffee, and was lucky to get a little writing finished before Charlotte got home and they had dinner. He'd stay up late after he finished watching the show Charlotte had picked out and fallen asleep during the first ten minutes. It'd be easy to turn the TV off and work, but once he started a story, he had to hang in until it was finished. He felt the same way about books. No matter how boring the book, he'd force himself to read until the end.

The X-Files theme played in the bedroom. Normally he wouldn't answer his phone, but it might be his agent, and he hadn't given her an excuse for not having anything new. Plus, he wanted to let Charlotte sleep as long as she could. She wasn't the most hospitable person when she woke up in the mornings, and definitely not while nursing a hangover. He walked back into the bedroom and unplugged the phone from its charger. The number didn't look familiar, but the 478 area code did. The hairs on the back of his neck stood at attention and his arms broke out in goose-flesh when he thought about home.

Not home, but where he was from. It'd never be home again. He slid his finger across the screen and sighed into the speaker.

"Hello? Mr. Blackwell," an unfamiliar voice said.

"Yeah. Speaking."

"Yes, hello. My name is Hank Roper." There was a pause, allowing Adam the chance to remember him, before the voice continued. "Mr. Blackwell, I am your—"

"Father's attorney. Yes, I know who you are. What can I do for you, Mr. Roper?" Adam interrupted. He didn't care what he could do for him. It was a reaction like when somebody asked you how you were doing, and you automatically said good, or well for the grammatically correct speakers. Adam was growing impatient with the southern attorney's slow drawl, and he'd hardly spoken.

"Well, I hate to be the one to tell you this, but under the circumstances, I guess it makes the most sense. Son, your daddy is dead. They found him in the lake three days ago. I'm sorry to be—"

"Okay. But why are you calling me, Mr. Roper? Brian should be able to handle everything."

Adam stood in the doorway to the bedroom, watching Charlotte sleep.

"Well, aside from being the right thing to do, I'm also calling to inform you that you're the sole beneficiary on your father's will. The land, and everything on it, is yours."

"I can't believe he didn't change his will," Adam said, and hit the case molding. This was the last thing he needed. It wasn't that he didn't have time to deal with it. He didn't want to deal with it.

"That's what your brother said as well. Course, he used a bit more colorful language. Anyway, seeing as you'll probably be here for the funeral on Monday, I'd wanted to see if you wouldn't mind stopping by so you can sign the papers."

"I don't want the land or anything to do with it."

Grace Ann died in the lake because of his father. Why would a good father want anything to do with the house or the land after that?

"You don't have to keep it. It's none of my business. What is my business is to make sure you're apprised of the situation and take initial ownership. What you do with it after that is up to you.

Luckily, your daddy was able to keep his head above water and not take out any extra mortgages and paid the farm off a few years back."

Adam smirked at the unintended pun. The lawyer didn't seem to notice.

"Alright, Mr. Roper. I'll see what I can do."

"Don't you even want to know what happened to him?"

"Not really. But go ahead and tell me so I won't have to act surprised when I get down there."

"He didn't leave a note, but everybody said he was still pretty broke up about ... well, he'd been depressed. The only thing that's weird about the whole situation is your brother found him caught in the wiring up by the dock, but it looked like he'd been tossed around in those rapids for quite a while."

"That is weird," Adam said and hung up the phone before the lawyer could reply. Charlotte stirred under the overstuffed comforter. Adam walked to her side of the bed and tripped over her shoes lying on the floor. He avoided falling on top of her and cracked his knee on the nightstand for his efforts.

"Damn it," he screamed and flopped down on the bed. Roused from her sleep, Charlotte slid up the bed and leaned against the headboard.

"What are you doing?" she asked.

She rubbed her head and blinked the sleep from her eyes.

"I was trying not to wake you," he said and traced the side of her face with his hand.

"Smashing job. Who was on the phone?"

"Yeah, we need to talk about that. I have to leave for a few days."

Charlotte sat up straight.

"What do you mean you have to leave?"

He walked out of the bedroom into the living room. He liked Charlotte, maybe even loved her, but this was going to cause a fight, or she was going to end up crying. She was a great person, but she had separation issues and caused a scene every time he had to leave town. She always wanted to go, even if she knew she'd be closed up in a hotel room while he attended a convention. Charlotte walked out of the bedroom, pulling her robe around her.

"You can't leave right now, Adam."

"I have to."

He walked to the kitchen and came back with a glass full of ice and a bottle of Johnnie Walker Red Label. Black Label was too smoky for him, and the others were too expensive. He fell into his recliner, banged the glass on the table, and poured four fingers. Some splashed off the ice and onto the end table. He mumbled under his breath and emptied the glass in one gulp and poured another.

"Who was on the phone? Why are you so upset?" she asked and pulled her robe tight across her chest.

"I'm not upset."

She was getting mad. Now was not the time for him to be aloof.

"So it's perfectly normal for you to have your first and second drink before breakfast?"

Adam sat the glass on the table and leaned back in his chair. He tried to smile, but he forced it, and he stopped.

The TV was on from the previous night. They had only muted it before continuing to the bedroom. Even without the sound, Adam knew they were talking about the latest string of murders in Chicago. Every weekend felt like more random acts of violence. Though they probably had their reasons. Was anything ever truly senseless? The glass was almost empty again, and it was too early in the morning to be this cynical.

Adam didn't even like to watch the news with no sound. They were always fear mongering no matter their political slant. A small town like Scarsville had negligible crime, but stuff did happen, though it was typically domestic or neighbor disputes. The only thing he had to compare it to was the time when The Suicide Killer terrorized the city of Crystal Valley, an hour south of Scarsville. Though nobody believed it could happen in their small town, they watched the noon and six o'clock news. Some said they started locking their doors at all times. The worst part was that the guy was still on the loose and had stopped killing. People speculated he had been caught by police for something else, or had moved away, but every few months the news brought it back up and scared everybody all over again. It was like they didn't want anybody to feel comfortable.

The news cut to sports and the Cubs latest winning streak followed by the White Sox latest losing streak. When he moved to Chicago, he converted from a Braves fan to a Cubs fan. Magic flowed through the stark white pinstripe uniform with the red C that looked like it was eating ubs, circled in blue. There was also magic in the feeling of Wrigley Field on game day. It was magic Adam needed in his life.

"I've been thinking about home a lot lately. I don't know if I've been expecting that call or what," he said and sipped his drink.

"Home?" she asked. "But you are home."

He laughed.

"I don't have much of an accent, but you know I'm not from around here."

He laughed again and took another sip from his drink. She looked from his smiling face to the emptying glass. He knew she didn't care for his laughing or his drinking scotch this early in the morning. The amber liquid spilled into his mouth as he tilted the glass back. He spit a piece of ice back into the glass and grabbed the bottle to pour another drink but decided against it.

"I knew it the first time you told me you were fixin' to get dressed. You never want to talk about your past and you've never called it home before."

"Maybe that's the scotch talking."

"What's the matter with you? Who was on the phone?"

She was waiting for a response, but he couldn't give her the one she wanted. Her sweet face implored him to tell her about his past. He loved her, or at least he thought he loved her, but he didn't want to let her into that part of his life. The part he left in Georgia. He didn't leave; he ran. Picked up and left. Adam cut off contact with everybody from Georgia. He completed the divorce from Mandy through the mail and her lawyer.

He tried to see the situation through Charlotte's eyes but couldn't. The view left him as confused as she looked. He tried to imagine her as one of the characters from his stories. A character he could develop and only knew what he wanted her to know. He tried, but somebody else had already written it, and he didn't like the ending.

That reminded Adam about the short story he finished last night before they went to eat at Giordano's. He had more than enough stories for a collection. It'd help pay the bills until he completed the book he was working on. He'd have to remember to call his agent later. Hopefully it'd keep her off his back for a little while longer. Going to Georgia would delay the writing he was already putting off even longer. Writing had become a job, something he had to do to eat and keep a roof over his head. He knew it would all come down to it one day, but he hated it. Adam was a mid-list pulp writer and with online adjunct jobs, most months had no issues keeping the lights on. Before he left Georgia, he had sporadic success publishing stories in a saturated yet shrinking market. The second novel he wrote was the first one he published. His first novel sat in a wooden box on the shelf with copies and special editions of his published work. He would never publish Black Rapids. It had too much blood on the page, and he didn't know he'd been bleeding when he was working on it. He wrote it two years before Grace Ann was born. The box resting on the shelf behind Charlotte's head drew his attention. Mocking him.

Charlotte sat in her grey robe, pulling at the tangles as she ran her hands through her hair. He knew she didn't know what to say. At the moment, Charlotte looked like one of his characters. At the age of ten, she was the lone survivor in a car accident that killed both of her parents. Charlotte's aunt, who didn't want any kids of her own, took her in. The aunt didn't want to care for her sister's kid either, but the life insurance money helped ease the transition. Charlotte paid her own way through college by working at the local pizza joint. Now, she taught fifth grade on the low-income side of town. She was one of the few teachers who weren't thinking of a career change or counting down the days until retirement and had won teacher of the year for her troubles. The plaque proudly hung over her desk at school, and she got the closest parking space to the school. She routinely cleaned spitballs off the reflective gold surface of her award, but the parking spot was nice because of the extra security she felt when she worked late. In the real world, she was an inspiration and a hero. The literary world would consider her generic and trite. Maybe she wasn't like one of his characters. She was better.

Adam looked out the window and stared at the motionless sky. He almost longed for the open country air and the fresh scent of loblolly pine. Images of cows lazily grazing in his father's pasture as the gentle song of the whip-poor-will floated on the breeze flooded his mind. The sound of the slow-moving water crept into the background. At first it was as soothing as the scotch he drank. Dark water crashed on the horizon behind the cows. It flowed faster at his notice. Small rapids with blue caps crashed onto the banks. He barely heard his father's voice over the rushing water. *She was pulled in. Somebody help me. I can't see her. Adam, she's in the water.* He tried to move, but was unable, and he tried to scream with the same result.

"Adam? What's wrong with you? You're scaring me," Charlotte yelled.

She shook him, and his glass fell from the arm of the chair. The remaining ice cubes and watered-down scotch splashed onto his lap and pulled him back to Chicago. He dug his nails into the coarse fabric of the chair and his heart pounded as he fought for breath. Charlotte picked his glass up and set it on the coffee table and grabbed his hands.

"What's the matter, Adam? Who was on the phone?"

"I'll tell you. I'm not trying to hide anything. But first, will you get me some more ice? And a towel?"

She hesitated but relented and walked into the kitchen. He ran his hands through his greasy hair, sat down and looked back out the window. This time he didn't see the cows or the lake. Black clouds loomed on the horizon. Charlotte threw the towel in his lap and thrust the glass into his hand. The ice rattled as he poured his drink with unsteady hands.

"What do you know about me?"

"I'm not in the mood for this. Just tell me who was on the phone."

"I will. Once you tell me."

She blew an exaggerated breath from her mouth.

"I know you're from a small town in Georgia named Scarsville, and that name sounds like it should be a made-up town in one of your books. Not a real place."

"Yeah, it's very fitting. What else?"

Her lips tightened, and her teeth clenched. There was a good chance she was going to lose her cool. Instead, she stood up straight like she was collecting herself and continued.

"I know you lost your mother when you were six. I know you had a daughter, and she was your entire world and she died. And then you moved to Chicago because you wanted to get away from the world you shared with her," Charlotte said and hesitated before continuing. "I know you're an amazing writer and deserve all the attention you get and more."

Adam was staring at the cherry oak box sitting on the shelf behind her. She followed his gaze and when she focused on him, her face was twisted, and her eyes threatened to rain down.

"I know you have a weird hang-up over your first novel and won't let anybody read it. It was your first, but it couldn't be as bad as you think."

"It's pretty bad," was his only reply.

"Most nights you have nightmares, but always say you don't remember them the next morning."

"I don't," Adam said too quickly.

"I think you're dreaming about what happened."

"Couldn't tell you."

She was making him squirm, and she knew it. He felt like one of her students being grilled over who shot the rubber band. But he'd asked for it.

"Can you tell me who called?"

"It was my father's lawyer."

She was good, but knowing how to get him to talk about something he didn't want to didn't make her girlfriend of the year.

"What did he want?"

"My father died three days ago."

"Oh, Adam, I'm so—"

"You know my daughter died, but you don't know she drowned, and my father was the one who was supposed to be watching her."

"Why didn't you ever—"

"Tell you?" he laughed. "I am tired of reliving it every day."

"What happened?"

"It was Memorial Day weekend, and we were all outside cooking out. Grace Ann and my father were riding the Polaris in the pasture. I looked away for a moment and the next thing I knew, my father was screaming she'd fallen in the water." Tears rolled down Adam's face. "By the time I got there she was gone. He showed me where she went in the water and said she never came back up. The water wasn't deep, but I couldn't find her. Five days later, the police called off the search. After the funeral, I left and haven't been back or spoken to anybody there since. I was supposed to be with her. If I had been right there, I would have been able to save her. Hell, I wouldn't have let her anywhere near that damn lake."

"But what does your father's death have to do with your daughter?" she asked.

The sky had grown dark, casting a shadow over Charlotte's face. Neither reached for the lamp. Thunder rolled, and a streak of lightning shot across the sky like a river cutting through the clouds. Charlotte didn't seem to notice.

"They think he threw himself into the lake and drowned. He didn't leave a note, but everybody who knew him told the police he never recovered after Grace Ann's death. Maybe he got drunk and fell in. I don't know. They said it was weird because they found him near the dock tangled in old wiring, but it looked like his body had been tumbling in the rapids at the end of the lake."

"What's so weird about that?"

"The rapids are at the bottom of a thirty-foot pit. There's no way out."

"Oh," was all she said. Her hand moved reflexively to her face. She always touched her face when she was upset.

"I don't know what happened. The only thing I do know is I have to leave soon."

"But why? Why can't your brother deal with it if you don't want to go back?"

"And the plot thickens. Evidently, my father never changed his will, and he left me everything. I have to go back and get it ready so I can sell it."

"Why can't you do it from here?"

"Because I'm sure my brother still lives there, and he's not going to be too happy about receiving an eviction notice."

"Let him have it or sell it to him and be done with it. You can't kick him out."

"I have to go back and deal with this."

"Wait until Wednesday and I'll go with you."

"No. I need to go now. There's no reason for you to go."

"I don't understand any of this. When will you be back and what about the funeral?"

He got up on shaky legs and walked to her. He put his arms around her, held her tight, and kissed her head, but never answered her question. Instead, he walked to the bedroom and packed.

Chapter Three

Adam merged onto I-90 and headed east. Traffic was light. If he had left an hour later, he would have ended up stuck in an interstate parking lot, huffing exhaust fumes. His brain raced with thoughts of his father and home. But it was no longer his home. A song he'd never heard came on the radio, and he flipped the volume knob higher than usual. The heavy drums and drop-tuned guitars rumbled through his body. He kept calling it home when it hadn't been his home for two years, and it wouldn't be his home ever again. He wanted to get there, take care of business, and get out as soon as he could. Grace Ann was also there, somewhere. The only thing he had to visit was an empty box in the First Baptist Church graveyard. His chest tightened, and he changed the radio to a station that only played the blues. Nina Simone's smooth voice slid from the car speakers and Adam hoped it would help his brain shift to neutral. He was thirty minutes into a fourteen-hour drive and didn't want to cry this early in the trip. There would be plenty of time for crying later.

When he left, Charlotte had been upset. She didn't understand why he had to be the one to make all the arrangements if he had nothing to do with anybody in Georgia. She was right to think his brother could take care of everything. It would have been easier to sign the house over to Brian and be done with it, but the house and land were worth a lot of money. Money would go a long way to help them with bills if he had a dry spell with book sales, or they had an emergency. The transmission shifted hard and jerked the car forward onto the I-65 exit ramp.

He engaged cruise control and forced his thoughts to his latest book. The story was halfway to becoming a novel, but he had no idea where it was going. It started off promising, but dwindled the last few days. Then he got the call. His creative energy was depleted, and he didn't know if he'd be able to save the book. The deadline was rapidly approaching. Abandoning the story and starting over wasn't an option. He rarely plotted his books, but he might as well try to get as much use out of the next seven hundred miles as he could.

When Adam pulled into the Kentucky rest stop, his book had not gotten any further than it was before he left. He was thinking too hard. Trying to concentrate on his story to block out all the other thoughts only succeeded in giving him a migraine. He wasn't ready to stop and rest, but if he remembered correctly, the rest stops in Tennessee were few and far between. Was there even one on this stretch of I-65 or the upcoming I-24? He couldn't remember, but there was no reason to take any chances.

Parked as far as possible from the building, Adam looked out across the empty parking lot. He wanted to make sure no suspicious-looking cars were near him in case he took a short nap. Under normal circumstances, Adam would have made the drive straight through, only stopping for gas, but going back to Georgia unexpectedly, and early morning scotch had drained his energy. When he went back to Chicago, it'd be an escape, and he'd drive the whole way wide-awake.

He kept the car running and set the air conditioner on high. The oppressive southern humidity was not something he missed, and it got worse the further south he went. Luckily for him, the AC worked great in his car. His sinuses would also get worse. The mucus was already thickening. By the time he got to the Tennessee border, it'd be sliding down the back of his throat and

Georgia would bring the boot heel to rest on his chest. He'd have a sore throat for days from all the drainage. When he was up north, he breathed better. He had to contend with the smog, but that was any major city. Relief from sinus pressure had been a bonus he'd not expected. That alone was reason enough to leave Georgia.

The seat laid back and stopped before touching the back seat. He popped his head above the steering wheel. He had forgotten to check the trucker parking lot. There were four giants in the back lot idling like they were waiting to make a quick escape if needed. Truckers were creepy. Or maybe it was the big ominous trucks that rolled down the road to far destinations. The unseen drivers were dirty vagabonds along for the ride waiting for their chance to take out an unsuspecting stranger in a run-down rest stop in the middle of nowhere, Kentucky, or to try to run smaller cars, that wouldn't allow them to change lanes, off the road and send them careening into a ditch or off a bridge. Of course, all of this was in his head, but that's how it typically worked. He needed to rest, and his brain decided it wanted to be creative now. He laid back down and, after checking on a few cracks from breaking tree limbs, fell asleep.

Grace Ann ran through the backyard. It was dark outside, but Adam saw everything. It looked like a movie where the film was supposed to be at night, but the set had been lit with artificial lighting. Adam lit the grill and prepared to cook hamburgers and hotdogs.

"Can I go with Grandpa? He's going to ride in the pasture," Grace Ann said.

"If he says it's okay, and he's going to watch you, then it's fine with me."

The little girl squealed and ran off. Phil pulled up in the Polaris, and Grace Ann curtsied. He dismounted and gave an exaggerated bow. Grace Ann twirled and put her hands to her mouth.

Phil waved to Adam.

"I've got her. We won't be gone too long."

"Good. I'm about to put the burgers and dogs on."

"Why don't you come with us?" Phil yelled back.

"Yeah, go with them. I'll take care of the grill," Mandy said as she materialized out of nowhere. She hadn't been there before.

Adam handed the spatula to Mandy and tossed her his favorite apron. He didn't need the apron, but he liked that it said, "Your Opinion Wasn't in the Recipe." Grace Ann skipped around the vehicle while waiting for Adam. When he arrived, she twirled to spin her dress like a dancer. The edges of the fabric glowed with the movement.

"How was that, Daddy?" she asked as she tried to keep her balance.

Adam spoke, but his words were slow and hollow.

"That was great, sweetheart. Be careful. You don't want to get too dizzy."

"I won't, silly," she said and jumped on the Polaris.

They rode through the rutted pasture. The cavernous echo of Grace Ann's giggling as she reached out and tried to grab the grass that lined the path was the only audible sound. The grass bent as a sweeping wind blew across the land. The black lake demanded Adam's attention. The water flow reflected in the moonlight, causing a blue hue to follow the ripples. Phil stopped the Polaris and got out.

"I need to check the wiring on the dock. One of the calves came up to the barn today and had a burn from her neck all the way to her tail. It looked like she got wrapped up in something. Brian thinks some of the electrical wiring came loose on the dock and she got caught in it. Amazing the calf knew to come to the barn for help."

Adam didn't say anything. He pulled Grace Ann close and watched Phil walk to the dock. Grace Ann struggled in his arms.

"I want to get out, Daddy."

"I don't want you getting out anywhere near the lake or the dock."

"But I need to get out."

"No, you don't. Didn't you hear Grandpa? Do you want to end up like the calf?"

"That won't happen to me—"

Grace Ann continued, but Adam had stopped listening. The woman in white walking across the pasture grabbed his attention. She walked slow and determined and wore a long flowing nightgown. From this distance, he couldn't tell who she was, but it wasn't Mandy because she was wearing blue jeans and a tank top. Without thinking, he left the Polaris and followed the woman.

"Hey, Dad. Keep an eye on Grace, would ya? I'm going to see if this lady needs help."

"Okay, but what lady are you talking about?" Phil yelled back.

Adam didn't answer. He kept walking like a man possessed. The woman was almost to the falls when Adam called out to her.

"Hey, ma'am. Are you okay? You look lost."

The woman didn't reply. She turned to face him and shook her head. He didn't recognize her, but the soft glow radiating from her distorted her face. The woman continued walking, and Adam ran to catch up. He blinked, and the woman stood at the top of the falls. She walked to the edge, looked to the sky and spread her arms wide.

"Hey, come down from there. You're going to fall," he yelled.

He reached the foot of the hill that led to the top of the cliff overlooking the falls and the woman fell. She didn't jump, she just stopped holding herself up and went over the cliff. Once raised to the sky, now her hands led the way in her swan dive of death. She didn't scream on the way down, but there was a scream. At first, he thought it was him, but realized it was too high pitched to be his voice. He turned and saw Phil running toward the lake. Ripples ran across the surface of the water like a large fish had jumped trying to catch a more exciting dinner. Phil yelled to him, but Adam didn't understand the words. He waved his hands, motioning for Adam to come back, and pointed at the water. Adam looked at the empty Polaris and panicked.

"Grace."

He took off running toward the ripples. The tall grass slapped at his cheeks, trying to slow him down. He covered his face and tried to ward off the attack. When Adam reached the end of the vengeful grass, he fell. His boot sank into a mud hole. The sudden snap back made him think he broke his ankle. He struggled to free his foot and sat down and laced his fingers behind his knee and pulled. There was no give, and he continued to pull. The mud gave and slurped at his heels as he pulled his foot free, but the ground kept his boot.

Adam jumped up and ran as fast as he could while wearing one boot. Phil was pointing to the water. When he looked at the water, it was deathly calm. He had never seen the water as smooth before. It looked like a sheet of tinted glass.

"It pulled her in right there."

"What? Why aren't you looking for her?" Adam screamed.

The calm of the water didn't bother him for too long, and he jumped in. It was thigh high, and he splashed around, arms and legs kicking and reaching under water, trying to find Grace Ann. He walked out further until the water reached his waist.

"Don't just stand there. Get in and help me."

Phil didn't move. Adam saw the fear in his father's eyes. At first, he assumed it was because of the emergency, but as Phil stepped back, Adam realized his father feared something in the water.

Adam crouched down under the water and prepared to stand when something tough and leathery wrapped around his arm.

Adam woke screaming and tried to pull the steering wheel to his chest. Sweat covered his face and soaked through his shirt. The air conditioner was still on high, but he was panting like a dog in search of shade and water. He wiped the sweat from his face and killed the engine. It was dark outside. How long had he been asleep? He didn't remember the time when he parked, but the sun had been out and not close to setting. He jumped out of the car and ran to the rest stop building and tried not to draw the attention of the people in the few cars that now dotted the parking lot.

He burst through the door and continued to the restrooms. A couple looked at him with mild interest, then went back to arguing over what they wanted to share from the vending machine. The restroom looked like every rest stop horror movie he'd seen and a couple he'd written about. The fluorescent lights above the two sinks blinked slightly out of time with each other. There was no way to tell if the black grease on the tile floor was dirt and grime, or dried blood. He decided he didn't care and kicked the stall door to get to the sink. The single hinge the door hung from protested the intrusion. A slight gurgling came from the first faucet, like the water wanted to come out, but it never did. He moved to the sink against the wall. Gray water trickled into his cupped hands. He patiently waited for them to fill and splashed his face and repeated the cycle. He needed to piss, but looked at the brown water in the clogged toilet and the urinal covered with a clear garbage bag and decided he'd wait.

The couple continued to argue in the lobby when he stumbled back through and caught himself on the round table in the middle of the room covered in various attraction brochures and state maps. They looked at him like he should make the decision for them, so he did.

"I'd go with the zingers," he said and staggered out the door.

When he made it back to his car, he fell into the driver's seat, turned all the air conditioner vents to face him and laid his head on the steering wheel.

Chapter Four

By the time his body temperature had returned to normal, he was already far south of Nashville on I-24. He hadn't seen any rest areas, but the last one left him in no mood to pullover. If the gaslight hadn't made him stop, his bladder would have. The burning intensified while he waited for the gas pump to click. Bouncing his weight off each foot didn't seem to help the issue either. Could he get bladder cancer from holding it for too long too many times? He didn't know, but he'd have to remember to look it up later. It wouldn't surprise him. Everything caused cancer. Why not your body's waste too? The pump clicked and shut off. He was lost in thoughts of his own mortality. The stinging sensation made itself known, and he realized he was staring off. Adam slammed the pump into its slot and tried not to waddle as he moved toward the store.

The bell chimed when he walked in, drawing the clerk's attention. Adam nodded and tried to grin. The disinterested clerk looked back to his magazine. Adam walked to the restroom in the back of the store, and turned the handle, but paused, remembering the last restroom he went in. Grey water ran behind the door and Adam refused to look down for fear the water would seep from under the door and reach out for him. Nature won the battle, and he flung the door open.

Nothing unnatural occurred while he went to the restroom. He emerged feeling like a new man and left his nightmare and cancerous thoughts behind him. The Georgia border and Scarsville city limits were the last thing on his mind as he eased his car back onto the highway and set cruise control.

The Now Entering Georgia sign didn't bother him like he thought it would. It might have been because the real one was miles down the road. I-24 crosses into Georgia and back into Tennessee before heading to Chattanooga. This stretch of road always baffled Adam. The road always felt like the car was going straight. There might be a few slight curves, but somehow, he'd leave one state and after a few miles, he'd be back in the state he recently left. It was all in his head, but the section of highway was the straightest meandering road he remembered ever driving.

"We're Glad Georgia's on Your Mind" loomed ahead of him from the real Georgia welcome sign. It was funny because Georgia had been the furthest thing from his mind since he left. However, the events that happened there never left him. Grace Ann's death wasn't tied to the state or even the town. It was tied to Phil and that damn lake. With Phil gone, the only thing left was the lake. He couldn't kill it, and the underground spring feeding it made sure nobody ever tried to drain it. The next best option was to sell it and never return.

Menacing dark clouds accompanied the assuming sign. It looked like the rain started as soon as he crossed the state line. Like it had been waiting all this time for him to return to take him home. The raindrops fell hard. Worn wipers smeared the black raindrops across the windshield.

Adam didn't mind driving in the rain. Worrying about all the other drivers and what they were doing bothered him more. Some drove too fast. It wouldn't be surprising if they were sitting at home and saw the darkening clouds and decided it'd be a good time to go flying down the road faster than they would have under normal safe conditions. Then there were the ones who genuinely got to him. The ones who slowed way down and turned on their flashers. Wasn't it illegal to drive with your flashers on? Or was it something people said, like being illegal to drive with the dome light on? If they were driving with their lights on, they'd be as visible as the annoying flashing lights. It occurred to him the most aggravating drivers were the ones who weren't doing anything dangerous, but he didn't care. The worst part about driving in the rain was he had never figured out how to use the defroster to defog the windshield correctly. He never knew when to use warm air or cool and had to guess every time and every time it seemed like he chose the wrong one.

Fog crept in from both sides of the glass. He switched the vents to defrost, blasted the air, and didn't bother to see if the vents were pushing cool or warm. The circulation fed the fog, and it swarmed to the middle of the windshield like a frozen sheet of ice. He leaned to the passenger's side, slammed his hand against the glass and tried to wipe it away before it completely obscured his vision. Traces of smeared fingerprints and smudges from what-ever he had on his hand trailed across the windshield. With hands at ten and two, he hunched over the steering wheel to get a better view. He tried wiping again, but it made the mess worse. The smears caused shadows to appear in the corner of the glass. They looked like smaller creatures looming from the grassy median while the larger, more threatening ones attacked from the other side of the road. They reached long, spiny fingers for the tires and scraped down the side of his car.

Adam tried to push all thoughts of monsters from his mind. Now was not the time for him to let his imagination play. He looked down at the console and flipped the temperature gauge in the other direction. The air tore through the fog at the base of the windshield and spread like a boat's wake on a flat lake. Earlier, Adam had mostly been concentrating on the creatures from the right side of the road. Bright lights from an oncoming car lit up the median and a flash of white fabric flapped toward his car. He slammed on the brakes, and the car slid across the pavement. The front tires raced across the rumble strips on the shoulder, and he spun the wheel and over corrected. The rear wheels pulled to the left and caught on the lip of the shoulder and mud at the onset of the median. Adam turned the wheel again, and the rear tires caught the grass. The back end of his car slid out from under him in slow motion. Then everything sped up, and the car spun through the grass. He gripped the steering wheel and held on, but he didn't try to turn it because he didn't know which direction he was going and didn't want to be the reason the car crashed into oncoming traffic and took out a happy family on their way on vacation. All this flashed through his mind, and the car slowed its spin. It came to a stop before it made it to the other side of the divided highway.

Adam's skin tingled with fear. The woman from his dream with the flowing white nightgown had walked out in front of him and caused the wreck. But she had jumped to her death, and besides, that had all been a dream. Or had it been a memory? Hesitantly, he looked out the back window. He couldn't see anything in the dark. There was no woman walking toward him or lying dead in the road where he had taken her out with his car as he swerved to avoid her. Maybe she made it to the other side and disappeared into the forest. Or maybe she never existed and being back in Georgia was making Adam crazy or paranoid, or both. With all vacationing families safe, he slumped over the center console and closed his eyes.

A loud knock woke him up. Through bleary eyes, he squinted into the morning sun and saw a hand beating on his passenger side window. The memory of his spinning car came back to him and he sat up straight, and the knocking stopped. The wide brim of a Georgia state trooper's hat replaced the hand, and Adam rolled down the window.

"Side of the highway's not really the safest place to be taking a nap."

"Sorry, officer, I was driving, and something ran out in front of me and I swerved to miss it. I was a little rattled and closed my eyes for a minute and must have fallen asleep."

"Must've," the trooper said. "I'll need to see your license and registration."

Adam pulled his ID out of his wallet and searched the glove box for his registration. It wasn't there. He slowly opened the center console as the trooper looked on. Electric pulses flowed through his veins. He hoped he had taken the pistol in the apartment the last time he got out of the car and forgot to grab it when he left town.

"Everything alright?"

"Yeah, yeah. Everything's fine. Still a little groggy," Adam said and slammed the console open like he was ripping off a Band-Aid so it wouldn't hurt as much. Lying on top of miscellaneous cables and old car phone chargers, he found the registration, but no gun. He exhaled, grabbed the paper and handed it and his license to the trooper.

"Chicago."

The trooper said it like a statement, but Adam knew he meant it as a question. What he meant is what the hell are you doing all the way down here?

"Yes, sir. But I'm originally from Scarsville. I'm coming back home for my father's funeral."

The officer shifted his feet, and his features softened a little.

"My condolences ... Mr. Blackwell. Hang tight and we'll see about getting you on your way."

"Thank you. Do you mind if I get out and stretch my legs?"

"Sure. Just stand toward the middle of the median here. I don't want to have to call an ambulance and a tow truck out here."

Adam's body tensed. He had tried to be as nice and respectful to the trooper as his tired body would allow him, and he was still going to have his car towed. And for what? He hadn't caused any damage. Adam pulled himself out of the seat and watched the cars pass from the opposite direction. The front bumper of his car sat six inches away from taking out a reflective red sign that read wrong way. Adam smirked and looked at his car. The rear wheel was buried in mud and tangled in long grass. He looked sheepishly at the trooper and walked toward the waist high grass in the middle of the median and waded in. The state must have been short on trustee prisoners to cut the grass.

He tried not to appear impatient. He spun his watch face to his wrist, so he wouldn't check it, but he had slept or passed out for the entire night and lost a lot of time. The worst part was fighting the urge to put his hands in his pockets, so he wouldn't spook the trooper. It was a natural reaction for him. He didn't know what to do with them and felt awkward if they weren't contained.

He wasn't sure where he was in Georgia, but didn't think he had made it too far past the border. There wasn't a schedule to keep, but he wanted to get to Scarsville, take care of business and get back home. While trying to waste time and act like he was stretching his back, he followed the thick muddy trail his car made when he spun through the grass. Something bright orange with white material flapping in the wind stood by the guardrail a little before the spot his car left the road. As he approached, he realized it was an orange construction barrel with a sheet of thick white plastic waving in the wind. Was a piece of plastic all he saw last night? He swore a woman darted out in front of him. But why would anybody be alone on the side of a major highway at any time, let alone the middle of the night with no vehicle? It was weird there was only the one barrel on the side of the road, and it didn't look like any road construction had been going in a long time. Adam walked back to his car and after eyeing the trooper for a few minutes, he finally emerged from his cruiser.

"Well, you don't seem to be wanted anywhere. I went ahead and radioed in for a tow truck to come and pull you out. It'll be here directly. Next time you might want to pull over at a rest stop or hotel if you get tired," the trooper said and handed Adam back his license and registration.

"Thank you," Adam said.

He didn't feel like trying to explain what he'd seen, especially since he wasn't sure it wasn't just a plastic sheet. And besides, the officer let him go without giving him trouble. No use in starting any now. He got back inside his car to wait for the tow truck. Fifteen minutes later, the truck crested the hill in front of him.

The truck made a wide U-turn across the highway and backed up to the front of Adam's car like there weren't any other drivers on the road. The driver jumped down out of the cab of his flatbed tow truck with far more grace than Adam expected after seeing the man's large frame and larger gut. He hitched fingers in his belt loops and pulled his pants up one leg at a time, like everybody else. Years of caked on grease made the leaping deer logo barely visible on his hat.

"Name's Darryl. Nice ta meet cha."

"I'm Adam."

A big grin tore through Darryl's thick beard.

"Ole Terry over there don't too much care for people mud bogging through the median. You must've caught him on a good day," Darryl said and tipped his hat to the Terry who waved, but didn't look like he'd be getting out to join them in the heat.

"Must have," Adam said.

Darryl unspooled the winch mounted to the back of his truck, climbed under the car and looked for a good place to connect. Darryl kicked his legs to maneuver for a better angle, kicking his feet dangerously close to the white line on the road. Adam stepped closer to warn him when a gruff cough came from under the front bumper and Darryl pushed himself to his knees.

"They don't make 'em like they used to I tell ya that," Darryl said, pulling himself up and transferring the red clay mud from his hands to his pants. "You've gotta climb all the way under cars nowadays just ta find a damn place to hook 'em. And it ain't just them foreign cars neither. 'Merican ones do the same way. You hook the wrong place, and you damn near rip the whole front end off of 'em."

"Guess it's cheaper that way."

"Cheaper for who? Damn prices keep going up. I'm surprised they haven't figured a way to make you pay more for the car after you done bought it."

Adam didn't reply. He stayed silent, hoping the uncomfortable conversation would end there. It wasn't what Darryl was saying that made Adam feel awkward, it was the feeling of talking to somebody he didn't believe he could have a conversation with without being an outsider. Like Darryl would call him out for being different from everybody else. He felt that way his entire life until he moved north and away from southern hospitality. He didn't believe northern people were somehow ruder and more attractive to be around. There was a thin line between being hospitable and over sharing, and in the south, the line seemed to blur a bit more than he was comfortable with.

The whining of the steel line wrapping around the spool saved Adam from further conversation. The winch pulled Adam's car out of the mud like it was a toy.

"I'm going to pull her up on the back of my truck so I can see better. Make sure there ain't anything wrong with her undercarriage," Darryl said and cackled and nudged Adam with his elbow.

A toothpick Adam hadn't noticed in Darryl's mouth before poked out from his wiry beard. He rolled it between his lips as the car rolled onto the platform. Darryl stuck his head under the rear of the car. When he finally stood, a new layer of mud joined the built-up grease on his hat.

"Everything looks fine to me, but you're going to want to take her to a carwarsh with one of those high-powered hoses so you can get this mud out of everything," Darryl said. "If you don't, it's libel to rattle your teeth right out of your head while you're going down the road."

Adam checked his watch and looked down the road in the direction he should have been going.

As if reading his mind, Darryl started, "there's one at the next exit back the way you came. You'd be backtracking, but you have to go that way to turn around, seeing as you can't go crossing the median again. I have to head up there anyway, and your car is already on the truck. I can drop you off so you don't have to drive so slow."

The thought of climbing into Darryl's truck was nauseating, but he didn't see any other way around it.

"Sure. That'd be great, if you don't mind."

"Ah. It's no problem t'all. I'll go let Terry know his break is over and we'll head out," Darryl said.

Adam pulled the passenger's side door open and slowly climbed into the truck. The cleanliness of the truck surprised him. At least on the passenger side of the cab. The seats and dash shined like they had been freshly rubbed with Armor All, and the slight scent of a pine tree punctuated the air. He had expected mud flap girls and support single mother bumper stickers plastered everywhere and a plastic hula dancer on the dash. The driver's side door swung open and Darryl climbed in. Relief flowed through Adam when Darryl didn't speak. Instead, he moved back onto the highway as haphazardly as he had left it and picked up the CB.

"Hey there, Garage, this is Big D. Anybody listening up there?" Darryl said into the CB.

He laughed and turned to Adam. "It's not just a clever nickname, either."

"I hear ya loud and clear, Big D. When you're finished up on the highway, Clint needs you to head up to the Rodgers' house before there's another domestic. Hank's truck broke down in the front yard, and Sheryl told him last time it better not happen again."

"Well, hey there, Darlin. It sure is good to hear your voice. What're we doing when we get off work tonight?"

"I'm going home ... to my husband."

"Ah, I see. Playing hard to get," Darryl said into the radio and then to Adam, "That girl don't know what'd happen if I got her over to my house."

"Go get the damn truck and bring it back to the shop before Sheryl gets home. Over and out."

"She wants me. She's afraid if she had some of Big D, she wouldn't want to go back home. I keep trying to tell her."

Despite its clean interior, the truck suddenly felt dirty, and Adam didn't want to touch anything. Sexual harassment didn't seem to exist in small town America.

Luckily for Adam, he saw the green exit sign in the distance. As the truck rattled down the highway, the white letters became clear in the reflected sunlight. Adam leaned forward in his seat. If the belt hadn't snatched him to a stop, he would have slammed his face into the dash while he read the sign.

"Wire Road?" Until this point, it hadn't occurred to Adam to ask where he was. He assumed he was somewhere in North Georgia.

"Yeah. You know the place?"

"I only know of one Wire Road, but it's outside of Scarsville."

"Well, yeah. This is the one. You're fifteen minutes from Scarsville. Where did you think you were?"

All the blood drained from Adam's face. Disorienting blobs floated around his head. Somehow he had lost three hours drive time between stopping for gas and driving into the median last night. He wiped the sweat from his brow and willed himself steady before he passed out. The manly man beside him wouldn't let that go.

"I uh, I wasn't really sure where I was at. I didn't realize I had made it this far south yet. I don't remember driving through Atlanta."

"Damn boy, that must have been some nap you were taking back there. Are you sure you didn't hit your head on something?"

"No. I don't think so," Adam said.

He ran his hands over his face and through his hair.

"I don't know how anybody could forget coming through Atlanta. Traffic's horrible no matter what time you do it."

Darryl swung into the carwash and got out of the truck. Adam pulled down the sun visor and looked at himself in the mirror. Aside from the shock of finding out he lost three hours of his life and didn't die, he looked fine. He slowly climbed out of the truck and walked around to the back with Darryl.

"Alright, I got you unloaded. Make sure you spray her down real good, and she'll let you ride her all the way home."

"Thanks. How much do I owe you?" he said, looking at the landscape like it was some alien soil, even though he and his friends drove up and down this highway countless times in high school.

"Uh. That'll be sixty, cash. There's a three percent charge if we have to call the garage with a card number. Not sure the exact price of that one. They'd have to calculate it for you."

"No worries. I have cash," Adam said, and pulled the money from his wallet.

"Thank you," Darryl said and patted his shirt pockets. "Hold on there. Before I leave you, I'll give you my card, so you can call us if you have any more trouble."

Darryl climbed into the cab of his truck and searched for a business card. It sounded like a cat attacking a ball of paper, sliding from one side of the truck to the other. Adam averted his eyes before he saw the full moon and fed money into the carwash. Darryl returned with a creased card with rounded off edges. The card had light brown smears across it from where he tried to clean off the grease before he gave it to Adam.

"All right now. You have a good one. Give us a call if you have any more problems and I'll be along directly."

Adam nodded his head and held up the card in a thank you for this gesture. He tossed the card on to the passenger's seat. He wanted to throw it away but decided if he did have another problem in this area, he didn't want to take a chance of another truck driver being worse, and he doubted there was another towing service around, anyway. A strong stream of water shot from the high-pressure hose and cut through the caked-on mud.

After he cleaned off all the visible red clay on his car, he pulled back on to the highway, feeling a little better about his situation. He hadn't run anybody off the road except for himself, and he was right outside of town. At least he hadn't driven in the wrong direction and ended up somewhere on the other side of the state.

As he entered the Scarsville city limits, a sudden feeling of dread passed over him. It felt like a black wave crashed down on him and he couldn't breathe. When the water receded, he took a large gulp of air. He almost became the first man to drown in his car and be nowhere near water. He pulled in large breaths of recycled air and tried to calm himself, but the heavy feeling of anguish did not leave him. Instead, it settled in his stomach and crushed any butterflies floating in there.

The last clump of mud slung off one of the tire rims and distracted him from the aberrant feelings. The hose had worked at getting most of the chunks of southern sludge off his car, but he had missed some stuck inside his rims. Adam drove the last few miles with clumps of dirt throwing the tires off balance before being hurled against the bottom of the car and falling to the hot asphalt. After the final piece smashed into the car, Adam held his breath. He thought it was the final piece that would finally break something in his car, and he'd have to get towed for the second time in one day. He continued holding his breath until he passed Blackwell Place. There were a few things Adam could do before he forced himself to drive down the old dirt road. The Blackwell family farm would be there at the end of the road, waiting for him to return. And so would the lake.

Adam braked hard at a new stoplight. *Ole town is moving up.* The yellow light flashed to warn drivers that soon they'd have to stop. In a town this small, everybody knew about the new light and had their own opinions on what to do with the money instead of wasting it on an intersection that didn't need a red light. The County Commissioner had been trying to get one for years, and it looked like he finally succeeded.

Adam drove around the town square and pulled into the parking lot of what used to be Mama's Diner. A new vinyl banner strapped across Mama's old wooden sign said Darlene's Kitchen. He wasn't hungry, but he should eat since he hadn't had anything since breakfast yesterday, and it allowed him to put off the inevitable for a little longer.

An electric chime rang as he walked into the diner.

"Welcome to ... well, hello there, stranger. It sure has been a while," Darlene said.

Everybody turned to see who had walked through the door but treated Adam's intrusion like a car accident they didn't want anybody to know they were looking at and almost turned away instead of rubbernecking.

"Hey, Darlene. What happened to Mama's?" Adam asked, pointing at the under new management sign in the window.

"Oh, Mama was getting too old to run the place. Got herself into a little trouble with the IRS, so she had to shut the other place down and I had to rename it. We still got the same menu, and she's in the kitchen cooking as long as she can stand it 'fore she sneaks out the back door."

"Everybody's snuck out of Darlene's kitchen at one time or the other," a man yelled from the back and everybody laughed.

"Oh hush, John Williams, before I call Margaret and let her know the last time it was you doing the sneaking."

There were a few muffled laughs, and the restaurant fell silent again.

"You just sit right here and let me know what I can get for you, honey."

"Thanks, Darlene. I'll start with a coffee for now."

"Sure thing, sugar," she said and walked away.

Darlene chastised John when she reached the end of the bar. She continued to use a playful banter, but if nobody were around, she wouldn't have been as lighthearted. Darlene said the menu was the same, but he didn't think she meant literally the same menus. It looked like somebody had cut up a bunch of slips of paper and written Darlene's Kitchen on them and stuck it over mama's name and laminated it. When he looked up from the menu, she was playfully swatting John with her bar towel as she walked back with his coffee.

"Here you go. Have you decided on what you want to eat?"

He was about to order when the door chime interrupted him, and he turned to see his old friend, Dan, walk into the diner. A smile erupted on Adam's face. He hadn't seen or spoken to Dan since he moved to Chicago.

"Hey, Dan. Have lunch with me and we'll catch up."

"No, I gotta go. I'm not hungry anymore."

The smile dissolved.

"Ah, come on, Dan. You still pissed I left town? I had to get out of here."

"Yeah, everything was so damn hard for you. I'm sorry your dad died, but don't think you can come back to town and everything will be like it was before you left. You weren't the only person who was hurting, you were the only one who left."

"I didn't know you had feelings for me like that. Maybe if you'd told me I would've stayed," Adam said to a few snickers.

"Fuck you, Adam," Dan said and turned for the door.

"Hey, Dan, my daughter died. I hope you never have to go through something like that if you ever have kids."

Dan hesitated for a moment, but the only response he gave Adam was the door chime as he left.

"I'll have the hamburger steak with mashed potatoes and green beans, please, Darlene."

Darlene shook her head.

"Bless your heart. You have no idea what's happened since you left."

"No, I haven't heard anything. I tried not to think about this place."

"Well, it's not my business to be telling, but you might want to talk to him."

"Doesn't look like he has too much to say to me. But like you said, it's not really your business," Adam said.

"Well, I was just trying to be helpful. I'll have your meal out directly," she said and walked to the kitchen.

Adam waited for his meal and ate in silence. He felt bad for the way he talked to Darlene and tipped her double. He acted like the scene with Dan hadn't bothered him and he took it out on the wrong person, even though she did sound like she was on Dan's side. Darlene was collateral damage because of Dan's unwillingness to talk to him. If he had sat down, he could have tried to explain why he couldn't stay in Scarsville anymore and why he had left so suddenly. He would have tried to explain it to Dan, but now he wasn't sure he could explain it to himself.

His first meal back in town hadn't lasted as long as he would have liked, but he couldn't hold off going to the funeral home any longer. The Barlow family owned the funeral home, like every-thing else in town. When old man Barlow moved to town with his wife in 1952, they quietly settled down and established them-selves as farmers. By 1961, they owned a used car dealership, a feed and tack store, all the buildings on the town square where Mrs. Barlow had her antique shop, and most of the good farming land in Scarsville and the surrounding area. The one large farm they hadn't bought up was the Blackwell farm, but it wasn't from lack of trying.

When Barlow died in '82, his eldest son, Vernon, took over the family business and Stephen, the youngest, went to school, came home and bought the funeral home from the Shepard family who left town shortly after. About the only thing they didn't own or repeatedly try to buy was the sheriff's department, and some people around town thought they had owned a couple of them over the years.

The façade of the funeral home looked like a larger version of the old mausoleums that scattered the graveyard between the funeral home and the First Baptist Church of Scarsville. He stepped out of the heat and into the cool parlor and felt like he entered an actual mausoleum. The building had four visitation rooms and adjoining chapels. It was a bit much for such a small town, but if they ever needed it, one family could have the two rooms in the front of the building while another family had the two rooms in the back. The administrative offices separated the two sides and created a semblance of privacy while the family grieved.

Adam approached the room on the right side of the hallway and looked in. The last funeral he'd been to didn't have a visitation because there was nobody to visit. They only had an empty casket in the church sanctuary. It was an empty symbol, but it was better than a picture in a cheap gold frame. Tomorrow or the next day, he'd be in one of these rooms, but with past tensions between his family and the Barlow's, he expected to be in the back room whether another family were using the front or not.

A booming voice startled him.

"May I help you, sir?"

"Holy shit. You could try not sneaking up on somebody like that," he said.

"I'm sorry, sir. I can assure you I didn't mean anything by it. Mr?"

"Blackwell."

He wasn't sure why Stephen Barlow talked like he was some highly educated Englishman, when he was part of the same backwoods redneck family as his brother Vernon. Going to mortician school didn't give you culture and it sure as hell didn't make you British.

"Ah, Mr. Blackwell. I was told you might be stopping by. I'm sorry, I didn't recognize you at first. Your brother has adequately handled all of your father's funeral arrangements."

"I'm sure he did, but I wanted to make sure everything was taken care of."

"Yes, all is paid in full. Would you like to see your father?"

"Nah, I'm fine with seeing him at the funeral."

"Are you sure? I understand you have been gone, and it has been a few years since you've seen or talked to him. While you think you don't want to see him, the first time might be a bit overwhelming, and the privacy today could be helpful for you."

"Damn. My brother has a big mouth. Can't wait to tell everybody our dad died, and I wasn't here because I ran off."

"Not his exact words, but it is a small town, so it's not really much of a secret."

Blood rushed to Adam's face. He bet Stephen already saw the red splotches that marred his skin when he got upset. He didn't have any desire to see his father before he died, and he didn't have a desire to see him now that he was dead. Stephen was probably full of it most of the time, but he could be right about Adam fighting his feelings. The last thing he wanted was to start blabbering at the funeral like some prodigal son who returned too late.

"I guess I'll go ahead and see him now and make sure you got the right guy."

"Your brother already did a formal identification, but what-ever you think is best," he said and held out his arm, indicating the way to the basement door. "Then you can get back to other matters. There's a rumor going around you have come back to kick your brother out of the house and sell the land."

The splotches on Adam's face glowed. He wanted to punch Stephen in his smug face but held himself back. The last thing he needed was to be arrested for assaulting one of the Barlows, whether they deserved it or not. Instead, Adam turned around on Stephen fast enough to make him think he was about to hit him and stuck his finger in Stephen's face.

"I don't know how you get off spreading that shit, but I'm not kicking my brother out of the house. And if I am selling the place, I can tell you right now it won't be to your greedy brother."

Stephen threw his hands up in surrender. An office door opened and Stephen's son, Eric, stepped out.

"Everything's fine, Eric. Just a little upset over the loss of his father. No worries. Right, Mr. Blackwell?"

Adam remembered Eric from high school. He was a hothead, but that was mostly because of his little man syndrome. He got worked up over the smallest things and he'd want to fight and ended up getting his ass kicked. It didn't look like he'd grown up much since the last time Adam saw him, and he wanted an excuse to fight. Adam could take him or at least hold his head until he tired out, but he decided to force a sad look on his face and nod slowly before adding a bit of flair.

"Yes. Yes, it's true I'm very distraught over the loss of my father. What ever shall I do?" Adam said and threw his arm over his face, letting himself fall in the direction of the door.

The chill of the basement mortuary quieted him. They had somehow made it even colder down here than in the rest of the building.

"That was a bit on the dramatic side, don't you think?" Stephen asked.

"What? You don't think he bought it?"

Stephen didn't look amused. He pushed his way past Adam

and walked down the stairs to the storage room. Aside from the temperature, the white tile and stainless-steel tables made the room feel cold and antiseptic. Adam hesitated at the door as Stephen walked to the wall of drawers and opened the middle one in the third row.

"You seem to have lost your sense of humor."

"Nah, I was trying to be respectful of my father," Adam said, but that wasn't true. He didn't care about his father. The thought of seeing his daughter on one of these tables drained any humor from his body. Is it worse to see the dead in a place like this or never have the chance to see them at all? Either way, the person was gone, but did knowing where their remains were provide any closure? Adam wanted nothing more than to know where his daughter was, though he doubted he'd ever have the chance to find out if knowing helped the healing process.

Stephen pulled the white sheet back from Phil's face and let it rest halfway down his chest.

"Take all the time you'd like. I'll be in the next room and will close up after you leave."

"Thanks. I won't be long."

The door closed behind him, and Adam wiped his mouth on the back of his arm. His dry and cracked lips burned in the cooler temperature. He stood by his father's side and wanted to feel bad. He tried to summon some sort of emotion, but the scar tissue was too tough. The old man was sixty-three, but the sallow skin and sunken eyes made him look like he had aged twenty years since the day of Grace Ann's funeral. It was probably the guilt of letting his granddaughter drown that caused him to age so quickly. It was no doubt what caused him to jump off the same cliff as Adam's mother had thirty years earlier. Time and distance from his father had not soothed the hatred for the man. He wasn't glad his father was dead and hated he killed himself. It robbed Adam from the satisfaction of knowing he had to live with his incompetence and be reminded of it every day when he woke up and saw the dark, churning grave of Grace Ann.

Adam followed the Y incision on his father's chest until it

disappeared under the sheet. He was tired of trying to elicit an emotion besides hate toward the man who let his world die. It was time to leave.

The sheet twitched as he turned away, and the courage he built up from hating his dad evaporated.

He must have hit the sheet when he moved. The sheet trembled again. Adam looked around the room, waiting for somebody to bust in laughing, but nobody came, and the sheet continued to move.

Adam willed himself to the table and stripped back the sheet and revealed the entire stitched Y on Phil's chest. The movement came from under Phil's skin where the point at which the two arms of the Y met with the stem. The tight stitches were being pushed from the inside. There was something sewn inside Phil's body. All the feeling left Adam's body, and he felt lightheaded. The pulsing continued until what looked like the tip of a black tail forced its way through the stitches. Adam stepped back and prepared to turn and run out the door.

He took one step and his father's hand reached out and grabbed his wrist. Adam shrieked and tried to pull away, but the grip on his arm was too tight. He felt the nails pushing into his skin. The hand held firm as he tried to pull his arm free.

The black tail pushed its way through his father's chest and whipped through the air, lashing out at Adam. Two more tails ripped their way out toward him and joined the first. He continued to fight to free his arm and Phil sat up. The black eel like creatures ripped through his chest and landed on the table and on the floor. They squirmed and gnashed their razor-sharp teeth as the flopped on the white tile.

Adam kicked one of the fish flailing on the floor and it flew against the stainless-steel wall with a moist thump. It laid still like it was dead, and it started writhing again.

Adam tried to yell for help, but all of his words came out a jumbled mess. He hoped Stephen would hear him, but doubted he'd be able to help. He'd probably fall over dead and some of those things would bust out of him too. *The town was cursed.*

Phil slid his legs off the side of the table and let go of Adam's arm. Adam fell to the floor and landed on his ass. Lightning bolts of pain shot up his spine and threatened to come out the top of his head. He put one hand in front of him to defend himself in case any of those things tried to attack him and pushed himself back. Adam's scream stuck in his throat, cutoff, when Phil spoke.

"You think it's all my fault," Phil said.

It sounded kind of like his voice only a waterlogged version of it. Water rattled in Phil's chest as he spoke. Black streams ran down his chin when his mouth moved. Black water poured from the incision in his chest and splashed on the floor reaching out for Adam.

"You think it's all my fault. You told everybody it was my fault."

"It was," Adam choked out.

"You told her it was my fault."

"Told who?"

Phil stood up and took one jagged step toward Adam.

"You told her it was all my fault, and I was the one to blame, but you lied and you know it. You're the one to blame. It was all your fault, and I told her the truth. She knows everything and now, she's coming after you."

"No. It wasn't my fault. You killed her. You killed her you bastard," Adam yelled.

Phil laughed. More of the black fish fell from his sternum with each hideous cackle. They snapped and shrimped their way toward Adam.

He let out a long guttural scream and the door to the room burst open. Adam cowered against the far wall covering his face. A hand grabbed him by the arm and he screamed again.

"Mr. Blackwell. Please, calm down. It's okay. I know it's hard when a loved one passes before we got to make amends."

"He's not dead. He's not dead. That's not him."

"I understand, Mr. Blackwell. This is why I wanted you to see him before the funeral. Now come along and we'll get you some water."

Chapter Five

Adam stood at the wrought-iron gate that led to the town cemetery. He finished the last sip of water in the cone-shaped cup, crushed it, and threw it at the no littering sign hanging from the cemetery gate. The cup bounced off a cartoon bug saying, "don't be a litterbug." The bug looked like a hunched old man waving his walking stick at all potential violators. Adam walked to the closed gate and stuck his face between the bars. He hadn't asked if it was a graveside service or if everything would be in the chapel. He hoped the service was going to be in the funeral home and they would bury him later, but he didn't think he'd be that lucky.

The thought of walking through the cemetery and seeing Grace Ann's empty grave sent a chill down his neck that settled at the base of his spine. The sweet scent of honeysuckle filled the air. Adam took a deep breath to enjoy the fragrance as it floated on a hot breeze, taking him away from his thoughts of death. As he became nose blind to the saccharine flower, he recoiled at the thought of the death and decay they covered.

He had spent enough time at the funeral home, and he didn't want Stephen or Eric to come outside and check on him. Before he got into his car, Adam trotted back to the cemetery gates and picked the balled-up paper cup off the ground.

Small blobs of wet Georgia clay fell from the bottom of the car door. Adam smeared them across the driveway and slipped into the driver's seat. He wasn't ready to go to the house yet, but he couldn't stay at the funeral home any longer. The car engine revved like it wanted to move, and then it died down. Adam could feel the hesitation but turned right and headed to Blackwell Place. There wasn't much in the town to begin with, and even less he wanted to see.

Adam pulled his car off the main road through a cloud of dust left by someone else. Were they coming or going? If it was Brian, he hoped he was going. The longer he put that meeting off, the better. There was a time when he knew every pothole and washed-out spot on the road. He could maneuver his car with his eyes closed, avoiding every obstacle with a quick twitch of the wheel. When his father annoyed the county enough so they would pour new dirt and grade the road, he would start his mental map over, beginning with the spots where loose sand would gather in the curves. The car bumped and jostled its way slowly down the road, and he realized that had been another time. It didn't feel like anything had been down the road since he left. They had allowed it to almost deteriorate to the point of needing a big truck to make it to the driveway.

The Blackwell house was the only one on the road. The Barlows owned some of the surrounding land but didn't have access to it from the main road. As people moved away, Phil bought the land facing the road. Nobody wanted to sell to Vernon Barlow. He was the reason most of them ended up leaving, anyway.

The house didn't have a traditional driveway. Suffocating trees lined the road on both sides and if it weren't for the abrupt dead end twenty yards past the entrance, most cars would keep driving and never realize they missed their turn. When a car pulled into the yard, the driver had to be careful not to clip the mailbox. Adam always said they should move it to the other side of the driveway, but Phil liked it where it was. He said it was easier to get the mail from the driver's side window when he went into town and that the only people that would hit it were the ones that didn't know about it and didn't have no business at the house, anyway. Adam had sideswiped it three times before he was eighteen. Even though it had been two years since he'd been there, Adam gave the mailbox a wide berth as he swung into the yard.

Worn patches of grass and dirt pointed out where to park your car. Adam came to a stop in the same spot he used to park in when he lived at the house. They didn't have assigned spots, but everybody always parked in the same place. Except for those times he and his brother wanted to piss the other off. Neither one ever said anything about it, but they could always tell the other was mad. Phil's beat up truck sat in the same spot it always did under the pecan tree in the front yard. Sitting behind it was a new truck Adam assumed belonged to his brother since it was in his spot.

The house didn't have much curb appeal, but there weren't any curbs out there for the Blackwells to care about. The two-story house was deceptively large. From the outside it looked like a small cottage home that might have three bedrooms, but inside it opened up into a foyer with a den and living room off the to the left. On the right was a dining room with a large country kitchen off the back. Straight down the hall from the foyer was the master bedroom, a smaller bedroom, and the guest bathroom. There were four bedrooms and another bathroom upstairs. Adam and Mandy had the master bedroom with Grace Ann in the room across the hall, and Brian and Phil's rooms were upstairs. There were a lot of people in the house, but they never felt crammed in. That's the main reason Adam never pushed for them to get a house of their own. He and Mandy always said they would build a house somewhere on the property one day. Mandy had her heart set on the three-acre pasture to the left of the main house. Phil had said hundreds of times that he was going to fence it in and let the cows eat it down, but there was always something else to do and he'd end up bush hogging it and let the grass grow back. The pasture was too close to the main house for Adam, but it was also too close to the lake.

He climbed the warped steps and stood on the porch that wrapped around the corner of the house, making the shape of an L. There were a few spots around the window where the white paint flaked off the siding in large pieces. Three gallons of haint blue paint sat by the door. The house definitely needed a fresh coat of paint, but he hoped they hadn't planned on changing the color to light blue, and with so few cans, he hoped they hadn't started painting the back first. He made a note to ask Brian about that and decide if he would need it painted before he tried to sell the house. If he did have it painted, it would be the same color white and not some crazy shade of blue. Under the window beside the door, an area of the porch looked like a puddle of water sat long enough to grow mold on the wooden boards and move up the wall. There were also two small spots on the bottom windowsill. Adam hoped there wasn't a leak in the roof. That would be one more thing he'd have to check into. The longer he looked at the puddle, the more it looked like two tiny footprints were in the middle. That was probably where Phil or Brian had left their wet boots on the porch and it stained the wood.

He pulled his keys out of his pocket, but realized the door was probably unlocked and turned the knob. The door squeaked as it opened. Neither Phil nor Brian ever locked the door, even if they left the house and nobody would be there. They always felt safe and never thought anybody would walk into their house uninvited, despite the state of the world outside of their little town. Uninvited guests didn't visit in their town. At least that's what they always said. The truth was, things like that did happen in their town, but they didn't want to believe it would happen to them. Adam shut the door behind him and locked it. He didn't feel unsafe, but always locked the door because he didn't like the thought of somebody being able to walk in while he was in the shower or the bathroom. He didn't want to die naked or with his pants around his ankles because he didn't hear somebody trying to break in the house.

Adam stood in the foyer and yelled, "Hello? Is anybody home?" A sigh of relief escaped his lips when nobody answered. He wasn't ready to deal with his brother yet. Hopefully he was out working in one of the back pastures and wouldn't be back until later. Adam opened the pantry door, hoping to find something to eat. The shelves were bare except for a few can goods. Cardboard boxes and heat conducting trays crammed the trashcan. A few lay scattered on the floor. Adam's ex-wife, Mandy, was probably the last person to cook a meal in the kitchen. He walked to the freezer and pulled out a box that said it was supposed to be Salisbury steak. After careful deliberation, he threw it back in and slammed the door before it could fall out.

The humidity hadn't waned any when Adam stepped back onto the porch. Like earlier, his shirt stuck to his back, reforming the created bond. The sun sat low in the sky. There would only be an hour or two left of sunlight, and Adam had something he needed to do first.

The barbwire sagged between posts like fruit rusting on the vine. Two rolls of new wire lay on the ground against the posts. It looked like another one of Brian's projects was stacking up. It was obvious that Phil hadn't been of much use lately. Adam pulled tangled horsehair from one of the barbs and wondered how many more projects were ready to go, but Brian would never complete. He lifted the wilted wire and stepped through. The last time he had been in this pasture, the grass stretched halfway up his thigh. The cows must have eaten the grass too close to the ground and were now in another pasture where they could eat. He walked unimpeded in a straight line toward the lake and could see a couple spots of faint yellowed white light, but not as many as there should have been.

The large barn stood watch over the pasture like a sentry station sagged from the years of duty. There was a flicker of white fabric from the side of the barn. Adam watched for more movement and kicked a few black objects on the ground like a child pretending not to be paying attention to what the grownups were doing. The movement reminded him of the plastic attached to the traffic barrel the night before. When it didn't reappear, he assumed he was seeing things again.

He thought he had been kicking rotted mushrooms, but when he looked down, he realized he was punting dried horse apples, as Phil called them, around the pasture. He would then remind Phil that no matter what you called it, like life, in the end it was still horseshit. They used to have conversations all the time that went back and forth like that. Eavesdroppers might think they were arguing, but that was part of their relationship and bond. How they told each other they loved the other. But that was before.

"Hey, brother."

The sudden voice startled Adam. He turned and saw his brother forcing himself out from behind the steering wheel of the Polaris. Brian had always been a big guy, but he looked like he'd put on thirty or forty pounds since Adam saw him last. Brian hitched his pants and scratched his belly. At thirty-four, he was two years younger than Adam, but looked and acted ten years older.

"Admiring the view? Beautiful, ain't it?

"Over there's where I saw my little girl drowned. You sound like dad. No matter what happens out here, it will always be 'God's Country,'" he emphasized the moniker with air quotes.

"Aw, come on Adam. I didn't 'mean nothing' by it," Brian said and used his own air quotes.

"There is no god here. Never has been."

"I'm sorry. I just... I just haven't talked to you since you left. I didn't know what to say. I'm mean shit. Daddy died going over the cliff over there. We all know it's dangerous."

"Maybe you're right. Maybe there is some redeeming beauty in this place," Adam said and started walking closer to the black lake.

"You don't have to be such a dick all the time. Daddy wasn't perfect. None of us are."

Adam wanted to grab Brian by his shirt collar and scream that it was their father who killed his daughter, but he saw the tears Brian was fighting to keep back. Speaking ill of their father's memory probably wasn't the smartest thing for Adam to do right now. He didn't want to fight with his brother. Besides, Brian loomed over him in size, and spent his day sweating in the sun fighting with cows and horses, while Adam spent his day in the air conditioner thinking of reasons not to type. He'd only gotten into one fight with Brian growing up. He couldn't remember what it was over, but he remembered the ass whooping he got, and then the ass whooping they both got from Phil because they were brothers and shouldn't be fighting each other.

Brian sniffed and pulled his cap from his head and rubbed his arm across his face like he was wicking away sweat instead of wiping tears. Adam helped him out by distracting himself with inspecting what remained of a half circle of solar powered garden lights.

The day Grace Ann disappeared, Adam was manic. The sun set behind a distant forest, and he screamed she was afraid of the dark and they needed to find her. Brian put his arm around him and tried to console him. Adam pushed his brother back and punched him in the mouth. He towered over Brian as he lay on the ground rubbing his jaw and told him not to touch him again. Adam went to the house and ripped every garden light that illumi-nated the path to the swimming pool out of the ground. Every-body watched in a sympathetic awe as he forced the plastic steaks in the ground, all while shouting that she was afraid of the dark and needed a nightlight. The nightlights soon became a sad vigil and a reminder of where she went into the water. Now there were three of the eight lights left. Adam kicked the top of one of crushed ones, and it rolled into the lake. The light didn't make a noise and there were no ripples in the water. Adam thought it strange and walked toward the water when Brian stopped him.

"Them damn cows go wherever the hell they want to. Don't care what they trample. Daddy told me to get some more lights last week, but I hadn't done it yet. Meaning to though."

"No worries. I'll pick some up tomorrow at the hardware store. Speaking of which, what's up with the paint on the porch. He wasn't going to have you paint the house blue, was he?"

"No. It was weird. He asked me a couple weeks ago to paint the ceiling on the porch that color. I hadn't gotten to it yet. I had planned on painting it the day he died. Not sure why he wanted it that color, though."

"Some people believe that ghosts are afraid of water, so they paint the ceiling that shade of blue to scare them away from the house."

"Daddy wasn't the type to believe in stuff like that."

"No, but all the ghosts around here seem to like the water, anyway."

Brian furrowed his brow and ticked his head to the left like a chicken would turn its head. Adam knew that look. That was the look he gave when a statement confused him, but he wanted to make it look like he was thinking it over. When he decided he'd thought enough, he would change the subject or leave, like nothing was ever said.

"Hey look. I hate to run, but I gotta date tonight. Well, it's not really a date, but she wanted to cook me dinner seeing as how I was the only one out here. I wouldn't have said yes had I known you was going to be here, but I didn't expect to see you."

"Nah, don't worry about it. Go ahead. I probably wouldn't be much company, anyway. Who's cooking for you?

"Candy Barlow," Brian said and looked at the ground.

"Seriously?"

"Come on, now you know they ain't all like that."

"Close enough."

"I know, but she's so pretty, and you know I've had a crush on her since school."

"I know you have. Just be careful. We have some things we need to talk about tomorrow."

"Okay, then. I'll see you tomorrow. But I done took care of everything for Daddy. There's nothing for you to worry about," Brian said.

Adam watched as his brother ran off like a kid who was just told he could go out and play with his best friend. It was true. He didn't think Candy would try to talk Brian into anything he didn't want to do, like selling the land to her uncle. But it was strange that she had an interest in Brian now that their father was dead. Of course, if she were after the land, she'd be in for a big surprise when she found out Brian didn't own any of it. By the way Brian was acting, Adam would have guessed that he didn't know what their dad's will said either, but Mr. Roper had said Brian wasn't too happy when he'd found out. Brian was acting comfortably content in assuming that everything would be his since he stayed at home. It wouldn't surprise Adam if Phil had told Brian all of that and then never had his will changed. He was glad that conversation was going to wait until morning. He still hadn't figured out what he was going to tell his brother.

The Salisbury steak tasted like the cardboard box it was entombed in, and he was sure there was a piece of the plastic film that was MIA. He washed the fork he used, put it back in the drawer, and threw away his Diet Dr. Pepper can.

There wasn't much for him to do, so he decided to find a place to sleep for the night. Phil and Brian had converted the bedroom he and Mandy shared into a storage room. It was weird Phil didn't decide to use the bigger room as his own when Mandy moved out, but he probably didn't want to sleep across the hall from Grace Ann's old room. The more Adam thought about it, the more he was glad there wasn't a bed in there. He turned the light off and shut the door.

Adam wiped the tears from his face and rubbed his hand across her name stenciled in neat letters in a crooked line at a six-year-old's height on the door. A black wave of emotion flooded his body and Adam realized this had been a mistake. He shouldn't have stayed here. He didn't know why he thought he could, when he had fled the house for the same reason. It was too late to try the one motel in town, and it always reminded Adam of the Bates Motel. Maybe he could have stayed with Dan if he had tried to explain to him and apologized instead of being a jerk. Adam stomped up the stairs and opened the first door on the right. Luckily, his father still kept it as a guest room. If the only bed to sleep in had been Phil's, Adam would have taken his chances with Norman and his mother.

Adam lurched awake. Sweat poured down his face. He had the reoccurring dream about the day Grace Ann fell into the water. Except this time, she didn't fall in. Something long and black snaked its way over the bank and through the tall grass. When she looked up to call for her him, it snatched her into the water and held her under. It moved her to the other side of the lake, and he couldn't find her when he jumped in after her. The creature didn't let Phil off the hook. He still should've been watching her. If Phil knew that thing lived in the water, Grace Ann's death was still his fault and he'd been putting everybody in danger every time they were close to the lake.

Whatever kind of animal it was, it didn't look like the ones he saw earlier at the funeral home, but what if they were both hiding in the lake? Adam shivered at the thought. But that was crazy. Those things were a hallucination brought on by stress, and the black thing was a dream. They didn't exist, and Phil didn't get up off that table.

Maybe he was crazy.

There wasn't anything in the lake. Nothing big enough to pull anybody into the water and hold them under at any rate. There was one more difference between the dreams. While Adam was thrashing around in the water, there was something running through the pasture. The swish of the dry grass sliced through the air and cut through the din of splashing water as it brushed against the approaching person. At least he had hoped it was a person. Then he heard the solid thud of feet pounding the ground as they drew closer. The thud morphed into the sound of feet running on hardwood floors.

A door slammed downstairs, and the crash echoed through the

house. Adam choked on his spit and wrestled free from the bed sheets. Somebody was running around in the house. Maybe Brian was home and making a lot of noise after a few drinks, but the steps were too close together. Whoever it was had a short stride. Maybe Brian had brought Candy home.

There was a quick flash of movement by Adam's door. He jumped back, and the headboard slammed against the wall. Hadn't he closed the door when he went to bed? The person making all the noise had been quiet enough so he couldn't hear them when they came up the stairs. There was a high-pitched squeal that made Adam flinch, and then the feet ran down the hall.

Adam jumped out of bed and slid across the floor and fell back against the bed. His feet were wet. He clicked on the lamp beside the bed. Waterlogged footprints were all over the floor. He jumped back on the bed and pulled his feet off the floor in case somebody was waiting under the bed to grab him. When he went to bed, he only pulled back enough of the comforter and sheets for him to slide into one side. He slid his arm to the other side of the bed and yanked it back. The place where his arm had been was a puddle of black water that looked like the partial outline of a body. The pool of water moved and reflected a blue sheen in the light of the lamp. Adam looked at the pillow beside his and saw the dirty outline of a child's head.

Adam's heart pounded and threated to burst through his ribcage. The rapid blood pressure made his head throb. His breath caught in his throat. He didn't know what to do or where to go. A loud scream pulled him from his internal fight-or-flight argument.

Whatever had slept in the bed beside Adam ran down the hall toward the stairs and his room. He jumped to his feet and ran to the door. Had he thought about it, he would have stayed where he was. His feet hit another puddle, and he slid into the doorway. Now the intruder was running down the stairs. He was going to lose them, but scared he might catch them, too. If they left on their own, no reason to call the cops, and he'd talk to Brian about locking the door when he came in at night.

He pulled himself through the doorway as a thump followed by shattered glass filled the house. They were going out the front door. Adam forced himself to move faster down the stairs and surged through the open door to a symphony of country crickets.

The trunk on his car was open and sheets of paper floated gently on the breeze and littered the ground. He didn't remember bringing a manuscript with him to work on. Adam ran out into the dew-covered grass and caught one of the floating papers and read it. His legs went limp and the same tingling pinprick sensation a person gets when their arm or leg falls asleep covered his entire body. Adam had been scared plenty of times in his life, but this was the first time something terrified him to the point of paralysis.

Adam snatched another one of the spiraling pages from the air. *Eventually, the Black Rapids will claim us all,* covered the sheet of paper on both sides. A strong gust of wind blew from the direction of the lake. It picked up the scattered papers and swirled around Adam in a paper tornado. Through the freight train chugging around him, Adam could hear a faint voice rising. At first, the voice was unidentifiable, but as it grew in volume, he could tell it was the voice of a little girl giggling like the typhoon surrounding him was a practical joke. Tiny fingers swept across the back of his neck and flipped his hair. When he turned around, the only thing he saw was the swirling paper surrounding him. He recognized the laugh. It couldn't be her.

He tried to push through but pulled his hand back. A piece of paper sliced across the lifeline on his palm. He wrapped his hand in the tail of his shirt and tried to squat and create a lower center of gravity when the papers stopped circling and flew on the wind to the lake. The flying papers whipped across his exposed skin and sliced like tiny razors.

Adam collapsed. Through half-closed eyes he saw the silhouette of a little girl spinning in her dress. He knew it couldn't be her, but reached for her and called out, "Grace Ann," before passing out.

Brian found him in the same spot when he returned the next morning.

Chapter Six

Eric Barlow killed the rumble of his engine and jumped out of his monster four-wheel-drive truck. He had to be careful to clear the drop step on his way down. One drunken night led to an emergency room visit when he made it home without too much incident, only to have his hip catch the step on the way down. The bump changed his off-balance trajectory and his head collided with the step.

The next morning, he woke up in a hospital bed with a concussion. Uncle Vernon waited beside the bed while his father sat in the corner. Stephen worried about his son's health and the impending prognosis of the violent hit he'd received.

Vernon towered over his nephew, showing him how small he was and told him he was lucky he'd made it home and hadn't knocked himself out cold climbing out of that ridiculous truck at the bar or gas station.

Eric didn't remember the gas station, but he didn't really remember much from that night. Everything was hazy and loud. He did remember one thing from his hospital stay. Vernon threatened to send him away and cut him out of any family business if he did anything to embarrass the family like that again. Stephen stood to object, but Vernon turned on his brother with the same venom and he cowed him back to the corner.

Now Eric stood on the porch of the bright white plantation home and ran through the events of the past week trying to think of anything he did or didn't do that would get him summoned to his uncle's house. He leaned back against a column as he waited for the housekeeper to get to the door.

The door slid open on lubricated hinges. Maria was almost as old as his uncle and had been with the family since she came to this country forty years ago. Eric couldn't remember where she was from, but assumed it was from Mexico. It was all the same to him. She was a bit slow moving, but she still kept a clean house and as Vernon told everybody, she had never stolen from the family and trust was worth more to him than how hot his dinner was. Eric believed him, but he also believed Maria would be out of a job if the house wasn't spotless when somebody showed up, invited or not.

"Hello, Maria. It looks like I have been summoned by the master of the house again."

Maria didn't laugh. She looked over her shoulder and said, "Good morning, Mr. Eric. Your uncle is in the dining room having his breakfast," and moved out of the way to let him in.

Eric took his boots off at the door. He felt like he was in school again being called to the principal's office and didn't want his detention changed to suspension because he got dirt on the rug. His feet sank into the plush hallway runner. It was still the same dark burgundy as the day they laid it in the hall when he was a child. There weren't any stains or worn patches from heavy traffic on it anywhere. Eric stood outside the oak framed doorway to the dining room and gave himself a few more seconds to come up with an excuse for something he didn't know he shouldn't have done.

"Damn it, boy. Get in here. The master of the house can't talk to you if you're in the hall, and I don't feel like yelling. I haven't finished my coffee yet."

The weight of worry increased as he realized Vernon had heard him at the door. Hopefully, the suspension wouldn't turn into expulsion. He took a deep breath and walked into the room. Vernon sat at the end of a long dining room table that had enough place settings for fourteen people. A dish of eggs over easy, and a plate of bacon and a large bowl of grits crowded his end of the table. He tore a biscuit in half and sopped up the remaining egg yolk on his plate.

Uncle Vernon always reminded him of one of the heckling critics from the Muppets. He thought the Muppet's name was Statler but couldn't be sure. The name didn't matter. Eric enjoyed the visual. It distracted him from the continuous onslaught of insults and diatribes from the man. The old man shoved the biscuit into his mouth and slurped from his coffee cup. Eric hadn't had a chance to grab anything to eat before his dad called to tell him Vernon wanted to see him right away. There was more than enough food for him, but he knew Vernon wouldn't offer and there was no way he was going to ask him.

"Didn't think I could hear you, did ya? I may be getting old, but my hearing is as good as it ever was. I knew it was you when I heard that damn truck of yours."

"I'm sorry, Uncle—"

"I don't care none for what you got to say. I only called you here, 'cause I got something for you do to."

Eric stood quietly, waiting for the assignment he knew he wouldn't want to do but didn't have a choice.

"I'm sure even you have realized that your new tenant down at the funeral home is Phil Blackwell."

"Yes, sir."

"I'm also reasonably sure you know that I've tried to buy his land many times over the years, and he wouldn't sell it. Wasn't too nice about how he said no either."

"Yes, sir."

"Well, I need that land. I called Earl Roper yesterday, and he told me Phil left everything to his boy, Adam. Your daddy told me he spoke with Adam yesterday, and he didn't think there was any way he would ever sell it to me."

"Probably not, but I don't know what I can do about it."

"You went to school with him, didn't you?"

"Yeah, but we weren't friends. We didn't really get along."

"And I'm sure it was all his fault for not liking you, huh?"

"I—"

"It don't matter none, no way. He don't know me 'cept by reputation, so he's not even going to talk to me. He might at least open the door for you. I need you to go over there and talk to him for me."

"He's not going to listen to me. I don't know how to negotiate."

Eric gripped the top of the backrest on the chair nearest Vernon.

"Hell, boy, I know you don't know how to do too much of nothing. I don't need you to strike a deal with the man. You liable to end up selling everything I got to him. I need you to convince him to hear me out. Just get him to the table. I'll do the rest."

"How am I supposed to do that?" Eric said, leaning over the backrest, pleading with his uncle.

"I don't much care how you do it. Talk him into it. Muscle him into it. You're scrappy for a little fella. It don't matter. Just get him here. Now, go ahead and go, I gotta feed the hogs. Maria went and made too much food again. I ought to start taking it out of her pay."

Eric wasn't finished with his uncle. He felt like yanking him up out of his chair and throwing him across the table for the shot at his height. The comment about the food was for him too. While he had him on the table, he would pour the bowl of grits over his face and shove the rest of the eggs down his throat. Vernon slid back from the table and walked out of the room. Eric wasn't finished with his uncle, but his uncle was finished with him.

Chapter Seven

Charlotte didn't sleep well. She kept tossing and turning while thinking about Adam and his father. When she met Adam, he was lying on a park bench beside her parking spot outside the school. At first, she thought he was like all the other homeless men who frequented the area until the school resource officer chased them off. A high squeal escaped her mouth when he sat up quickly and startled her. He apologized for scaring her and went to leave when she stopped him.

"Hey, you don't look like you're from around here," she said, kicking herself for not jumping in the car and locking all the doors. Downtown Chicago wasn't the place to talk to random strangers lying on the benches, but he was cute. She then chastised herself for thinking he was cute, because downtown Chicago was definitely not the place to be picking up strange men.

"No, I'm not. I was just taking a walk and got lost, so I thought I'd sit and watch the birds for a while. Guess I fell asleep," he said and smiled.

It was a sad smile, and he was forcing it a bit much. She could barely pick out the hint of an accent, but she couldn't tell where it was from.

"Well, this isn't exactly the best part of town to be taking a nap in. Where do you live? I'll see if I can give you directions."

"I'm new to town. I'm staying at the Radisson."

"Oh, I think that's a few blocks away. I can give you a ride if you'd like."

What was she doing? This is the craziest thing she had ever done. This town was full of crazy people, and she was about to let one of them into her car. She ran-skipped around to the driver's side and opened her door, so she could make a quick getaway. But she paused before getting in the car.

"That's nice of you, ma'am, but really, I'd hate to impose, and I sense you're a little hesitant. I don't want to make you uncomfortable. You could just point me in the right direction if it makes you feel better."

Ma'am? He called her ma'am. He definitely wasn't from around here. His politeness won her over, and she waved him over to the car. He was too polite to be a psycho-killer. So was Ted Bundy, but this guy wasn't asking for help. She slid into her seat and waited for him to join her.

In the end, he wasn't Bundy, and he invited her to join him for dinner in the hotel restaurant. She didn't see his room that night, but she did two nights later and now here she was cleaning his writing desk. It amazed her how a man who strived to keep himself clean and washed his hands religiously and had a place for everything could be such a slob when it came to his work area. She mopped around the legs of his desk and tried not to knock off the stacks of books he had on each corner. Two empty pop cans, piles of papers and junk mail he planned on shredding and an empty coffee mug that said "Stop looking at this mug and write something," above a person bent over a typewriter, crowded the laptop computer that sat in the middle of the desk. The coffee cup had a mildew smell and fuzz in the bottom. But she was not going to try to straighten up his desk again after he got so mad at her the last time.

She was just going to clean around it as much as she could and plead with him when he returned to clean it up a bit. When he returned? If he returned? That was the question she didn't want asked. She knew it didn't make sense to him when she told him he couldn't leave. The unasked question was in his eyes. He thought she sounded crazy, and maybe she was, but she had a bad feeling about him leaving. Call it intuition is what she would have said if he'd asked, but paranoid is what he would have called it. He probably thought she was jealous that he would meet up with his ex-wife who, though they were divorced, didn't have closure with their relationship.

She didn't worry he would try to rekindle a flame already burned out, or in their case, a wick cut off at its base. What she was worried about was his propensity to run away from his problems. Their relationship had been rocky lately, but it was always peaks and valleys with Adam. The death of his daughter caused him to drop everything and run away, and recently, he dropped his agent because he didn't like the way he was doing things. He didn't tell him why. He just fired the guy and moved on. He was lucky he found another agent so quickly. He said it was because his guy was burning a lot of bridges lately, and other agents were circling his client list like sharks waiting for somebody to fall overboard. There were also a few online colleges he was adjuncting for that wanted him to return, but he decided not to go back to them. Now that she had time to think about everything, she realized some of those were a bit of a stretch, but she also didn't believe that should diminish her feelings of abandonment when he first told her he was leaving for a few days.

It might have been the fumes, but cleaning always made her think clearly. She liked the scent of bleach. It made everything smell clean. After mopping under his desk, Charlotte stood on her tiptoes and stretched her back as far as she could. It felt great to finish mopping and force the pain from being stooped over from her body. She raised her hands over her head and closed her eyes. The sudden movement made her lightheaded, and her head rocked like an unmoored boat on the ocean.

She waited for the feeling to pass but lost her balance and fell back against the wall. The impact of her body against the thin wall rattled Adam's brag shelf, and it fell, spilling all of his published books onto the floor. She cursed herself and began picking the few up that landed on the floor. Luckily for her, she had moved the armchair against the wall earlier, so she could mop under it, and most of the books fell on it.

She picked the board up off the floor and placed it back on its wall hangers. She told Adam to screw the boards to the hangers when he hung the shelves, but he said they'd be fine. There was a slight bow in the middle of the board from the weight of all the books he stacked sideways, and now it wouldn't lie flat on the hangers. Instead of trying to balance the heavy books on the ends of the board, she decided to look for some screws and the drill and fix it herself.

The edge of the cherry wood box caught her toe as she walked by the chair. She held in a deep breath and fought to hold back the building scream. Her chest burned as she held in her breath, realizing what she kicked. The air slid through her parted lips as she picked up the box containing the manuscript for Adam's first book. It was the one book of his that he would never let her read. He said it scared him. Considering how horrific his other books were, she never wanted to read it if it scared him. He said it felt like parts of it were coming true and from another part of his life that he'd blocked out.

She bit her lip as she inspected the box. It was a shame for nobody to read it, ever. Maybe if she read it and it was really good, she could figure out how to let him know. That might be what he needed to get out of his funk for good. Still, she felt like there was a betrayal on her part for reading something he never wanted anybody to read. She sat down with the book in her lap and read.

Eventually, the Black Rapids will claim us all.

Chapter Eight

ootsteps crashed down the hall. Adam opened one eye toward the closed bedroom door. Somebody was running through the house again. Like last night. Adam sat up in the bed. He was in the spare bedroom upstairs and still dressed in his clothes from the night before. How did he get there? The last thing he remembered was paper swirling around him. Somebody was running through the house. Like they were doing right now. He jumped out of bed and ran to the door and put his ear to it. He strained to hear the footsteps again, but they were going down the steps. The steps sounded different. They sounded like heavy boots walking heel to toe, and not like little feet scurrying on tiptoe, right? Or was that what he was telling himself so he wouldn't feel ridiculous in the daylight? He thought he'd seen Grace Ann, but whoever broke into the house wanted him to think he was going crazy. Maybe it had been one of Vernon's guys trying to scare him so he would hurry up and sell to him and go back home. Anger overtook the fear.

The hallway was clear, but someone was banging around in the kitchen. Adam crept down the stairs and grabbed an unopened bottle of whiskey from the dining room buffet. He rushed into the kitchen, poised to strike the intruder.

Brian leaned against the kitchen counter, eating a bowl of cereal.

"You plan on taking me out with that?"

Caught by surprise, Adam froze. After the few seconds it took to recognize his brother, Adam sheepishly looked at the bottle and lowered his weapon.

"No. I was going to take out whoever broke into the house last night."

"Well, I didn't do no breaking and entering. I just used my key. Surprised I still had it on my key ring."

Adam sat the bottle on the counter.

"Last night somebody was running through the house and woke me up. I chased them outside. I thought I saw ..." *Grace Ann* "I thought I saw them, but couldn't tell who it was or what they looked like. When did you get home?"

"I ain't the one that beat you up."

"I didn't say I got beat up."

"I got home early this morning, and you was laying out in the front yard. Your face and hands were all cut up, so I put you to bed," Brian said, and slurped the milk from his cereal bowl.

"I was laying in the yard?"

"Yeah, it was strange too, 'cause I had to help Daddy out of the yard like that the day before he died. He was babbling about seeing somebody too."

Brian shifted his weight and wouldn't look at his brother. Adam knew there was something he wasn't telling him. If somebody had done the same thing to his father, maybe they were after the house like he thought. Anybody could look at the place and tell it was going downhill. Maybe they were trying to rush the inevitable so Phil would sell. Brian was still fidgeting at the sink.

"What aren't you telling me?"

"Ah, it's nothing. Daddy was drinking a lot before he passed. He was seeing a lot of things that weren't there. It's really nothing to worry yourself over 'cause it's not possible."

"If it's no big deal, then it shouldn't bother you to tell me."

"Well, just remember, Daddy was sick. Like I said, if he hadn't jumped off that cliff, he would have drank himself to death soon enough."

"Okay, I get it," Adam said. He was starting to get impatient with his brother, like he was trying to drum up suspense by holding out on him. A growing fear was fighting its way out from the pit of his stomach and spreading like a cancer to the other parts of his body as he anticipated what Brian was about to tell him.

"Fine, I'll tell you. But you can't get upset with me. I told you he wasn't right."

"Scouts' honor," Adam said, holding up the Boy Scout salute.

Brian rolled his eyes.

"The morning I picked him up out of the yard, he was going on about seeing somebody, but he wouldn't tell me who it was. Finally I'd had enough with pleading with him, so I put him to bed, and right before I walked out the door, he told me it was Grace Ann he'd been chasing, that she was back, and wasn't happy with him or you and she would get you back home."

All the air rushed from Adam's lungs. He felt gutted and stumbled back into the dining room and fell into a chair. Phil had similar experiences before he died. Adam didn't know how to process this new information. Last night he heard somebody running through the house, and when he followed them outside, he thought he saw his dead daughter. Adam squeezed his fingernails into his palm. The nail of his ringer finger slid along the edge of the paper cut on his palm. The harder he squeezed, the deeper the nail slid under the flap of skin. The stinging sensation made him stop and look at his hands. Blood welled up around the newly opened cuts and ran down his wrist.

The sight of the blood reminded Adam of the paper tornado. Somebody had driven his father crazy, and now they were trying to do the same thing to him. But nobody had ever read his first book except for him. There was no way for them to know what the first line was. He moved his hand to his cheek and ran his fingers delicately across the slashes on his face. They were as real as the ones on his hands. The dull ache he had since waking flared with a rising heat.

Brian walked into the dining room with a wet washcloth.

"Here. Clean yourself up before you get blood all over the place."

"I gotta get outta here, Brian. I can't stay here with everything that is going on. This place already drove Phil crazy. I can't let it do the same thing to me."

"Just calm down and try to relax. You're probably worked up because the last time you were here you lost somebody you loved and now, you're back because of somebody else you loved."

"No, that's not it. I hate Phil. He was the reason I left and now, he's the reason I'm back. Either way, it's his fault."

"It was an accident. Dad never would have done anything to hurt her, and you know that," Brian said, standing over Adam.

"If it wasn't his fault, then why did he kill himself?" Adam asked, stepping up to his brother.

"You're right. Dad's death wasn't no accident. He died 'cause you left. All he ever wanted was for you to forgive him. It weighed on him."

"That might be true, but we have a bigger issue we need to talk about. Right now, we need to talk about what to do with the house."

Brian took a step back like he was preparing to take a hit, and then he squared his shoulders for an attack. This wasn't how Adam wanted all of this to play out. He hoped they'd be getting along, and he could break it to his brother easily, instead, somebody had broken into the house and caused an argument and now he was going to have to bring it up like a slap to the face. It didn't matter how you did it, either way it would sting.

"What do you mean, what we're going to do with the house?"

"I need to sell the house."

Adam took a step toward Brian in an act of consolation, but Brian bucked up and bowed his chest out.

"You can't just come in here and sell the house because you want to."

"Actually, I can do that. He left everything to me."

Brian wiped tears from his face.

"Dad wouldn't have done that. He wouldn't have left everything to you and left me with nothing."

"I guess he forgot to cut me out of the will. Or he did it as a way to force me to come back to Georgia."

"Looks like he succeeded," Brian sneered.

"I guess so, because I wouldn't have come here for any other reason than to sell this place and let it be somebody else's problem."

"That don't make sense. I did everything for him. I kept this place running while he hid from the world," Brian yelled, pointing his finger at Adam. "And you. You just ran away from everything because you want to blame Dad and God and everybody else for her death. You walked out on your wife."

Adam put his hands up, palms out, and walked toward Brian.

"Look, you need to calm down. This isn't doing anybody any good. Just have a seat and let's talk about this."

"Don't fucking tell me what to do. You don't give a shit about this place and you don't give a shit about me. You only want to sell this place 'cause it's one more way for you to stick it to Dad now that he's dead. You blame me too, don't you? That's why you want to kick me out. You want to go back to Chicago and leave me down here homeless because I didn't blame Dad for everything that happened.

"That's not true."

"The hell it's not. You blame everybody for your problems, but you don't realize you're the one that's everybody else's problem."

Adam put his hand on Brian's shoulder to try to comfort him, and Brian knocked it off.

"I don't blame you for anything and I don't plan on leaving you on the streets. I want to sell this place and split the money with you."

"I don't want no money. I want to live here and work the farm like I always have."

"This place is too big for you to take care of by yourself. You could get a smaller farm anywhere you want with the money we could get for this place."

"It's not too big."

"Brian, you have to be realistic. Look around here. You have rolls of barbwire piled up waiting for you to fix the fence, and they're already starting to rust. The barn doors look like they're about to fall off and you have paint waiting on the porch. It might have been a weird request from Dad, but you still hadn't gotten to it and the rest of the house needs painting too. And those are only a few of the things I've noticed since I got here yesterday."

Brian walked through the dining room and stood in the foyer. He put his hands on his hips and looked down at the ground. Maybe something he said knocked around in Brian's big head long enough for it to make sense. He didn't want to do anything to hurt his brother, but Brian wasn't being logical about the situation, he was being emotional. Adam had always been the logical one of the two. He liked to have fun as much as the next country boy, but he liked to think things through before he jumped. Not Brian. He wanted to go in hard and figure things out later.

When they were younger, Brian and his friend Davy Andrews could have been killed while they were playing on a rope swing at Davy's house. The boys threw the rope around an old tree limb that hung over the creek that ran through the Andrews land. They both taunted Adam when he wouldn't get on the swing and splash into the creek. He didn't think the tree limb would hold any of them and there was kudzu covering the bank, working its way up the side of the tree that anything could be hiding under.

After teasing his older brother for a few minutes, Brian knew Adam wasn't going to do it if he didn't want to. Brian jumped on the rope and swung out over the water. On the way back, the limb snapped. The rocky bank knocked all the air from Brian's lungs, and he couldn't move. He landed beside the kudzu and a foot away from a coiled cottonmouth. The snake raised and showed the boys it's soft white throat. Adam ran toward the snake and kicked it like a soccer ball as it prepared to strike his brother. The day was over after that. On the way home, Brian swore Adam to secrecy. Their parents had warned them hundreds of times about the dangers of playing in or near large areas of kudzu. Later that evening, after they settled their nerves, they sat down to watch Phil's favorite movie, *Lonesome Dove*. Everything was fine until Sean O'Brien became the first to die on the cattle run when he got tangled up with a nest of water moccasins. Both boys started to cry and hug each other. Phil never said anything, only shook his head.

Adam stood in the foyer behind Brian and cleared his throat. Finally, Brian looked up at Adam and said, "What did you even come for? You could have destroyed everything on the phone like you did with your marriage. Candy was right about you. She said you were up to something, otherwise you wouldn't be here."

"It's dangerous."

"What?"

"The lake. It's dangerous. We've always been told to stay away from it. And every time we've gone near it, something bad has happened."

"There's nothing wrong with that lake. All water can be dangerous if you're not careful."

"You know that's not true. You know there's more to that lake than just water."

Brian opened the door and turned back to his brother.

"If it's so dangerous, why would you want to put that on anybody else by selling it to 'em? Sounds like your typical selfish bullshit to me. You blame Dad for Grace Ann's death, but it's your fault he's dead."

Brian walked out the door and slammed it behind him.

Chapter Nine

Adam decided to skip the visitation. He didn't feel like listening to people he didn't know say, "I'm sorry for your loss," and "he was a good man," or any other cliché they could come up with. Most of the time, people used those phrases because they didn't know what else to say. But that was only part of the reason why he didn't want to go. The other part, maybe the biggest, was that he was afraid. He didn't want to admit it, but he was afraid that Phil would come after him again. He was afraid Phil would climb out of his coffin the way he climbed off the mortician's steel table and come after him with those black things squirming inside his body and pushing their way out of his incisions. It would be bad enough to see everybody's reaction, but what if nobody else reacted? What if he was the only person who saw them? If you're paranoid, they can still be after you, so did that mean even if you were the only one to see them, they could still hurt you? Everybody would think he was crazy. Maybe he was. Either way, Adam wasn't taking any chances.

He skirted past the visitation room and hid in the corner of the vestibule while the friends and mourners filed by to wait for the family procession in the chapel. There were a lot of people. A lot more than he had expected, anyway. He recognized many of the faces as they funneled into the chapel, which was one of the side effects of living in a small town.

He caught a glimpse of one familiar face he hadn't expected. At first, it was only the radiant reflection of her corn silk hair bouncing off a sea of black fabric threatening to swallow her up. He pulled himself up straight and did a comical job of hiding behind a drooping peace lily as his ex-wife, Mandy, passed. She was the last person he wanted to see while he was down here. Until now, the thought of having to see her or interact with her at all had not crossed his mind. The last time he saw her, she was sitting on the top step of the porch, in a summer dress that he thought was way too bright and sunny for the storm they were facing, with her head in her hands crying because he was leaving. She didn't see him wave goodbye.

Adam flipped the lily bloom out of his face and headed for the door. Brian stepped out of the visitation room with their great uncle Marty. Or was it Murphy? He couldn't remember what his name was, nor was he sure the guy was a great uncle, only that he was a distant relative he'd met at a family reunion when he was a child.

"Surprised you made it. I figured you'd be too busy talking with a realtor to bother showing up for the funeral. Can't say I blame you for not coming to the visitation. Might be awkward having to talk to people who still loved Daddy."

"You're right. That's why I didn't come. And now I've realized it was a mistake to come here for the service too."

"Yeah, but that ain't on a count of everybody being here. I saw you hiding behind the plant over there. You was hiding from Mandy," Brian said with a laugh. "Bet you didn't expect to see her, did ya?"

"No, I didn't, and I really wouldn't like to talk about it right now."

"You ain't nothing but a little bitch, you know that Adam? Always running away from your problems even when you was the one that caused 'em," Brian said to Adam and then to the man he was holding up, "Sorry for my language Uncle Cliff, he just gets me so riled up."

Cliff? He was way off. He never would have guessed. Uncle Cliff absentmindedly patted Brian on his forearm.

"Look, it was a mistake to come here. I see that now. I need to leave. I'll see you later. We still need to talk."

"What you need to do is show some damn respect. Man up and go in there and sit with the family. You don't have to talk to nobody."

Brian was right. He needed to man up. There was nothing for him to be ashamed of. None of these people had been through anything like he had. None of them except for Mandy, and she wasn't going to welcome him with open arms. Brian was also wrong. Adam had no reason to show any respect to the man who let his daughter die. Phil was gone, and while he wouldn't say he was happy about it, he sure as hell didn't care. Adam made his decision years ago. Now he needed to go in there and prove to them, and himself, that the decision was the right one, and it didn't matter what they had to think or say about it.

The chapel was quiet as Adam walked down the middle of the pews. He was at the end of the procession and ninth in line. The only sounds in the quiet room were Uncle Cliff's shuffling feet and the distant buzz of a dust clogged box fan. Mandy sat on the end of the fifth row. Adam didn't turn to look at her as he passed, but he could see her turn and do a double take when she saw him. There was a small amount of relief in knowing she had seen him now and the shock was over, and he didn't have to face her directly. He only had a chance for a quick peek, so he couldn't easily read her facial expression. Did she look mad? Sad? Or was it simply a look of shock? It certainly wasn't a happy look.

There was only room for eight people per pew, so Adam ended up sitting in the second row, alone. He propped his arm on the carved oak armrest and the felt reserved for family flag fell to the floor. He felt everybody's eyes on him as he contemplated whether or not it would cause a scene or distraction if he reached out in the aisle and picked it up. The preacher stood and began to speak, and Adam snatched the placeholder off the ground.

Under normal circumstances, Phil would have had a graveside funeral, but the gravedigger the Barlows used had to go out of town suddenly due to a family illness and the back-up digger was on vacation in Biloxi, Mississippi. The regular guy would be back in the morning and bury Phil. A slight embarrassment for Stephen Barlow, and if it hadn't been for the chance to mortify a Barlow, Adam wouldn't have cared, but if he saw Stephen, he would play it up to be a bigger deal just to see the guy squirm.

Grace Ann's funeral was held in the chapel as well, but it wasn't because a laborer's mother was in the hospital and his drinking buddy was trying to hit it big in a casino. It was because they never found her body. They didn't need to have a graveside service. Mandy had a tombstone put in front of a plot bearing Grace Ann's name in case they found her, and so Mandy would have somewhere to visit.

Adam had never seen the tombstone. Dan and two funeral home employees dragged him out of the chapel during Grace Ann's service. He had stepped up to the pulpit and carefully unfolded the eulogy he'd written for his daughter. His fingers slid across the edge and gripped the polished wood like he was about to dig in and deliver a fire and brimstone sermon that would make Jonathan Edwards proud. Hundreds of faces packed the room. There were even a few he didn't recognize. Funerals for children always brought extra people out, especially if they'd died in a horrific way. They were there to show their support, but Adam saw them as rubberneckers at a car accident.

Sweat fell from his forehead and smeared some of the ink, creating a black pool of his words. Everybody in the crowd was crying, but Adam didn't want them to see him cry.

"Thank you all for being here today." The knot in Adam's throat slipped tighter and threatened to cut off his air. "The outpouring of love and support is humbling. I'd also like to take this time to thank the tireless efforts of the Scarsville first responders and to the first responders of the neighboring counties who worked tirelessly to find our little girl."

Adam paused to scan the room. He focused on faces he didn't know to slow the flow of tears and fight the strain he felt in the back of his throat from holding back the full brunt of his emotions.

"We gather here today not to bury our daughter, but to remember and celebrate a little girl who was the light of so many people's lives. She touched the life of every person she came in contact with, whether it was a giggle she hid behind her hand or the twirl of her dress."

Adam stood up straight, choked back the tears and wiped his face with the back of his hand. Tears fell and the pool of ink turned into a pond.

"Like most ... like most parents, we had hopes and dreams for our daughter. And we struggle to understand how a young life ... how such an innocent life can be taken away. But with Grace in our hearts, we can all be sure that she was loved, and that we were all loved."

The deluge of tears hitting the paper flooded the pond's dam and created a roaring black lake. There wasn't a dry eye in the chapel or in the overflowing vestibule. A loud stuttering cry pulled Adam's attention to the family pews, where he saw his father crying uncontrollably in a seizure of pain. Adam looked down at his paper as a tear fell from his eye and the inky black lake swallowed Grace Ann's name on the paper. He gripped the pitted wood and squeezed his eyes shut. He shouldn't have looked at his father. What right did he have to be here and crying and carrying on the way he was? It was his fault. He was the reason they were all here instead of sitting by the pool while Grace Ann played. To hell with it. Everybody loves to see a car wreck.

"I can't do this. I'm up here fighting to hold myself together and he's down there like a babbling idiot."

Adam paused, unsure of himself. Aside from a few sniffs, silence worked its way across the crowd. When Phil didn't look up at him, it enraged Adam. He balled up his notes and threw them in Phil's direction. The pastor who sat behind him, rereading scripture he knew by heart, closed his bible and stood. Adam sensed the movement and pointed his index finger behind him.

"One minute, Brother. I'm not finished here. He's the one to blame."

A woman Adam didn't know gasped, and the preacher rested his hand on Adam's shoulder.

"That's right, lady. I bet you didn't know that. My father, Phil Blackwell, is the reason we're all here today. It's his fault my little girl is dead," Adam said and pointed at Phil.

"That's enough, son," the preacher said, tightening his grip on Adam. Brian and Dan stood up.

"The hell it is, Brother Michael," Adam said, shrugging off the preacher's hand. "That bastard knows the lake is dangerous and he still let my little girl go near it."

Brian and Dan walked toward the stage.

"Don't worry boys, I'm almost finished. He ruined my life and took the only thing that made it worth living away from me. It should have been him."

Mandy wrapped her arms around the quaking Phil and was saying something to him.

"So you're on his side with this, Mandy? Did you not hear me? He is the reason our little girl is dead. It should have been him. The lake is dangerous."

Brian and Dan stormed the stage. Each of them grabbed one of his arms and tried to lead him to the steps, but he wrenched back and pulled his arms from Dan's grip.

"Adam, you're finished. Come on down. You're causing a scene," Dan said.

"I will not. I'm not finished with him yet. Everybody needs to know what a piece of shit he is. The lake is dangerous. They shouldn't have been near it."

Dan grabbed his arm again, and he and Brian pulled Adam down the steps. He tried to snatch away from them and started swinging his feet.

"Don't make us carry you out of here," Brian said through gritted teeth.

"It's going to take more than you two to do it."

Everybody was standing. Some were shaking their heads and turning away from the fight, but others watched in amazement. Funeral home employees came into the room to calm the crowd and to intervene with the three people who had their phones out trying to film the action. Two Scarsville Sheriff Deputies came down the center aisle. Adam kicked out at them, and one grabbed his foot. Adam realized he was losing this fight and turned his attention back to his father.

"It should have been you, *Dad.* You should have been the one to die, not my little girl. I hope your guilt kills you."

With Adam's focus on his father, the deputies were able to grab both of his legs. The four men carried Adam while he twisted and thrashed to get back to his father, all the while yelling, "it should have been you."

They carried him to the visitation room on the other side of the building and threw him in a chair. He jumped up trying to leave, and one of the deputies pushed him back into the chair.

"I suggest you stay in that chair, Mr. Blackwell. You've caused quite the scene in there."

"I was just getting warmed up."

"I know. That's why we had to intervene, the only reason I'm not arresting you right now, is because I know you're going through a hard time and this isn't like you."

"Arrest me? Why don't you go and arrest him? He's that one that killed my daughter," Adam said and moved to stand again. The deputy stepped in front of the chair and pushed his knees against Adam's keeping him in his seat.

"I don't want to do it, but if you don't calm down right now, I will arrest you. Do you understand me?"

"Yes, *sir*," Adam said as he saluted the deputy and leaned back in his chair.

No charges were ever filed. They pitied Adam, and the last thing he wanted from any of them was their pity. They made him wait until the funeral home was clear before he could leave. That night Adam packed what little belongings he cared to take and left town.

At Phil's funeral, the last notes of Amazing Grace faded and everybody in the first pew stood. Adam realized they were all looking at him because they were waiting for him to lead the precession out the door. He stood and looked around at faces he hardly knew and locked eyes with the only one he recognized.

Mandy gave him a sad smile and cocked her head to the left. The hand on his arm made him jump into the middle aisle. He walked down the worn carpet runner, not thinking about timing his steps with the rest of the family members. When he reached the vestibule, he headed straight for the door. Brian called his name as he pushed the double doors open and the sticky heat engulfed him once again.

He stood at the entrance to the graveyard contemplating whether or not he wanted to go in and find Phil's plot and piss on it or if he wanted to wait until they had him in the ground. He decided to wait and bumped into Mandy as he turned around to go find his car.

He grabbed her arms so she wouldn't fall down and said, "hey."

"Hello, Adam. It's been a while."

"Yeah, it has." He could tell this awkward small talk was going to be painful. He tried to focus on the smell of the honeysuckle wilting on the vine behind him.

"I'm sorry about your father."

"Don't be. It's been a long time coming."

"Adam, you really need to get over the hate you have for him. It was an accident," she said and pulled her hand back as she reached out for him. When Adam didn't respond, she continued. "You still haven't gone to her grave, have you?"

"It's not a grave. It's a stone with some dates on it."

"I think it might help you. At least let me show you where it is. You don't have to stay if you don't want to, but at least you'll know where it is."

How nice she was being surprised him. He ran out on Phil

and the lake. But he had also run out on her, and she had every right to hate him. Brian and Dan were obviously still mad at him.

Adam and Mandy quickly fell back into their comfort with each other and walked side by side through the cemetery without saying a word. The trail wound between families like a dividing line to keep score.

Mandy walked off the trail toward a gravestone in the shade of Japanese red leaf maple tree that looked more like a bush. The rose quartz headstone shined in the sun. The hard stone encased a picture of Grace Ann running through a field and looking back at the camera in her navy-blue dress with the ruffles flying in the wind. Below it the inscription read, *Beloved Daughter Grace Ann Blackwell. Forever in our hearts, and resting in the arms of Jesus, our Savior.*

"Some savior," Adam mumbled as he wiped tears from his face.

"This area seemed a little empty and Mr. Barlow was nice enough to let me plant this small tree here."

"How much extra did that cost you?"

"Don't be so cynical. It didn't cost anything. There were a lot of people that were good to us. You would have known that if you'd stuck around."

And there it was. Shots fired. She had held out longer than he expected. He looked back the way they had come.

"Don't leave. I didn't want to start an argument, today. I'm sorry."

"I'm not leaving. I was looking to see where he was going to be buried."

"He's going to be closer to the path with your mother."

"Another empty grave that's probably his fault too."

"That's not fair. You can't blame everybody's death on your father."

"Not all of them. Only the ones in the lake."

Mandy moved to his side, and they both looked down on their daughter's headstone. The area around the stone was clear of any leaves or debris that might have blown around the cemetery, and there were fresh flowers in the permanent stone vase. Adam could tell Mandy came out here a lot and took care of the area. It was obvious from the graves he'd seen on the way in that it wasn't a caretaker keeping the cemetery clean.

"Adam, I'm worried about you."

"Don't be. Everything was perfect and then it was a gone. One minute, I was a father and the next, I wasn't."

"You'll never be happy if you're waiting for life to be perfect again. You'll only be happy when your life has purpose."

Adam stepped back from her and pointed at Grace Ann's tombstone.

"My purpose died two years ago."

"When was the last time you went to church? I'm sure Brother Michael would talk to you, if you let him."

"Church can't help me," Adam said and threw his hands in the air in mock resignation to a god he no longer believed in.

"You use your love for her as a way to protect your heart. You can't keep going like this."

"It's a poisonous protection."

"What does that mean?"

"It means that it protects our heart while you still have them, but when they're gone, it poisons your heart."

"I lost her too, Adam. And then I lost you."

"I know you lost her, and yet, here you are berating me because I haven't moved on like you."

"It's been two years. You have to allow yourself to heal. And you were the one who moved when she died," Mandy said and stepped back like something had stung her.

He could tell she hadn't meant to bring that up, but it was the second time she had since they came out here.

"Do you even hear what you're saying? I think you have a poisoned mind," Adam said and recoiled at his own juvenile retort, but he had to finish what he was saying. "So, why don't you go back to Father Michael or Brother or whatever relation he's called and his church and let them fix you. Unless it was them who made you this way."

Mandy opened her mouth to say something, but then closed it. She turned and started walking back toward the funeral home. She stopped before she got to the path and said, "I've read your books since you left, and they are so much darker and angrier than they used to be. You need help, Adam."

"Oh, you read my books, now? Don't try and make nice with me now that I'm rich and famous. I'm seeing somebody. See? I can move on."

Tears finally formed in her eyes. That wasn't what he had been trying to do. He hadn't been waiting for a chance to hurt her again, but that's the way it seemed. He wished he could take it back. They stood there looking at each other until she finally brushed her windblown hair behind her ears.

"I got married last year."

Adam was not expecting that. His mouth moved, but no words came out. He didn't know what to say, anyway. When she turned from him, he found his voice again.

"I thought I heard her last night."

Mandy stopped, but didn't face him.

"I stayed at Phil's house and I thought I heard her laughing and running through the house. I jumped up and chased her outside, but when I ran outside, there wasn't anybody there."

Mandy slowly shook her head and walked away, leaving him alone in the cemetery. He called after her a few more times telling her that he'd heard their daughter, but Mandy didn't stop.

Chapter Ten

It wasn't his best work, but what did she expect? It was his first book. Far from a pastiche, she could easily see his influences. Charlotte poured hot water over the waiting tea bag and walked back into the living room. Steam rose from his Green Bay Packers mug. She felt like a trader to her Bears, but that was his favorite mug and she wanted to feel closer to him. Of course, if she really wanted to feel closer to him, she should go down a bottle of Johnnie Walker and call it a day.

He said he didn't like the book or try to get it published because it hit too close to home, and he felt like he had somehow predicted the death of his daughter by writing it. Adam didn't like to talk about his past much, so she wasn't sure how close it was to anything that transpired.

So far, the story followed Charles (Charlie to all his friends) Ransom. Charlie's six-year-old daughter, Macy, fell into the river and drown. They were fishing with Charlie's father, Bill, and Macy fell in while Bill was supposed to be watching her because Charlie fell asleep on the bank. They never found Macy's body. Charlie became estranged from his family and became the town crazy for a few years until his wife disappeared on the same stretch of river. Charlotte wanted to keep reading but had already been fighting to keep her eyes open for the last ten pages. She didn't want to miss anything and decided to call it a night.

The story was eerily similar to what happened to Adam and his daughter. He always blamed Phil for Grace Ann's death, but the book made it look like Charlie was partly at fault. Did Adam blame himself deep down? It would make sense with the way he went into deep depressive states. It was one thing to lose a child, but Charlotte couldn't image shouldering the blame for the child's death.

Charlotte put her lips to the rim of the mug and blew the steaming tea. She took a sip and picked the story up where she left off the night before.

It was his fault. Charlie hadn't been there for Gina, and now she was gone too. He sloshed through the muddy bank of the river and cut the kudzu and finger thick vines with his machete. It'd been days since he'd had a drink and his hand trembled with each strike. A wall of lush green foliage blocked his path. Charlie pulled back and prepared to run his rival through.

He thrust the blade forward, and the wall retreated. Charlie stumbled into an open field he'd never seen before. The river cascaded straight down a waterfall ending in a fog-covered pool.

Charlie walked to the edge and stared into the churning water below. The waterfall wasn't new, but the searchers never mentioned it to him. No wonder they never found his daughter. Had they even looked? A pulsing glow emanated from the center of the pool, making the fog look smoky-blue.

A strangled voice boomed, "Just one more step and everything will be over."

The sudden noise startled Charlie, and he almost fell over the cliff. He wiped the sweat from his brow and scanned the trees for the source of the voice. The voice sounded familiar.

"I ... I don't know what you mean."

"You have come searching for your wife, have you not?" the voice asked.

Charlie spun around in the opening, but only managed to make himself dizzy.

"Yes. Do you have her?"

"I do. I also have your daughter," the voice thundered.

Charlie cowered.

"What do you want from me?"

"The only way you will ever see them again is to jump into the water below. Do that, and your wife and daughter will live."

"If I jump, I'll die, and I won't see them."

"This is not a negotiation. Jump or don't. It matters not to me."

Everything had come to this. He now recognized the voice from his dreams or delusions. It had been calling him here the entire time. The voice disappeared when he quit drinking, but here it was again, telling him there was a chance to see his family again.

Charlie stepped to the cliff, and Gina ran out of the brush. Her bright red hair was dark and tangled like she'd been sleeping in the woods since she'd vanished. She fell to her knees and called out to him.

"Don't do it, Charlie. Please, don't jump."

"Stay back, Gina. I have to or he won't let you go."

"Macy is dead. She can't come back."

"I have to try. I have to try and save my little girl. It's my fault she's dead. If there is even a chance I can bring her back, I have to try. There is nothing here for me anymore. If I can't be with her, I don't want to live," Charlie said.

He turned back to the rushing water and jumped before Gina had a chance to say anything else. The water rushed by, and he hit the water. The impact bent his leg back, and his ankle snapped. Water forced its way up his nose and down his throat.

Charlie hit the bottom of the river and pushed toward the surface. He pierced the top, and the waterfall poured down on him. He cleared his vision and saw Gina looking over the edge. Her hand covered her mouth.

It dawned on Charlie that he survived. He jumped and now would be able to see his daughter again. He tried to wave to Gina, but she didn't see him. He swiped the water away and saw Macy standing beside her mother. He no longer could tell if it was tears or *the water blurring his vision. Gina didn't know Macy was home. Charlie yelled to his family.*

Something under the water grabbed Charlie's leg and dragged him under. He fought to the surface and saw his daughter standing over his wife. He tried to yell again, and whatever had his leg pulled him under for the final time.

Charlotte dropped the manuscript and covered her mouth. If Adam worried the book had predicted his daughter's death, did he think the rest of the book was just as prophetic? Or had he been knowingly foreshadowing his own death all these years? She had worried about him going to Georgia. He had a habit of running. They were in a good place in their relationship, but she knew there was always something that wouldn't let him commit. She'd always thought it was his ex-wife. From what Charlotte could gather, their relationship was fine until their daughter died. There was no reason to think their marriage would have ended if their daughter were still alive. Adam would never have come to Chicago, and she wouldn't have found him on a park bench in an area he had no business being in. He told her she saved his life twice that day. If Chicago hadn't killed him that night, he would have ended up doing it. Now he was back in Georgia facing another crisis, and she'd be lying to herself if she said there wasn't the slightest twinge of jealousy in her gut at the thought of Mandy being the one to pick up the pieces.

But jealousy wasn't the reason for wanting to jump on a plane and go to Georgia. It would be one thing to pick up the pieces, but the ending of his book unsettled her. He hadn't put up a huge fight about going back. He'd put up a bigger fight about her staying behind. When he left, he was in a daze that she originally discounted as mourning for the loss of his father before he could make amends. There was always tomorrow until tomorrow never comes. What if the reason he didn't want her to go was because he believed that stupid shit about his first book and didn't think he would return? What if he thought he was going home for the last time, and like Charlie Ransom, he was going to jump off the cliff to bring his daughter back, to show the world with one final act how much he loved and missed his daughter?

Charlotte wiped the tears from her face with the back of her hand. She had to go to Georgia and stop him before he did something stupid. He always thought of the worst-case scenario possible for everything. She hoped he hadn't convinced himself that his damn book was the reason everything had happened and there was no way for him to fight his destiny. She slid out of her chair to the floor and shuffled the scattered manuscript into a messy stack, not bothering to see if the page numbers were in order. When she brought him home, to their home, they were going to burn the book together. It had weighed over him like a pregnant cloud waiting to deliver its final shower for far too long. She knew it wasn't healthy for him to be that way, but she hadn't realized how bad it was and blamed herself for not doing something about it.

She grabbed her cellphone and sent a text to her favorite substitute, Amanda. Out of all the substitute teachers she'd used over the years, Amanda was the best at handling the kids and they always seemed to behave better for her than the others, if only slightly. Charlotte had asked her many times why she didn't become a full-time teacher, and she always gave the same answer. She'd rather work part time so she could spend more time with her own heathens. Charlotte also liked her because she was quick to respond and didn't mind being asked at the last minute.

Charlotte sat her phone on the dresser when she walked into the bedroom and it started vibrating S.O.S. in Morse code across the top, and true to form, Amanda was already responding that she would love to fill in for her. It was the last week of school and would be an easy few days and extra money before the summer break started. Hopefully Charlotte would only be gone two days and would be back for the last day of school.

She grabbed the first thing she found in the closet and stuffed it into her large overnight bag. In the bathroom, she grabbed her makeup and toothbrush and threw them into the bag. She didn't want to waste time packing when she still had to call the airline to get a ticket. It shouldn't be hard to get a ticket from Chicago to Atlanta, but she wanted to hurry in case the next flight was soon. She checked her puffy eyes in the mirror one last time.

"I'm not going to Georgia because I'm jealous. I'm going because I'm afraid something bad could happen to Adam if he's left alone."

In her heart, she knew that, but still felt like she needed to look herself in the mirror and say it. She believed the woman looking back at her.

Chapter Eleven

dam slid the plastic bags across the dining room table and took the brown paper bag to the kitchen. There weren't any double old-fashioned glasses, so he settled for an old coffee cup emblazoned with the Atlanta Falcons logo on a red helmet. It was Phil's favorite cup. Scarsville might be a backward town, but at least he could still get Johnnie Walker. He dropped in a few ice cubes and poured the amber liquid to the lip of the mug. A loud engine rumbled in the distance. Adam hoped it was somebody who turned down the wrong road and would turn around when they came to the dead end. He sighed and took a long pull from his mug as the driver gunned the truck up the driveway and killed the engine.

Adam went to the front door and watched as the driver sat in the lifted Ram. Maybe they wouldn't get out and would leave him alone. The driver kicked the door open, and Adam walked out on the front porch. Eric Barlow jumped carefully from his truck.

"Hey, Adam. How you doing?"

"Eric."

Of all the people who would show up at the house, Eric was the last he expected. Eric sounded pleasant when he spoke. It was fake, but he was trying. He wanted something. Eric stopped at the first step and looked up as Adam towered over him from the porch.

"I'm sorry I wasn't able to make the funeral yesterday."

"No worries. I didn't want to be there, anyway."

Eric's mouth moved, but no words escaped, like he was thinking through all the possibilities of what he could say.

"I'm sure it was a nice service."

"I couldn't tell you."

Eric put his hands in his pockets and kicked at a shuckworm-infested pecan. Adam wasn't in the mood to deal with somebody who clearly had something to say but couldn't work up the courage to do so. He should have stopped on the dirt road if he needed to do that.

"So what can I do for you?" Adam used his own fake nice voice.

"Well, we've known each other for a while, and haven't ever really been what you'd call friends."

"That's an understatement."

Eric wasn't money and land hungry like his dad and uncle. Adam tried not to hold his family against him when they were in school, but Eric had his own issues that made people despise him. The problem with Eric was he was five foot two and thought he had to make up for it with his attitude and apparently his truck too. When people mentioned his height, he would get twitchy, and his face would turn red like he'd just finished running laps around the baseball field.

The school board managed to kick him out of school his senior year when another student, Matt Daniels, overheard him boasting about his latest conquest. The one he was bragging about happened to be Matt's sister, Mary. Matt pushed his way into the circle of underclassmen, and everybody got quiet except for Eric. He continued with his story of domination. Matt finally spoke up and told the growing crowd that, "everything he says is bullshit. My sister went out with him because she felt sorry for the little guy." Eric's face changed many shades of red as Matt continued. "She said he tried to make a move in the movie theater, but his arms were too short, and he couldn't get them around her shoulder and he ended up looking like he was raising his hand because he had a question."

Everybody in the group laughed except for Eric. His face was blood red, and he was blowing air out of his mouth like a bull lining up to take a run at the matador. Eric went at Matt swinging but being a foot taller than Eric at six two, Matt put his hand on Eric's head, keeping him from landing any punches. Matt played the scene up by holding Eric with one hand while he checked the cuticles on the other. He quickly swapped hands holding Eric's head and checked the other cuticles. This stunt turned the whole scene into a slapstick comedy sketch, and the taunting crowd wanted more. Matt finally had enough and pushed Eric down in a puddle of water gathering by the drink machines.

When Matt turned his back to go to class, Eric jumped up and with an overhead arc slammed his backpack against the back of Matt's head. Matt crumpled to the ground and bright red blood poured out of the three-inch gash in his head. When they searched Eric's backpack to see what caused the damage, the only weapon they found was a heavy black stapler. The Barlow's fought the expulsion, but Matt Daniels needed to have his head stitched back together and suffered a massive concussion. Matt's mother worked as a clerk in the Sheriff's Department, so there was little they could do to keep Eric out of any trouble that time. In the end, the Daniels family dropped the charges and Eric finished high school at a private school in Crystal Valley. Matt finished his final year in a hospital bed.

Eric pushed his hands in his pockets and swiped at the ground again.

"I'm sure it would be a lot of fun to stand here and reminisce about how we were never friends, but as you can probably tell, I have a lot going on at the moment."

Adam motioned to the house with his mug.

"So it'd be great if you could just tell me what you want."

"Yeah, you're right. You always were a dick. I'm here because my uncle thinks you'd at least hear me out, where you wouldn't even open the door for him."

"I didn't open the door for you. I was coming out anyway. You could have just called."

Adam tightened his grip on the mug and took a gulp. He knew why Eric was here the second he saw him. Why was he entertaining this conversation? Why had he come outside? He should have stayed in the house and not answered the door. It didn't matter how much money Eric offered; he would never take it from a Barlow. The sooner he got the house on the market, the faster he could get home and out of small-town politics. He could have it all finished by this afternoon and leave for Chicago in the morning and not worry about returning to Georgia ever again.

Maybe Brian would come to Chicago and spend a little time with him. He hated his father, but that didn't extend to Brian, no matter what Brian thought. Brian in Chicago would be a hilarious site. The easier solution would be to give in and sell to Barlow, but he couldn't do it. Not even to spite Phil.

"Just the same, if you'd be willing to come to my uncle's house and talk to him, I'm sure you could come to an agreement that would make you both happy. And we don't call because we like to conduct our business in person. It's more personable that way."

And people can't hang up on you if you corner them at their house. The Barlows had probably forced many people into selling places owned by families for generations by showing up and intimidating them until they gave in to get away. All with a personable smile on their face, he was sure.

"Let me stop you there, Zacchaeus. I couldn't care less about your uncle's happiness or his money and the need for my own happiness is debatable most days, so that's not going to work on me," Adam said and took another sip.

"Come on, Adam. He'd be willing to pay you double what this place is worth. You could use that money to run as far away from here as you wanted."

"I didn't run away, Little Man."

The scotch made him drowsy. His head was light and fuzzy, and he started to sway on the top step.

"Look at you. You look like shit, and I bet that's not even coffee in that mug. What is it, 9:30? Sell to my uncle and you can go back to your hiding place and never have to return."

"You're a little fire plug this morning, aren't you?"

"Is that all you can do? Make fun of my height. I've been hearing the same shit from people my entire life. It doesn't bother me."

Adam looked over Eric's head and squinted at the blue Ram.

"Your truck says different."

"Damn it. Why are you being like this? Just go talk to my uncle or his lawyer if you don't want to see him. Get your money and go."

"I'll never sell to him. He's a land hoarding bully who is responsible for the downfall of this town."

"Bully? You can call him a bully, while you're picking on a grown man about his size?"

Eric was right. This wasn't like Adam. He was never the bully. He never let anybody bully him, either. Humor was always his way of dealing with issues. Some would call Adam a smartass, but he'd rather be a smartass than a dumbass. He would laugh and the person attacking him would, usually, get embarrassed and leave him alone. It didn't always work out the way he wanted, and he would push too far, causing a reaction he didn't expect. The problem was Adam knew what to expect from Eric, and he pushed anyway.

"Grown is a bit of a stretch don't you think?"

"I'm not going to keep listening to this shit. Go talk to him or not, I don't care. Sober up before you decide to run from your daughter's ghost again."

The mention of Grace Ann's ghost caught Adam off guard and made him think about her running through the house and the pasture the night before. She hadn't been there, but he thought she was. He needed to get out of town.

"What the fuck did you say?" Adam sat the mug slowly on the

porch rail with unsteady hands. "Don't talk about my daughter again." Adam ran down the stairs quicker and steadier than the alcohol should have allowed.

Eric took two steps back.

"You have the nerve to come to my house knowing I would never consider selling it or anything to Vernon Barlow, and then you're going to bring up my daughter? I'd rather keep it and let it rot then ever sell to him or anybody else in your family."

Eric's demeanor changed, and he almost looked sorry for bringing up Grace Ann. He had to know bringing up a dead relative was not going to get somebody to change their mind or calm down.

"I shouldn't have said anything. But this place is already falling apart. You're not going to get as much as you think."

Adam stuck his finger in Eric's face.

"You're lucky I'd never hit a kid."

Eric's face turned red.

"I'm tired of your shit, Adam."

Eric put both of his hands on Adam's chest and pushed him out of his face. Adam stumbled, but managed to catch himself before he hit the steps. Eric was still there yelling at him, but Adam couldn't make out the words. His head was swimming. He balled up his fist and turned toward Eric and swung. To Adam, it felt like he had cocked his arm back far enough to touch the ground. A subtle whoosh of air brushed his face as he followed through and connected with Eric's left eye.

Eric fell to the ground and held his eye. Sitting on the ground, he pushed himself back with his feet to escape Adam as he stood over him.

"You stupid son of a bitch. You'll pay for that."

"I'm sure whatever the price is, it will be worth it. Now, get the hell off my property and tell your uncle, I'll never sell to him."

Eric pushed himself off the ground. His eye was already turning black and would swell shut before he got out of the drive-way. He climbed into the truck and stared at Adam. The engine roared to life, and Eric pushed the throttle to the floor, revving the engine. The motor echoed through the trees and fell to a quieter rumble. Eric put the truck in gear and rolled toward Adam before turning in a wide arc and speeding down the driveway. He didn't stop at the entrance and floored it again, sending rooster tails of loose dirt into the air and fishtailing toward the forest on the other side of the road. Eric got the truck back under control and disappeared from sight. Adam could hear him all the way down the road and again when he gunned it onto the highway. He almost felt sorry, almost, but Eric pushed him. Still, he felt like he had been looking for a fight and hadn't found much of one.

Adam walked back inside the house and into the kitchen. He topped off his mug and grabbed the plastic bags from the hardware store. The sun beat down from overhead, but the scotch warmed his body. A nice breeze blew through his hair and crinkled his bags. It might have ended up being one of the few pleasant summer days in the south, but he had an emotional job to do and wouldn't be enjoying the temperature reprieve.

He staggered to the barbwire fence.

"Hello, my old nemesis." He grabbed the wire and shook it. "I don't think I'll be tangling with you today."

Adam toasted the wire fence with his mug and walked to the aluminum gate. He pulled the rusted bolt out of the loop and the fence swung in. On the other side, Adam pushed the gate closed with his hip and held it in place. The bolt slid easily but clanked when it hit the side of the loop. Adam pulled it back and tried to slide it again with the same result. Metal clanging against metal echoed as he pulled back and tried to slide the bolt home. Sweat ran down his forehead and stung his eyes. The answer finally dawned on Adam. He looked around the pasture sheepishly and hoped the only audience he had was a few birds or maybe a cow that had wandered back his way. He stuck his arm through the gate and lifted it with his shoulder, and the bolt slid into the loop like someone had sprayed it down with a can of WD-40. Under normal circumstances, Adam would have remembered the trick to closing the gate, but it had been a while since he'd been on the farm and he was already frustrated.

As he approached the lake, a large bird flew over the water. It looked like it had a massive wingspan, but Adam always got buzzards and hawks mixed up from a distance. Phil and Brian laughed at him every time he pointed out a hawk, but when they drew nearer to each other, it was only an ugly scavenger. He decided this bird was a hawk, but as he stumbled closer, the bird began a slow circle over the water. Every damn time. It was definitely a buzzard, but he couldn't think of a reason it'd be over the water. It wasn't going to swoop down and catch anything. Maybe something died on the bank. Hopefully, it wasn't a cow. They'd have to get a backhoe in here to take care of that problem.

When he got to the red clay lake edge, he dropped his bags of garden lights beside the three remaining nightlights. Nothing looked or smelled dead. Maybe it was on the other side of the lake? He took a gulp of his drink and pulled the remaining lights from the ground. The land was dry, but Adam managed to force the eight new lights into the soil, recreating the nightlight semi-circle for Grace Ann. Could the lawyer put in the farm purchase agreement the new owners would have to leave the lights up? He doubted it. It wasn't like the lights were a gravestone, but they did mark the last place Adam saw her alive. She died here; that should count for something. It wasn't hallowed ground, but it was haunted ground. Haunted by the memories of a playful girl who lit up every room she walked into. Adam wiped the tears from his face and stood up on wobbly legs that sloshed like they were half-empty canteens.

He walked to a dirt patch and picked up a handful of rocks.

"You're the reason my little girl is gone," he yelled, and threw a rock into the water.

The rock splashed, but not loud enough for its size and didn't make any ripples. He threw another, and it landed with the same muted splash. The water remained calm, like a smoothed out black bed sheet.

"Now you're mocking me. Won't even make a fucking splash."

He threw a handful of rocks and doubled over from the exertion. Still no disturbance in the water. A part of Adam knew it should scare him, but he pushed it back. He was too mad to let the reality of the situation bother him. He started picking up anything he could find on the ground and throwing it into the water, he didn't care if it was a rock, stick, or horse shit, it was going into the water. On his fifth trip to the water's edge, he threw a rock as far out across the lake as he could. It didn't even reach the middle, or at least, that's what he thought from the trajectory, but there was no evidence that it had even come down.

He looked up to the sky and screamed, "Why? Why did you take her?" There was no answer. The only thing in the cloudless sky was the circling buzzard.

"You want to mock me too. I see."

Adam picked up a rock and threw it into the air, but he was right under his target and the rock didn't go near the bird. He picked up another as the bird came back around and threw it into the air like he was doing a basketball granny-shot.

"You aren't a hawk. How do you like that? You'll never be a hawk," Adam yelled at the uncaring bird. "You're no hawk."

Adam threw rocks in the air and dodged them as they fell to the Earth. He pointed at the bird.

"You're no hawk. You're no hawk. You're no hawk. Bird of prey, my ass. You're no hawk. You're no..."

The black tentacle slipped out of the water and wrapped around Adam's calf. Tiny razor like teeth ripped through his jeans and into his skin. He managed a strangled yelp before it pulled him into the water.

The black water felt like being dropped into an ice bath when you were expecting a warm soak. Glacial water pushed the breath Adam swallowed from his lungs before the tentacle pulled him back under. He kicked at the thing holding his leg, felt it give slightly and razors slashed his leg. It was only adjusting its grip. He was running out of air and grabbed the snake—tentacle—creature wrapped around his leg. He pried it away and pushed off the bottom of the lake.

The circling buzzard was the first thing he saw when he breached the surface of the water. He took a big gulp of air, and the thing grabbed him again. Every movement was sluggish from the alcohol, but the world was slowing down too. As he fell back into the water, he realized he hadn't made a splash either, and the creature was about to pull him to the bottom of the lake.

The cold water seized him again, but he kept his breath. Adam thrashed and pulled but couldn't escape the monster that had gotten a better grip on his leg. He wanted to open his eyes to see what had a hold of him, but he hated going under the water even in the swimming pool. There was no way he could open his eyes underwater.

The animal pulled his leg again, and the water pressure around his face changed as something swam past him. Adam's lungs burned from the strain from not being used to holding his breath. He pushed forward again, and what felt like a tail brushed across his face. He forced his eyes open and the rank water attacked and forced him to close them again.

His drunken head cleared.

He was going to die.

The best thing for him to do would be to open his mouth and take a few gulps and fade away. Hopefully Grace Ann didn't fight too long.

She must have been so scared.

He forced his eyes open again and fought against the burn, but he could barely see anything. The water was as murky as it looked from the top. The sun was barely visible and created a blue halo on the water's surface.

A school of the black eel like creatures swarmed around him. Their sleek muscular bodies cut through the water like friction didn't slow them. They emitted a florescent blue light and would disappear and reappear like wraiths floating through the night. One of the creatures appeared beside his face and turned to face him. It opened its mouth and wrinkles formed around its jaws like ancient skin. The creature hung suspended in the water, and Adam realized where he had seen them before.

They were the creatures that ripped their way out of Phil's body. He pictured them slipping through the sutured cuts and landing on the floor with a sick wet mop plop. He pulled back, and the jaws snapped.

Seeing the creature cut through the inevitableness of death and a new longing for survival hit him. He bent and pulled at the thing wrapped around his leg, but it wouldn't move. His hands sank into the muddy bottom of the lake. It was hard to see in the water, but even the blue tint of what was visible disappeared when Adam raked through the bottom of the lake, looking for anything to help him.

He clawed his way back toward shore, but the creature pulled him deeper toward the middle of the lake. Mud sucked at his hand as he dug in deep. Something sharp slid through his hand and he fought a battle of tug of war with the mud.

When he pulled his hand free, he was grasping part of a broken bottle. The glass sliced into his skin. Flaps of skin surrounded the glass as he bent down and tried to slash at the tentacle, but his arm moved too slowly in the water. Stabbing was the only way he was going to move fast enough to cause any damage.

He moved his hand closer to his leg and thrust the glass forward into the thing. The glass didn't tear through the skin immediately. He pulled back, found a new spot and pushed and twisted the glass against the thick hide. The glass popped through the skin and Adam sliced down the tentacle. Blood poured out of the wounded creature and blue turned dark purple.

A screech rumbled from the depths of the lake and the tentacle let go of his leg. Adam kicked to the surface of the water. He was only ten feet away from the bank and tried to stand, but the mud pulled at his boots. He tried to walk, but the mud held fast. He pulled harder and the red clay bottom released his feet, but the lake kept the boots. Air caught in his throat and he couldn't cough. His chest tightened and his heart raced. Hell of a way to die. Survive being held underwater and fighting off a lake monster just to have a heart attack and drown before he made it back to shore.

When he was almost to the bank, he saw Brian riding one of

the horses in the pasture and called out to him. The horse galloped toward the lake after two quick kicks from Brian. Adam called out again, and another tentacle wrapped around his leg and pulled him under. He pushed back to the surface and stood in the knee-deep water. The creature pulled him again, and he stumbled.

Brian arrived swinging his lasso over his head. He released, and the loop flew through the air and ringed one of Adam's arms as the creature pulled him under. Adam pushed to the surface and put his head and one arm through the rope. "Now," Adam yelled and fell back into the water.

Brian kicked the horse. The rope tightened around Adam's shoulder and armpit. The rope burned red braid marks into his skin, and he winced as the horse pulled him from the water. Brian jumped off the horse and ran to him.

Adam coughed and vomited. The brackish scotch torched his raw throat. Brian leaned over and clapped him on the back.

"You okay?"

"Yeah, I'm fine."

Adam burped and retched again.

"I'm fine, but I don't remember eating that," Adam said.

The water was bad, but not like stagnant water bad. Adam had drunk from a still pool in a creek bed before when he was a kid. Phil popped him in the back of the head as he knelt beside the creek, and told him he would have done worse, but the aftermath of drinking that water would be bad enough punishment. Adam had been sick for a week after that. He thought he was going to die. More than a few times, he wished he had. That water had been bad, and Adam had thought that's what death tasted like, but he was wrong. This water from the lake tasted spoiled, like it had been sitting in the shadows for years and now brought out to quench the thirst of the land and all of those on it.

He watched the flat lake water with new eyes. The water still didn't move, but there seemed to be electricity in the air like the hum of a hot wire fence, and the water took on a darker blue-black appearance that glowed around the bank. The water remained undisturbed. It didn't even look like his brother had just dragged him out of the lake on horseback while he kicked and thrashed to get away from whatever it was that had a hold of him. Until now, it had never occurred to him the water never moved. Even a harsh wind didn't disturb the water's slumber. He couldn't remember ever watching the rain splash on the mirror surface. The sky wasn't threatening to open up now, but he'd have to remember to check the weather later and see if there was a chance it might rain. None of the family had ever mentioned the motionless water because they always focused on the waterfall and torrent of water being thrown against the pit walls.

"You don't look fine. What the hell happened?"

Adam shivered in his brother's arms as Brian helped him up. The black creatures were swarming around him again. He thought he was going crazy at the time, but now he'd seen them in the water. They must have wormed their way into Phil's body, sliding between his organs and nesting deep enough that no pathologist would find their hiding place. But could that happen? How could they hide from somebody rooting around in the confines of a body cavity? They were big. It wouldn't have been easy for them to stay hidden until Adam came to visit the morgue.

Brian continued looking at Adam, waiting for his answer. He needed to tell his brother the truth. He needed to tell him the water was dangerous, and they needed to sell the place or burn it all down. Either way, they needed to get the hell away from there as fast as they could and never come back.

But he didn't. He couldn't. Brian would look at him like he was crazy and making an excuse to hurry up and get rid of the place. Or he would think he was trying to tuck his tail between his legs and run. Again. Everybody thought Adam was a coward for leaving, but he obviously had the right idea. Brian wouldn't believe him, and Adam wouldn't blame him. Adam coughed and spit out a wad of something he hoped was phlegm.

"I came down here to put new lights up for Grace Ann, and I ... well, I made a drink before I came down here and made another one for the trip and I must have gotten too close to the water."

Adam shivered at the thought of the leathery tentacle reaching out of the water and ripping into his flesh before dragging him under.

"Damn, brother. You might want to take it easy on that stuff. You're liable to take yourself out. It looked like something had a holt of ya."

"Felt like it too." Adam looked at his feet. "I was stuck in the mud. My boots weren't so lucky, I guess."

"Your jeans look like they got the short end of the stick, too. What did that?"

Bloody cuts peeked through holes torn in the denim.

"Yeah, I guess so. There, must have been some kind of briar patch under the water and I got tangled in it. I cut my hand on a glass bottle at some point."

Adam held his hand out for Brian to inspect.

Brian put his foot in the stirrup and flung himself over the horse.

"Let me give you a ride up to the house. You need a shower. That water looks cold, and you smell like fresh roadkill cooking on the blacktop. Need to get something on those cuts too, so they don't get infected."

Brian wasn't wrong. Adam sneered and sniffed himself. The putrid smell filled his nostrils, and he thought he was going to puke again. The horse would get him to the house faster, but Adam didn't like horses. He used to love horses, until one day when he was ten, he was riding in the pasture and the horse he was riding got spooked and threw him. The rock he landed on broke his arm in two places. After that day he swore off horses but knowing what lay beneath the surface of the water, he supposed the horse had every right to be scared. He reached out for his brother's hand but pulled back as Brian extended his own.

"Thanks, but I think I'll just walk."

"Still scared of horses, uh?"

"Yeah, something like that."

The hot water invigorated his senses. The sticky grime washed from his body and swirled down the drain. After he finished scrubbing the dirt and memories of the lake off, he stood under the cascading water and relished the warmth as the cold fled. When the water went from just below scalding to lukewarm, he turned it off and stepped out of the shower. Condensation covered the mirror and metal fixtures. The walls looked like they were crying as large teardrops of water ran down the flower-covered surface.

Adam put on his underwear, gym shorts and a t-shirt and went downstairs. He stood in the middle of the foyer weighing his options. It was getting close to dinnertime, but he really wanted to sit down and relax. The overstuffed La-Z-Boy called to him. He walked into the living room and fell into the plush recliner. It was the only luxurious thing in the house, but Phil always said he deserved it after a long day's work. Adam agreed with the senti-ment and flipped the leg rest up. He laced his fingers behind his head and closed his eyes and ignored the rising blue mist on the lake. The large panel window glowed blue as he drifted to sleep.

He was floating in the air. It took a moment for him to realize what room he was in. Both of his parents lay in bed. Phil was fast asleep; only the gentle coo of his pre-apnea sleep could be heard over the restless tossing and turning of Helen Blackwell.

Outside the bedroom window, blue light glowed, casting shadows across the walls. Blue tinted frost covered the pane and a low, but terrifying voice with an ancient scratch called out to his sleeping mother. A hallucinogenic nausea rocked Adam when his mother woke and he could feel her dread, and pain like he was inside her body, experiencing her emotions and hearing her thoughts while he floated above her.

Helen ... Hel ... en ... Helen.

Whispers ricocheted around the room. The lake was calling to her again, and this time it wouldn't allow her to ignore it.

Helen carefully slipped out of bed. She didn't want to wake

Phil. The last time she tried to leave, he awoke and wanted to know where she was going. She lied and told him she was coming back from the kitchen. It hurt her to lie to him, but she had to. His sleep-veiled face looked like it believed her, but he didn't lie back down until she was under the covers with his arm wrapped tightly around her waist. It was like he knew something was wrong. But how could he? She had been hearing the waterlogged voice for weeks, even with Phil awake in the same room. Those times the voice scared her the most. It told her all the horrible things it would do to her family if she didn't join them at the bottom of the watery pit at the end of the lake. It told her they would rip the arms from her two boys and feed them to the black creatures that protected the water and then drown her husband in their blood and take her, anyway. It entered her mind and showed her. She fought back tears and tried not to frighten her family as the black water seeped into the room and gave everything an oily sheen only she could see.

She tiptoed through the room barefooted and took one last look at Phil. He didn't stir as she closed the door.

Helen, you're running out of time. You must come now, or I will take your children in your place.

She didn't dare go to her boy's rooms for fear of losing her nerve and grabbing them and running. But it would find her. It had told her there was nowhere for her to run, that it wouldn't follow. Tears streaked her face, and she started down the stairs, skipping the third step that would creak and wake everybody in the house. She hurried down the rest of the stairs and crossed the foyer. She stopped at the door and flipped the switch to turn off the outside motion-sensor floodlights and knocked Phil's keys off the key-holder beside the switch plate. They landed with a heavy clunk and fear paralyzed Helen. The house remained quiet as she carefully slid the deadbolt back and opened the door.

The night was uncommonly chilly for a Georgia summer. She wrapped her arms around herself and stepped into the grass. Morning dew soaked her feet and the bottom of her nightgown.

"I can't leave," she whispered, barely audible enough for her to hear. But it heard.

You have to. You know what the other option is. Decide now, or you won't like it if the decision is made for you.

Helen walked to the pasture and could see the inky black water. A blue light pulsed under the water and made the surrounding bank glow. She went through the gate but made sure to close it. Phil wouldn't need to track down the cows first thing in the morning. She crossed the pasture and stopped at the edge of the lake. The bottom half of her nightgown soaked through with dew, but in the watery glow it shined black, like she had washed it with colors. She looked across the water and stamped her feet to pull them out of the cold grass, if only for a few seconds.

Up here, Helen. You must come to the top.

The blue florescent light under the water brightened with the voice as it floated on the breeze. As she made her way to the top of the cliff, she heard the creatures jumping out of the water and their thick bodies splashing down.

When she reached the top, she looked over the edge. It looked like there were hundreds of them splashing around in the turbulent waters. The twisting, writhing creatures covered the surface like a spawning next except for three areas filled with bright blue dots. Lightening like lines shot from the orbs at each other. Rocks crumbled under her feet and she jumped back.

Now is the time, Helen.

"Time for what?"

Time for you to decide.

Helen looked down into the water and around the pasture to find a place to focus her voice.

"I don't understand."

A sacrifice must be made for peace to continue.

"But ..."

Jump.

"I can't.

You must.

"I won't. There has to be another way," Helen yelled.

She stepped back from the edge.

The only other way is for somebody to take your place.

The voice screamed and a bright blue light that looked like flames lit up her house. Helen covered her ears and fell to her knees.

"No!" she screamed. "Don't take them. Don't take them. I'll do it."

The blue flames slid back into the earth. Helen covered her face but did not move.

The time is drawing near, Helen. You must make a choice, or one will be made for you.

Helen stood on shaking legs and inched forward. She toed the edge and fought to move herself back. Something behind her would only allow her to move forward, but when she looked, there was nothing there. The crumbling earth fell into the pit exciting the creatures as they hissed and fought each other to the top of the water. Helen began to tire and weaken from the struggle and she gave in. A bright blue light lit up around her and she stepped off the ledge. As she rushed toward the water, she saw a child on the bank.

Chapter Twelve

Adam awoke covered in sweat. The woman he kept seeing in the white nightgown was his mother. It was the last thing he saw her wearing before she jumped. She hadn't abandoned them; she was trying to protect them from whatever was in the lake. Of course this was all a guess. Even now, he couldn't recall the memory of his mother walking to the top of the cliff and jumping. It had to be a deeply repressed memory that his six-year-old mind fought hard to hide.

Small feet running across the porch stirred him from his thoughts. He jumped up and tripped over the recliner footrest. Sharp pain ripped through his left leg and arm as he crashed to the floor. He sat up and winced as he flapped his arm like a baby bird, testing to see if his wing was ready for flight. Adam's wasn't. Using the arm of the chair, he pushed himself up.

Then he saw her. Staring at him through the window on the front porch. She giggled, and he knew it was her. He tripped his way through the living room and into the foyer. The mirror beside the door hadn't been cleaned in a while, but he could still tell he looked like hell. It couldn't be Grace Ann outside. She was dead. Another giggle came from behind the door, and he grabbed his chest and tried to calm his heart before it ripped through his chest. The door squeaked on its hinges as he inched it open.

And there she stood, swaying back and forth in her favorite navy-blue dress. She looked like his daughter, but she couldn't be. Memories of memories will distort the past; she looked the same, but there was something about her that was different. Maybe it was the way her hair was styled or the dusting of freckles on her nose that now seemed prominent.

The porch light flickered, and she was no longer his daughter, or at least, she was no longer how he thought he remembered her. Now, she belonged to the lake and looked like she had been living there even though she had not aged. Her hair was no longer radiant and parted on the left. It was dull and matted. Parted on the left? She always wanted her hair parted on the right. The blue dress she wore was soaked through and dripped into a large puddle around her bare feet. But the worst of it was her eyes. The beautiful green eyes he loved to watch dance and sparkle with every laugh were now a creamy blue. Phil once had a horse that was blind in one eye because a tree branch fell, and a limb stabbed the horse's cornea. Both of Grace Ann's eyes looked like that. Unseeing, yet seeing everything. He reached out for her, and she pulled away.

"It's your fault I'm dead."

Grace Ann's accusation caught Adam off guard, but the sound of her voice chilled the blood in his veins. She still had the same sweet innocent voice, but below it there was an ancient screech that knew no time or space.

"No. No, it's not. If Grandpa had been watching you like he was supposed to, none of this would have even happened."

Tears ran down Adam's face as he reached out to her and again, she pulled away like a defiant child. That wasn't like her.

"You have always blamed Grandpa, but everything was your fault."

"No," he yelled and stomped his foot on the porch. Grace Ann didn't even flinch. When she was alive, he never would have had a reason to do that, but if he had, she would have run off to hide.

"It wasn't my fault. Your grandfather should have been watching you. He knew that lake was dangerous. That's why they always kept us away from it, even when we were children."

"You knew too, Daddy. But you didn't know enough. Grandma was the sacrifice to keep the peace, and you saw everything," she said and pointed at Adam.

Adam's voice caught in his throat and only a high clicking sound came out. Scenes from his dream flashed through his head. He wasn't sure if he was thinking about the night his mother jumped from the cliff or if something was projecting it to him. He tried to clear his mind and failed.

"You saw her jump to save your life. You shouldn't have seen anything."

Grace Ann's voice rose in pitch as she spoke. A blue fog crept over the side of the porch and covered their feet.

"I was too young. I couldn't do anything to stop her."

No longer trying to hold back tears, Adam began to sob.

"You couldn't stop her. It was her job. But once you saw everything, you had to be the next sacrifice."

"But I didn't see anything. I don't remember anything that happened."

"No, you don't," she said.

Adam sighed in relief, but he wasn't sure why.

"You were protected because you didn't remember, and your fear of the water kept you away. You were too afraid for them to talk to you. They had to take me that night because you wouldn't do it. Now it's your turn."

"My turn for what? Grace Ann, baby, I don't understand."

She didn't sound like a child anymore. His little girl was gone and the thing controlling her was all that was left.

"It's your turn," she repeated and pointed to the cliff.

A bright blue light erupted from the top of the rock formation and shot into the air. Within the beam of light, he could make out the shapes of two people. The one in the back guided the person in front forward. The person in front wore a billowing nightgown that waved in the wind. It was his mother. At first, he couldn't make out any details of the figures, but as the woman turned to look at the house, he saw with perfect clarity the fear on her face and longing sorrow in her eyes. Helen's mouth moved, but he couldn't hear what she was saying. She stepped off the cliff and plunged into the murky water below. Across the cool breeze he heard his mother's voice and final words, "I love you all."

He hadn't heard her voice in thirty years, but he knew it. Even the most terrifying moment of her life she spoke to them in her soft voice. Adam convulsed, and he fell to his knees. He reached out to Grace Ann, and she backed away.

"It's your turn to do what you should have done before, but you ran away. He had to take Grandpa to call you home. His death was because of you too."

"He who? I don't understand."

"You don't have to understand. Just jump, Daddy."

Adam lowered his head. He couldn't face ... his daughter? Ghost? Demon? He didn't know what to call her, but she was trying to persuade him by sweetly calling him daddy. She was being sweet, so he'd kill himself; sacrifice himself for something he didn't understand.

"I can't."

"Just jump. Just jump," she said.

She jumped up and down.

"Come and join us, Daddy. Just jump. Just jump."

Grace Ann walked down the steps and headed for the lake. Adam chased after her.

"No. Wait, Grace. Don't leave. Stay here with me. You don't have to go back. You can stay with me and everything will be okay."

Grace Ann's face turned red and contorted. Her nose twisted further than he thought was possible, almost touching the crinkles around her closed eyes. She huffed once and stamped her feet like a spoiled child on the toy aisle.

"Just fucking jump," she yelled, and continued toward the lake.

Not my child. That's what all parents say, and until one day they hit that aisle and their child sees the one toy they cannot live without. Adam stopped his pursuit. He wasn't sure what to do, but he knew he wasn't about to go running up that cliff and take a swan dive three stories down into a pit of churning water and whatever those black creatures were. She was still screaming for him to jump when he ran behind her and grabbed her shoulder.

A bright spark between his hand and her dress flared and a bolt of lightning shot out of the stormless sky. The bolt moved in slow motion as it streaked toward Adam. A loud hum filled his ears, and the lightning bolt struck his shoulder. The blast separated him from Grace Ann, and he flew backward and landed on the ground with a dull thump. Everything went black.

When Adam came to, he kept his eyes shut tight. His head throbbed; bolts of pain shot through his head. Hopefully he wasn't having a stroke. Blaring sun assaulted his eyes when he opened them and realized he was walking toward the house. He tried to stop his legs, but dragged his feet another couple steps, and heard a distant voice.

A grey shower of water crashed over his head. He was in the water again. The thing in the water had pulled him back in, and this time it was going to keep him. Grace Ann led him back to the lake. He jumped to his feet and thrashed his arms above his head and blew water from his mouth and nose.

"Damn it, Adam. Let's go. I can't carry you the way I did Daddy."

It was like being at the bottom of a waterfall and fighting to hear what the person next to you was saying. He tried to focus on the voice but couldn't register who it belonged to. He hit the ground.

"Adam, listen to me. You have to get up and come inside the house. You can't sleep out here in the yard."

"You won't kill me. I won't let you. You killed Grace, but I won't let you get me. I'll drain the whole damn lake. You killed her. You killed her. You killed her," Adam screamed and began to sob.

A strong hand fell on his shoulder and shook him.

"Nobody's going to kill you. It's just me," the voice said.

The hand on his shoulder squeezed and Adam winced at the pain and stopped flailing around. He finally opened his eyes and saw Brian looking at him like he'd lost his mind.

"You know Daddy was acting the same as you right before he died. You might want to lay off the hard stuff for a while. This place is getting to you."

"No. No, it's not. It got to him, but it won't get to me. We've got to get the hell out of here now."

"We can't just leave the house. There's nobody to take care of the animals."

"I don't care. Turn them all out to pasture and let's go."

Adam thrust his finger at the lake.

"There's something wrong with the lake. Something is controlling it, and everybody that lives here. I won't be the next sacrifice."

"Sacrifice? What are you talking 'bout? There ain't no sacrificing going on. We don't even slaughter any cows or pigs."

Adam wanted to slap some sense into his brother but knew Brian would easily take him in a fair fight, and Adam wasn't in the best state of mind right now.

"Look. I know you want to stay here, but we can't, or it will get us too."

"What will?"

"Just listen to me. As much as I don't want to do it, I think it might be a good idea to sell the place to Vernon Barlow and be done with it."

Brian took a step back and put a cigarette in his mouth. He patted down both of the pockets on his shirt and all the pockets on his jeans. Then checked the left shirt pocket again and pulled out his lighter. Blue smoke escaped through his lips and nose.

"Now I know you've lost it."

"That's not what I really want to do, but maybe we should

think about it. He'll pay us double what this place is worth and then we can leave and get the hell out of here and never come back."

"Why do you think he wants this place and why do you think he would pay that much?"

"Because Eric was here, and ..."

"Eric was here? Why was he here?"

Brian threw his half-finished cigarette in the grass, leaving it to burn out.

"Eric came by and said his uncle would give us double what it was worth. I punched him in the eye, so the dollar amount might not be the same, but I know Vernon wants it."

"So now you're going behind my back and trying to make deals without talking to me first. I can't believe you," Brian roared and took a step toward Adam.

Adam didn't shy away from Brian this time and stepped forward on legs still wobbly from the lightning strike.

"I wasn't going behind your back. Eric came to me. I wasn't going to take the deal. And it doesn't really matter if I was going to because legally this place is mine and I'm letting you stay here."

"Oh, you're just letting me stay here? You just letting me take care of your cows and pigs and horses too?"

"I guess that makes us even for room and board. The lake is ..." Adam struggled to find the right word. He didn't know what was wrong with the lake, but he knew it wasn't right. "It's haunted, Brian. It's haunted. It killed Mom and Grace Ann and Dad. If we don't leave, we will be next."

There, he said it. The place was haunted, and the new possibilities scared him. The thing in the lake was easy enough to avoid, they'd been doing in their whole lives and never knew it. But he couldn't avoid Grace Ann. She hadn't hurt anybody yet, but that didn't mean she couldn't. She hadn't hurt anybody, unless she convinced Phil to jump like she was trying to get Adam to do last night.

Brian stepped back, pulled his hat off and ran his hand through his greasy hair.

"There ain't nothing wrong with that lake. Never has been. Momma and Daddy just told us that to keep us away when we was young. I know you're still upset about Grace Ann, but the lake didn't kill her or Momma or Daddy. And it sure as shit ain't haunted."

"You have to listen to me. Something's not right here."

"I used to go out fishing in that jon boat all the time and nothing ever happened to me."

"You aren't the one it wants," Adam said.

"What are you talking about?"

Brian stood tall and crossed his arms in front of his chest. Adam could tell he was going to take it personal and get defensive. This was how he would act when they were children. Brian always thought Adam was the favorite child.

"You didn't see it, Brian."

"See what?"

"You didn't see Mom jump."

"Nobody did," Brian said.

He turned his head toward the lake and blew air through his teeth, causing his cheeks to puff out.

"I did. I saw her do it. She didn't want to jump. Something's not right here. Can't you feel it?"

"I don't feel a thing. But I do see that something's not right here. First Daddy and now you."

"What do you mean?"

"A couple weeks before Daddy died, he was going on and on about the lake. He was drinking too much and started seeing things. I wasn't going to tell you cause I thought it would upset you, but he said he saw Grace a couple times.

"He saw her too?"

"Have you seen her?"

"Twice. Well, once for sure. She's the one that told me the lake wanted me. Don't you get it? We've got to get out of here."

"No. I think it's both of ya'lls grief and guilt that's causing all this. There's nothing wrong with that lake or anything else around here. You want to know what I think?"

Adam didn't care what he had to say. Brian wasn't listening to him. It made sense if Brian would think about it.

"Guess you don't care to know, but I'm going to tell you, anyway. I think this is one more way for you to push me away. First the lake wants Momma, and then it takes Grace because it wanted you. Why'd it take Daddy then? Cause you weren't around?"

Brian's questions roused Adam from his thoughts.

"Close. It killed him to get me to come home."

"You realize how full of shit and yourself you sound? Always has to be 'bout you. You're the only one that matters. You got the education. You had the perfect wife and perfect family."

"You forgot about the good looks. Grow up. Don't make this about childhood jealousy. I don't have time for that."

"You never have time for anything except for what you want."

This conversation was going nowhere. Brian would never understand. How could he? It wasn't that Brian was stupid. He wasn't the brightest, and there were obviously unresolved issues of resentment, but Adam didn't have time for that. He didn't plan to go anywhere near the lake; he needed to get out of Georgia. The lake pulled him in and tried to kill him, but he was able to get away, and then it sent Grace Ann to bring him to it. He wanted to go with her. It would have been the easy thing to do. Would everything have stopped if he had gone to the lake, or would it have come after Brian next? Adam didn't know the answers but didn't want to be around and let it decide to flood its banks and take him out.

But Phil had seen her too.

Brian said Phil saw her a couple times. Maybe she told him more? He might have known what was going on. Did he know how to fix it? He probably didn't know how to end everything, but he might have known more than Adam did.

"He used to always write stuff down. You remember? He would say it was for posterity. Maybe he wrote some of it down?"

Adam ran up the first few stairs and then slowed down as a wave of nausea crashed over him.

"Adam, hold up. Just leave it alone," Brian called after him.

Adam went through the door and to his father's room. He hadn't been in here since he'd come back. The room looked untouched since Phil died. The bed sheets were twisted and thrown on the mattress. Clothes lay haphazardly around the room, on top of the chest at the foot of the bed and hanging over his grandfather's rocking chair. An empty bottle of Waterwheel bourbon rolled across the floor and came to rest at his foot. Adam picked up the bottle and sniffed the open throat. He pulled the bottle away and inspected the label. The subtle hint of caramel and citrus floated through the air. Adam sniffed the bottle again as he combed through the mess of papers scattered across the dresser.

Brian stood in the doorway.

"I don't know what you're trying to find."

Adam knocked an orange prescription bottle to the floor. The pills rattled inside as the bottle tried to escape Adam's reach. He picked the bottle up and examined the label.

"Why was he taking Vicodin?"

"He threw his back out a couple months ago. I think mixing the pills and whiskey was part of his problem."

Adam thumbed the top from the bottle and shook a couple into his hand.

"Nah, I don't believe that. It was the lake that killed him," Adam said and dry swallowed two of the pills.

"Don't off yourself in the lake to prove you're right. I'll show you there's nothing wrong. I'm going fishing," Brian said.

Adam wasn't paying attention. He already decided he wasn't going to change Brian's mind and started searching to see if Phil had left a journal. The police had no doubt looked through his stuff for a suicide note, but they hadn't looked too hard. Brian probably told them everything they needed to know to rule it a suicide. Adam laid his hands on a beat-up spiral-bound notebook and heard the front door open and close.

Chapter Thirteen

B rian was pissed. He lit a cigarette, climbed into the Polaris and headed for the utility shed beside the dock. Ever since Adam had gotten home, all he was worried about was getting everything over with so he could go back to where he came from. Adam hadn't been the one to pick up the pieces when he left. Brian stayed home and took care of their father and even Mandy for a little bit, while Adam ran away from all his responsibilities. It was Adam's fault their father was dead. If he had stayed home and talked to Phil, he would have seen things differently. Instead, he caused a scene at Grace Ann's funeral and put all the blame on Phil. It was too much guilt for one person to take. It shouldn't have surprised anybody to hear he was dead. But Adam didn't even care. He was glad Phil was dead. And after everything that happened, Phil still left the house and everything in it to Adam. Surely, he was too distraught over Grace Ann's death and Adam's running away and forgot or ceased to care about his will. He wouldn't leave Adam everything after the way he treated him and disappeared, would he? If his plan was to bring Adam home and there would be a big family reunion and he would stay, that plan had backfired royally. Now, Adam was talking ghosts and selling to Vernon Barlow. He had gone just as crazy as Phil since they'd last seen each other. They hadn't even talked on the phone. That might have been okay for Adam, but Brian resented him for it.

He backed the Polaris to the rolling door of the shed and slid out of the driver's seat. It had been a while since someone opened the door. He feared it might be rusted shut, until he gave a tug and the door rolled up easily with only a few squeaks, like it had been recently serviced. The last time Brian used the jon boat, he had plenty of room and backed it into the shed. Cardboard boxes lined the small trailer and would have to be moved.

He flicked his cigarette toward the water and stepped in the shed. The scent of old rat shit baking in a tin can filled his nose. He pulled his shirt collar over his face and swatted at the dust floating in the air. An old fifty-pound bag of fish food sitting on a workbench started to rustle. Avoiding the bench, Brian worked his way around the trailer and kicked all the boxes to the far sides of the shed. He moved to the back of the shed and carefully opened a Rubbermaid cabinet; he didn't want anything jumping out and surprising him. There didn't seem to be anything alive in the cabinet, and he reached his hand past a colony of abandoned dirt dauber nests and pulled out his father's favorite spinning reel. Despite the condition of the cabinet, the rod and reel looked to be in good shape. He grabbed an old Plano tackle box and sat it and the rod in the bottom of the boat.

Brian backed the Polaris up until the trailer hitch hovered above the ball of the UTV. Sweat ran down his face as he cranked the hitch in place. It was too hot to be fishing, but Adam made him so mad he didn't care. He did wish he'd thought to bring some water.

The makeshift boat ramp crumbled in the grass to the left of the dock. Only fifteen or twenty feet from where Grace Ann went into the water. It was also the place where he pulled Adam out of the water. How did he fall in? He knew Adam had been drinking, but he was stone sober when he came out of the water. Of course, almost drowning would scare even the most dedicated drunk sober. Adam said something pulled him in and wouldn't let him go, and it had been hard to pull him out. Everything hadn't been great for a while, but Adam thought a piece of paper Daddy forgot to change meant he could take over. Now Adam was affecting Brian's thoughts. He sounded as paranoid as Adam, too. Adam always thought about the worst possible thing that could happen in any situation, real or imaginary. It was no way to live, and Brian wasn't going to buy into it.

The rocks crackled as the tires forced them together. Brian backed the boat into the water. A fish jumped. There were no ripples marring the surface, but it sounded like the fish might have been in the middle of the lake. He usually liked to fish along the banks, but it was hot, so the fish were in the deeper water. The middle was as good a place to start as any. The hand crank winch spun and released the boat to knock gently against the dock. Brian tied the boat to a cleat on the dock rail and pulled the Polaris forward enough to pull the trailer out from the water.

The boat rocked hard away from the dock and threatened to get away from Brian, leaving him to splash in the inky water below. He steadied himself, tied the boat closer, and attempted to step in again. He wobbled on unsteady legs and sat down faster and harder than he wanted. He expected water to crash over the side of the boat, but it didn't. It would take him a few minutes to adjust and get his sea legs. He didn't believe ghosts haunted the lake. He wasn't the type to believe in ghosts, but the lake did give off eerie vibes and made him feel like he was being watched.

Brian paddled the boat to the middle on a lake of glass.

He laid the oars down and picked up his father's rod and reel. The line was old and would likely snap if he got a bite from a decent sized fish, but he didn't care, he wasn't out here because he wanted to catch dinner. He was out here to prove a point to his brother. Sitting in the middle of the lake was lonely, but the lack of wind or sound from any animal magnified the loneliness. It was the quietest place Brian had ever been, and it terrified him.

To get his mind off the lake, he wrapped a length of fishing line around his hand and tested its strength. When it didn't break, he opened the tackle box and pulled up the three rows of collapsing shelves. The fish would be close to the bottom of the lake, so he decided to Carolina Rig an artificial worm, and see if he got lucky. He slid a few beads and a sinker on the line and tied a leader of line to the end. It amazed him how easily he remembered how to tie fishing knots as he twisted and pulled the filament. Brian rummaged through the different packs of plastic worms in the bottom of the tackle box. He selected a color called June Bug and opened the pack. The worms were still moist even though they had been in that shed for a while. He slid the hook through the head and turned it around and buried the hook into the black with teal and purple flaked body.

The lure plopped into the water. It hardly made an audible noise and created no wake rings. Brian slowly jerked the bait across the bottom of the lake. The sun beat down on the back of his neck. It didn't matter where the fish were. When he reeled in the cast, he was going to move closer to the bank so he could sit in the shade created by one of the trees hanging over the water. He had never been one for sitting still long enough to fish for an extended period of time, but he needed to stay out on the water long enough to show Adam there was nothing wrong with the lake.

The worst-case scenario in any situation was the first thing Adam grabbed on to, but he'd always been afraid of the lake, even when they were kids.

When they were younger, Brian was fishing from the bank and hooked a big one; at least he'd thought it was a big one at the time. A fish hit the top of the water somewhere to the right of where he stood. It sounded big. He needed to get his line in quick, so he could move and have a chance to catch whatever he'd heard. He reeled his line in faster than anything swimming in the lake could catch. The frog shaped lure skimmed the top of the water. It rotated on the line, and the chartreuse underbelly glowed like a meteor on a starless night. Then it was gone.

The frog disappeared, and Brian's line pulled taut. The reel snatched in his hand, and the skyward rod snapped to the water. He'd never had a fish hit his line like that before. It must have been a monster. He slowly turned the handle, but he only heard the click of the drag. The line didn't move. It was stuck on a branch. Brian jerked the line, and the branch shifted. His shoes slid across the dirt toward the bank. He pulled again and reeled in the excess line and lowered the rod to his waist and pulled, trying to dislodge his favorite lure from the tree. His feet started sliding again and Adam ran up and cut the line and sent Brian flying back to the rocky dirt. Brian wanted to beat his brother's ass, but he'd forgotten about the whole incident by the time the stone bruises had faded.

Adam swore something in the water grabbed the frog and was trying to pull him in, but Brian told him it was only stuck on a log. Brian had an active imagination, but it was nothing compared to Adam's.

The line twitched, and Brian nearly jumped to his feet. That would've been bad. He would've ended up swimming for the shore when he couldn't get back in the boat. It was just a nibble. He ran his hand across the back of his neck. His sunburn stung. Adam would have freaked out like a California hippie because it might be cancer. Everything in California caused cancer. Brian laughed, and the rod bent toward the water.

He snatched the rod to set the hook and reeled in the slack. The line went dead in the water. He probably got too excited and pulled the hook from the fish's mouth. The line started moving, but the fish didn't run against the strain of the line. It swam toward his boat. The change in direction surprised him, and he didn't think of reeling in the extra line until the fish went under his boat. The line pulled tight across the bow and turned the boat to face the opposite direction. Brian had never seen a fish act like that before. The line went limp. It must have been a sudden burst of strength that left the fish spent. He looked over the wakeless water and reeled in the line.

The first thing out of the water was Brian's worm. When attacked, the hook ripped from its belly and it slid up the leader line like it was trying to escape an inevitable death. He could barely make out the shape of the fish in the dark water. It might be a catfish, but he couldn't tell. The head bumped against the bottom of the boat, and Brian grabbed the line. Using the line as a guide, he stuck his hand in the water. If it was a catfish, he didn't want to screw up and grab one of the razor-sharp fins behind its head.

The fish stopped thrashing, and he slid his thumb into the mouth. The course sandpaper of the fish's lip pulled at his thumb. Something sharp and hooked in toward the fish's throat stopped his progress. It might have been the hook embedded in the lip, but fear flooded Brian, and burst through the dam of his tough guy persona. It wasn't a catfish.

There was a slight pull in the water as the animal gulped its prey and bit into Brian's thumb. Hot pain shot up Brian's arm. He tried to pull his hand out of the water, but it pulled him deeper. His mouth collided with the side of the boat and filled with warm blood. He spit pieces of his teeth into the water. Whatever was in the water released his thumb long enough to strike his hand again with laser speed and precision. It clamped down on his hand and fingers fell away. In anguish, Brian's scream was ragged as it escaped from his mouth. From the middle of the lake, it sounded like a small rodent caught in a trap. Adam would never hear him from in the house.

Brian trembled and pulled his hand out of the water. A long fish that looked more like a fat snake thrashed on the end of Brian's ruined hand. Its sleek black skin looked like tough leather, and it had to be at least five feet long. Brian fell into the bottom of the boat, and the creature released his hand. It flipped and writhed in the hull, trying to get itself back into the water.

Brian moved to the bow and put the middle bench between him and the creature. His fingerless hand throbbed, and he buried it his shirt causing another rash of sharp shooting pain. He wrapped his hand in the tail of his shirt and tried to calm his breathing before he hyperventilated. It didn't work. The creature's head popped in the air and landed on the seat with a dry thud. Momentarily neglecting its need for water, it focused on Brian and snapped its jaws. It tried to move off the bench and get in the hull with him, but it was slowing down.

A hard bump on the side of the boat and the creature stopped moving. The wind died, and the birds stopped calling to each other. Everything had gone quiet. Brian rolled in the hull. He used his elbow for leverage and moved to his knees. Another thump hit the boat. This time, the attack came from the bottom. The blue eyes of the creature on the bench began to fade. Another knock hit the boat and rocked it back and forth. The creature on the seat found its second wind. It chomped its sharp teeth, rolled off the bench and flopped into the water. There was no splash or ripple effect.

Something repeatedly hit the boat. Were there more fish? It sounded like he was caught in a hailstorm underneath a tin roof. Brian reached for an oar and plunged it into the water. He used the palm of his injured hand to steady and guide the oar. On the second row, a smaller version of the fish Brian caught jumped out of the water and snapped the oar in two. Another fish leaped out of the water and snapped its powerful jaws in his face.

Brian swung the oar handle and connected with the next fish that flew at him. There was a high-pitched shriek, and it fell back into the water and snapped at its own tail. The thumping contin-ued. There was no escape. He had one more oar, but he didn't want to risk that one getting bit in two, as well. Maybe they would get bored? He could fight them off, but his hand was still bleeding through his shirt. The ends where his fingers used to be, throbbed with every beat of his heart.

It was the middle of the day and the sun should have been high in the sky, but a darkness fell over the lake. The once motionless water jumped and splashed, matching the hailstorm on the bottom of the boat. Adam was right. Something was wrong with the lake, and he hadn't believed him. He wanted to show Adam how wrong he was, and now Brian was going to pay for it. Bright, soundless lightning strikes of blue and red filled the air. The bolts formed pockets of purple spheres where they crossed. He screamed. He screamed louder than he thought possible. Thick cords of muscle stood out as he yelled.

"God! Help me, please! Please! Help me!" he screamed to the dark sky.

Brian was lightheaded, and his head rocked with the waves. Red foam bubbled to the surface and attached to the hull of the boat. A blue lightning bolt struck the water off to Brian's left and everything went quiet again.

This was his answer. This was his chance to get away. When he got back to the house, he would pack and go anywhere Adam wanted to go. He'd go to Chicago if he had to. He could handle the city. They had the best pizza. He'd get used to it.

With trembling hands, Brian grabbed the oar. The rough water may have been over in the lake, but there was a tidal wave bouncing back and forth in his skull. He shook his head to calm the waters, but only succeeded in breaking the levees. He pitched to the left. Red saliva escaped his lips.

Brian closed his eyes tight, and a low rumble vibrated through the boat. The vibration strengthened, and his vision blurred. He rolled back into the center of the boat, and an underwater roar stopped him. It wasn't over. The storm was about to hit. He wasn't afraid, he didn't have the consciousness to be, but his bladder released when a large black tentacle pierced the bottom of the boat. Water trickled in until the tentacle withdrew from the hole. Water poured in like blood after the knife has been removed. Brian lost his balance and fell. His back hit the cold water and his entire body broke out in goose flesh. He could see the fish circling him like water buzzards. There were hundreds of them.

They attacked as a group. The first teeth sank into his cheek and neck. Blood filled his mouth as he tried to scream to the black and blue sky. The blood created a feeding frenzy, but the fish did not snap at or bite each other. They knew their place. Razor-sharp teeth plunged into every available piece of flesh. One of the fish burst through his stomach and thrashed as it became tangled in his intestines. Brian died when the next fish burst through his chest and fed on his heart.

Chapter Fourteen

Adam threw the bottle on the bed and sat down. Phil didn't have great taste in clothes, movies, or women, besides Helen, but he knew a great whiskey when he came across it. Adam would have to remember to grab some the next time he went to the store.

The cover of the notebook held on by a few paper tabs. It came off in his hand when he opened it to Phil's near indecipherable scrawl. Gooseflesh rippled up his arms and a shiver-inducing chill ran down his spine as he read.

I saw her. Grace Ann. I know it sounds crazy, and nobody will believe me, but she was there, I swear. I was asleep in my chair and when I woke up, she was standing on the porch looking at me through the window. Damn near broke my hip trying to get outta my chair. I had a little to drink, but I wasn't drunk. Just enough to take the edge off.

Another chilled flowed through Adam as he thought about Grace Ann watching him through the same window.

She blames me for everything. I don't understand how she can blame me. I told her I only wanted her to have fun. I wanted to tell her it was her daddy's fault, but I didn't want to talk bad about him to her. What am I saying? She's dead. I'm going to drive myself crazy thinking about her.

Adam felt the blood rush to his face. That son of a bitch blamed Adam for Grace Ann's death. A sudden urge to burn the house to the ground and run back to Chicago filled Adam. He picked a framed picture of his mother off the floor and set it on the bed next to him. The hatred buzzed in his ears and subsided to a low ring as he looked back to the journal. The writing became more erratic as it went down the page.

Phil had been drinking while he was writing. A large brown stain smeared the ink on the next page and made the writing indecipherable. He left the liquor there to pool because most of the remaining pages stuck together. Adam only deciphered out two lines from the smeared stains. At the bottom of the page, it read: *Where does the water go? I will find her.*

It didn't make sense, but Phil had been drunk at the time, and it probably didn't make sense to him either. He flipped the final fifty pages as one and a few sheets of paper fluttered to the floor. Adam expected more of the same ramblings from an old drunk when he picked them up. It took him a moment to realize what he was looking at.

The graphed map pages came from an old atlas. It showed the surrounding highway and roads leading into Scarsville. A black star represented the family farm. Beside the star was a black circle where the lake was. Deep depressions from the tip of the pen streaked the black lake. Adam could see the hints of blue on the map peeking from under the ink. Phil hadn't marked the lake. He made the water look as black as it did in person. To the right of the lake, there were four creeks circled. Three of them were on the Blackwell property, but if he was trying to find where the lake emptied out, only one of those had enough water flowing in it to make sense. The last creek circled was on the neighboring farm's land.

The other papers were a satellite view of the property and provided more detail than the atlas. The roof of the house was a grainy black spot on a light green background. Brian wasn't home at the time of the fly over because there was only a hint of Phil's pale blue truck sticking out from under the pecan tree. Adam hesitated when he turned to the next page containing the lake. It was a massive black mark and made the grass look greener around it. The most striking thing about the lake was the shape. From the aerial view, it looked fake. The outline of the lake made a perfect oval that ended in the dot of the pit. The banks were too smooth and perfect. It didn't look like a lake that had been washing away its banks to reinvent itself. It looked like a scalpel and steady hand cut a void into the ground.

Everything was black, except in the middle of the lake, where the water was a lighter shade of grey. It looked like a small blotch with lighter tendrils reaching out. Adam shivered as a chill ran down his spine. Had the satellite caught whatever pulled him into the water? It was small on the grainy printout compared to the lake, but it was still massive in scale. Adam's hands were sticky with sweat. He threw the page on the bed. There wasn't anything in the lake. The satellite didn't catch anything. The printer was probably starting to get low on ink, or some of the jets were clogged. That's why it wasn't dark all over. He wiped the sweat from his brow and scattered the remaining sheets on the bed.

There were six images of fields. Adam recognized one of the photos as the pasture behind the lake. It had a number two in the top left corner. The other photos looked like random pastoral pictures from the air. They could be from anywhere. Adam grabbed the closest one and saw a number three on the corner. He laid it beneath photo number two and searched for number one. It took Adam a while to realize picture four didn't connect to the bottom of picture three but lined up with the edge of picture one.

Adam stood back from the bed and surveyed the land from the house to the middle of the neighboring pasture. All the land around the lake was flat. On the opposite side there was a gentle slope that provided a view from higher ground, but there was nothing that looked like water had been flowing underneath it for years.

He gave up. There was nothing there. Phil had lost it and

started looking for Grace Ann and where the water came out after it left the pit. When he couldn't find anything, he killed himself. That was the only explanation. Adam had only been seeing similar things because of the stress created from being back in town. Similar or exact? He just needed a good night's sleep and to dry out. He resolved to this conclusion and slid the pictures into a stack. Phil may have been crazy, and the journal proved it, but there was something off about the whole thing.

The printed satellite images were bright white with no bent edges. A sick mind hadn't gathered and poured over them. The person who took the screenshots from various angles was meticulous in their work. All the fence lines and creeks matched up perfectly. It was a bit obsessive, now that he thought about it. Phil could still have been sick at this point, but it was a different kind of sickness.

The picture on the top of the stack was of the dead end beside the driveway, barely visible from the decades old deadfall was the end of a slight ridge. Adam quickly shuffled through the pages and lined photo four to the edge of photo one. The ridge didn't continue onto the next page. If that ridge had anything to do with the lake, Phil had been looking in the wrong direction. He should have followed it North, instead of going East and South. It would be strange for the water to flow north here, but with everything else going on, it was easily overlooked.

Adam closed the journal. What if the creek Phil was looking for was further north? It would be easy to pull up the satellite images and follow them north. It might be a waste of time, but he might find the right creek. But why did that matter to Phil? He could spend all that time looking for something that wasn't there, or even if it was, it probably wouldn't explain anything. Instead of running off and following crazy theories of a dead man, he should be getting the house ready to sell and get back home. There weren't any writing deadlines approaching, but there was something he could be working on that was productive.

He couldn't up and leave again. He ran away once when they needed him, and he didn't want to do that again. If he sold the place right now, he would be passing the problem over to the next person and he didn't want that hanging over him. Well, he might be okay with leaving the problem with Eric, but it would definitely be too big of an issue for him to handle and he'd get somebody else involved who would get hurt. Adam didn't want that on his conscious; look what it had done to Phil.

The doorbell rang. Adam wasn't expecting anybody. From the window, he could barely make out a black car with 911 printed in gold letters before the taillights. Eric had called the cops. That son of a bitch came to the house knowing he would stir things up. He'd made Adam punch him. Adam was in a state of ... state of what? It wasn't mourning. Temporary insanity. Did that still work? Temporary insanity from being back where his daughter died, and he'd just heard ghosts running around the house. But only heard the ghosts. If he admitted to seeing them too, the insanity wouldn't be considered temporary.

The doorbell rang again, followed by a knock that could only be described as copish. Adam hunched his shoulders and walked to the steps where he stood up straight and bounced down to the foyer and opened the door with a big smile on his face. No reason to look like a beat dog and let them know you're guilty. Let them prove it.

Sheriff John Brown stood on the front porch with his hand poised to assault the door again when Adam opened it. He stared off toward the lake and removed his sunglasses when he saw Adam.

"Hey there, Mr. Blackwell."

"Afternoon, sheriff. Is there something I can do for you?" Adam asked.

There was no reason for him to run. They had him if they wanted him. It wasn't like there was anywhere for him to hide. And why was he thinking about running? He'd never had any reason to run before. He also never assaulted a kid—man before, and especially not one he thought could have connections with the sheriff. Didn't think that one through. He wiped his sweaty palms on his shorts and reluctantly shook the sheriff's outstretched hand.

"I was hoping you might be able to clear something up for me."

Here it was. His right to remain silent was being revoked. He needed to clear up why he punched a guy who had the whole department on the take. He bit his lip.

"First, I'd like to give my condolences for the loss of your father. He was a good man."

"We weren't as close as we once were, but I appreciate it."

What was he waiting for? Why didn't he do it and get it over with? Take him down to the station and give him his one phone call. Who would he call? Charlotte? He hadn't thought about her since he'd been home. It was understandable. He'd been busy, but now that he thought about it, he should probably call her whether it's at the station or when the sheriff left.

"No, I don't suppose you were, going up north and all. But the reason I'm here is we've gotten a few calls about strange lights and noises coming from over this way and I was hoping you could sort that out for me."

"Strange lights and noises? That's weird. I haven't heard or seen anything. We're not really that close to anybody. You'd think I would have," Adam said and relaxed a bit. Maybe these reports were the only reason the sheriff was here? He didn't want to let his guard down and get caught in a trap.

"Yeah, that's what I was thinking too. That's why I came out here to ask you. I don't usually make house calls, but the complaints made it sound like you had a lion or some other kind of wild animal over here."

Adam laughed, then said, "No zoo here. I'm not sure what it could have been. Maybe coyotes?"

"Maybe," the sheriff scoffed, "I'm not really sure what to make of it, myself. We've been getting these calls for a while, and like I said, Phil was a good man, and when he told me he had no idea what it was, I believed him, but he had also been sick for a while. When we got another call 'bout thirty minutes or so ago, I figured

I'd head up here since you were back in town and might have a different perspective."

Adam didn't understand what the sheriff was getting at. He obviously didn't think Adam had anything to do with it since it was happening before he got here, but he didn't completely believe him either. The two men stared each other down. Adam squirmed in his shoes, willing the sheriff to break the uncomfortable silence. When he'd given up hope, he opened his mouth, but the sheriff spoke first.

"Well, I guess that's it. If you wouldn't mind, I'd appreciate it if you would keep an eye out for anything out of the ordinary. Maybe talk to your brother and see what he has to say about it."

"Yes, sir. You'll be the first person I call if a wild lion goes running through my pasture," Adam said and almost saluted.

John Brown's mouth moved like he was talking, but no words were coming out. Finally he squinted his eyes and said, "Thank you, I'd appreciate it," and walked down the steps.

Adam had his phone out opening the Google Earth app before Sheriff Brown made it to his car. He typed the address into the search bar. The Earth turned and like a 3d rollercoaster ride, Scaresville Georgia came rushing at him. A red pointer indicated where the house was as the camera circled the surrounding area. It was hard to ignore the lake. The house was the focal point of the location, but the black water was always there. Adam saw the same grey shape in the water reaching out toward the house. It wasn't the ink jets. He forced his attention from the lake and tried to focus on the house and noticed something he hadn't seen before. A heavy pang hit his chest and stayed there like somebody had stomped him and then decided to stay awhile and rest on top of him. His breaths were shallow and raspy.

There was a bright orange spot in the driveway. Adam already knew what it was, but zoomed in any way and could barely make out the pixelated shape of a car. It was Mandy's Challenger. She called it her Halloweenmobile because of the two black racing stripes down the center. Adam had loved that car, but they didn't keep it long because Mandy said they were going to kill themselves in it one day and she had a lot left to do. Like having kids. Satellite images were always old, but this had to have been at least ten years old. If that grey spot was whatever pulled him in the water, then it had been there for a long time and nobody knew about it. It could have grabbed anybody whenever it wanted. Mom knew. It had been in the lake for decades, possibly centuries. He didn't see the creature in the dream about his mom, but he had an overwhelming feeling it had been there, waiting. It is what the voice would have sent after her family if Helen hadn't complied and jumped off the cliff.

Adam scrolled to the deadfall at the end of the road and found the ridge. Trees covered the land north of the deadfall, and blocked the satellites' view, but Adam and Brian had explored those woods many times as kids and he knew there wasn't any water beneath the canopy of those trees. He continued moving north and finally came to another clearing. The ridge picked back up in the middle of the clearing and snaked its way across three pastures in varying shades of green until it approached a road.

He scrolled to the other side of the road and a thin black line escaped from under the road and mixed into a bright blue lagoon. It was massive. There were a few small boats out on the water and trucks waiting on the bank.

The black line had to be water flowing from Adam's lake. It was eerie how black and serpentine it looked as it stretched to its limits. That is, if it had any limits. It could be contaminating other waterways. There probably wasn't anything he could do about it, but Adam needed to find out if it was possible for the same thing to happen in the surrounding lakes. Maybe it already was? Adam followed the lakeside road until it met the highway. He thought he was covering a lot of ground when he was chasing the ridge through the pastures, but it wasn't that far. Maybe a fifteen-minute ride.

Chapter Fifteen

Adam dropped the boot-foot waders in the back of Phil's truck. He didn't plan to get in the water and didn't want to get anywhere near the water if his lake was feeding into it. There's no telling what else had slipped through over the years, but either way, he wanted to be ready. He threw Phil's journal on the bench seat and slid behind the wheel. The door squeaked like an old seesaw as it bounced on its hinges. Adam couldn't remember what year the truck was, but he knew Phil bought it before he was born. Phil never wanted a new truck. Always said they had too much technology waiting to break, so they could charge you to fix it. Adam smiled as he rolled the window down with the hand-crank. The air conditioner probably didn't work. Phil never would have had it changed over to new stuff. Upgrading the system would leave it open for more problems. The only problem Adam saw is that it was never cooler than hell during the summer. Fall wasn't much better, and what happened to winter? There were more than a few Christmases spent in shorts and sundresses. The car would have been more comfortable, but Adam didn't trust it not to fall apart on the bumpy dirt roads he was going to drive. Adam put the key in the ignition, and another vehicle pulled into the driveway.

He knew it wasn't Eric because he would have heard him coming. It better not have been somebody else from the Barlow family trying to buy the land. He may have softened to the idea of selling to them, but he didn't want them to badger him into it. That would only make him want to keep it out of spite. Of course, there would be a grim sort of satisfaction in knowing the lake could take them all out. Barlow wouldn't ever use the land for anything besides cattle, so he'd never come anywhere near it. There was always the chance that Eric was a fisherman, though he doubted it.

The minivan pulled closer, and Adam could see it wasn't a Barlow behind the wheel, but a Blackwell, or at least a former Blackwell.

"Hey. Does that thing still run?"

Mandy's sticky sweet voice penetrated Adam's shell. He had forgotten how much the sound of her voice could soothe him. The funeral wasn't a good day, and he barely remembered speaking to her. Memories of Grace Ann running through the house and across the porch clouded his head. Also, the last time he'd been in the funeral home chapel was for Grace's wake or remembrance or whatever you call it when the only visitation is for a kindergarten photograph. Adam cleared his throat and thoughts.

"I'm not sure yet. I was about to try and hope for the best."

"I stopped by because I didn't like the way we left things the other day. I wanted to talk to you before you left town again."

"Instead of running away from my problems, you mean?" he said and crossed his arms on the door. It squeaked under the pressure and he pushed it hard and made it louder before he stopped so she could speak. A breeze pushed the door, and he fought to keep it quiet while she patiently waited.

"That's not what I meant. I was just—,"

"Never thought I would see you driving such a mom-car," Adam said, cutting her off.

She turned to look at the silver van.

"Neither did I, but after driving it for a while, I got used to the idea. I like it now."

"Kind of a boring color for you too, isn't it?"

Adam didn't know why, but she was starting to squirm, and he was enjoying it.

"Yeah. Guess I'm over the flashy colors."

"Why—"

"Where're you going? Or trying to go?"

It was her turn to cut him off. There was something she didn't want to talk about. He would let her go, but that was because she had brought up his plans. The journal fell to the floorboard. He jumped across the seat like he needed to save them from the drowning dark of the truck cab. Bent corners poked out from the beat up notebook as he presented it to Mandy.

"This is Phil's journal."

"Okay," she said, still not getting the importance of his find.

"It has his notes. He was trying to find where the water goes after it leaves the lake," Adam said, shaking the notebook, imploring her to look at it.

She took the book and flipped through it. He could tell she still wasn't getting it. She was skimming through too fast.

"Most of these pages are ruined. How do you know what he was doing?"

He took the notebook back and showed her pages where the writing was legible.

"There are a few pages where you can read the writing and the maps in the back."

She narrowed her eyes and tilted her head. She thought he was crazy and was about to cross her arms. And then she did. He'd certainly seen that look enough times while they were together to know where this was going. He used to hate it when she looked at him like that, because she would also purse her lips. She looked like a confused duck. If he laughed, she would really think he'd lost it. He was getting too worked up over an old notebook.

"Okay, okay. Look at the maps. He had narrowed it down to these few creeks. He'd marked off the couple he'd checked already, but he missed one," Adam said, trying to not sound as obnoxious as he felt.

"So you want to go check out the one he didn't mark? Why? What was he looking for?"

Adam pulled out his cellphone and went to the Google Earth app.

"No. That's not the right creek either."

"I don't get it," she said.

"I am about to go to the one he didn't realize he missed. It's on one of the neighbors' land, but we still can get to it."

"We?"

"Yeah, you wanted to talk. So come with me. I've got some waders for me. I doubt you have any waders in your soccer-mom car, but Phil probably had some that would come close to fitting you."

"I'm not running through somebody's backyard to find where a lake drains. And I'm definitely not getting in the water."

"It's right by the road, see," he said, pushing the phone at her. "Ride with me. You don't even have to get out of the truck if you don't want to."

She stepped back and looked toward the lake. Adam knew she would go. She wanted to make it look like it was a harder decision than it actually was.

"Okay, but first you have to tell me what ya'll are looking for."

"Grace Ann."

———

The truck slid the final five feet over loose gravel to the stop sign.

"Don't you think we should call the police and let them search?" she said and sniffed.

"We will. But first, I need to know that's the right place. I can't call them and tell them I think my lake dumps out into somebody else's lake and I need you—" He paused, not knowing how to finish his sentence. He turned onto the highway and forced himself not to floor it. The cab was quiet, and he was struggling with what to say next, when she helped him.

"We went on our first date in this old thing."

"Yeah, I was so nervous that night," he said, relieved.

He had been nervous because he knew Mandy's dad was going to answer the door. Adam had run into him at the hardware store earlier that day. Her dad made it quite clear he wasn't happy about them dating, and he and her mother wanted her to date somebody who would get her out of the small town so she could experience life. Their relationship had always been strained, but if he were still alive, Adam wouldn't mind letting him know he had gotten out of the small town.

"Lot of good times in this truck."

"Yeah. Phil would probably roll over in his grave if he knew how many good times we had. Hell, Grace Ann was probably conceived in the back."

"Stop it," she said, and slapped his shoulder.

She never liked it when he talked about sex, but at least he was able to say Grace's name without everything going to hell.

"What? You were always a sucker for the ambiance of a cargo light."

"Okay, Adam. Stop."

"Why? We were about to have fun for a second. Is that it?" Adam said, looking at her.

"Just keep your eyes on the road. Whose land is this creek on?"

She was changing the subject again. She wanted to talk to him, but still wanted to stay guarded.

"About that. I know it's going to sound crazy, but it's a coincidence, I swear."

"Are you serious?"

"Yeah, but I didn't realize it until after I followed the road to the highway."

"You better not be taking me down here to start anything."

Adam flipped on the right blinker and the green arrow stayed solid as he slowed and turned onto Barlow Road.

Chapter Sixteen

Gas sloshed in the red plastic container. Its capacity was two gallons, but the sound and heft said it was probably half empty, at least. Last night, Eric saw Wayne's Gas Station through the dirt-crusted window of Sharky's Pool Hall, and remembered he needed to get gas. It was only eight, and they closed at ten, but Mary Beth Williams walked in and all bets were off. Mary Beth came in drinking and continued to throw them back hard, and he thought he might have a chance with her. The stupid bitch stood up on wobbly legs and told the wall above his head there was no way in hell she'd have anything to do with him and told him to run along home. That was at a quarter past ten. He'd thought about following her out to her car when she left, but she was slung around Vance Gaskell's shoulder, and even Eric Barlow knew there were some people you didn't want to tangle with. He'd seen Vance break a guy's jaw for spilling a beer on his boots in the same bar.

Luckily for Eric, it was the yardman's day to do the lawn, and he swiped some gas while his back was turned. He would have stopped at the gas station on the way, but if everything went to plan, he didn't need any witnesses showing up and saying he'd bought gasoline on the same day the Blackwell house went up in flames.

It was more than luck turning for Eric. If he'd stopped for gas, he would have over done it and would be trying to hike through the pasture with a full five-gallon container. The yardman's was probably mixed with oil for the weedeater, but it would still burn. It wouldn't take much to get that old house going. Divine intervention struck again when Eric crawled to the top of the final hill on his belly. The large white house sat silent, surrounded by cars. He'd had every intention to sit there as long as it took for Adam to leave the house, but it didn't take long. As soon as he got comfortable and wished he'd brought some snacks, Mandy pulled up and they both got in Phil's truck. That was weird, but he didn't have time to worry about it. They had given him the perfect opportunity, and he couldn't waste any time. Yes, Eric Barlow's luck was finally changing. Maybe after this was all over, he would get cleaned up and head over to Sharky's and try to hook up with Mary Beth's cousin, Leslie. She was hotter anyway.

Eric had tried, and mostly succeeded, to hold back the wrath of his anger before he got to the Blackwell house. It wouldn't have been good to get all riled up and have to wait in an empty field until the coast was clear. There had been a kindling in the pit of his stomach, but now the flames flooded his body as he stomped up the steps.

He sat the gas jug down and prepared to kick the door in but held back at the last moment. Brian hadn't crossed his mind. He pushed the jug behind the stack of paint cans and knocked on the door. If Brian were there, it would ruin his plan.

Nobody answered. He'd waited long enough for anybody in the house to get to the door and tried the doorknob. It was locked. Adam was definitely a city-boy now. Country people left their doors unlocked unless they were sleeping, and even then, some of them didn't think twice about checking the door before they went to bed.

Again, Eric prepared to kick the door, but thought better of it. Some of these old houses were sturdy, and he didn't need to bounce off the door. That would be embarrassing, even if he were the only one around to see it. He tried the window and forced it open on its warped frame.

On the way in, he hit his head on the window, fell to the floor and landed on a lamp wire. The glass lamp fell from an antique sewing machine and shattered, sending shards of glass across the wood floor. If there was somebody home, and they didn't know he was there before, they sure as hell did now.

He stayed on the floor listening for any movement, but heard nothing and climbed to his feet. He'd never burned down a house before, but it shouldn't be too hard, and he probably didn't even need the gas if Adam still didn't want to sell. An arson investigation would make it look like he'd tried to burn it down for insurance money, then Vernon would be able to get it for dirt cheap.

Eric walked into the dining room and grabbed the buffet. He wanted to flip it over and stomp it to splinters and bust up the rest of the house for the way Adam had treated him. Everything would have been okay if he'd just sold him the land or had at least been nice about how he told him to get lost. He didn't need to punch him, and he sure as hell didn't need to make fun of how short he was. Adam wasn't even that damn tall. He tilted the buffet on two legs but set it down. It wouldn't be good to wreck the house before he burned it. For one, he didn't know how long they would be gone and second, Adam could try to say somebody broke into the house and trashed it before they torched it.

Keeping a level head took away from the fun, but he would be glad he kept his cool later. He figured the bedrooms would burn pretty easily, so he could spread the gas around the kitchen and dining room. Before he left, he would set the drapes and bedding on fire in the bedrooms.

The gas was still on the porch, and it was getting late. He wished he had time to walk through the house and see everything he was going to destroy. Not the stuff. Everybody had stuff, and stuff could always be replaced. He wanted to see all the memories that would go up in flames. All the participation trophies from little league, mounted fish and deer they shot on their own land, pictures from weddings, from every birthday party and delivery room miracle. But those amounted to stuff as well. He wanted to watch doorways with height measuring pencil marks collapse; rooms where books were written and plans of forever were made fall in on themselves from the pressure; back porches that lead to patios where more than a few Blackwell men married their brides turn to ash. Most of all, he wanted to see Adam's face when he realized it was all gone.

Eric opened the door and smiled as he bent down to get his gas. A blue flash to his right caught his attention. He stood up straight and watched the barn. Something had moved, but he didn't think it was an animal. It didn't move like an animal. He kicked the top paint can off the stack and headed to the barn. He had come too close to turn back now. Maybe it wasn't a person. Maybe it was something flapping in the wind. If it had been Brian, he would have seen Eric and come back to the house to see what he wanted.

Eric walked toward the barn. A hand wrapped around the edge of the door followed by a second one, and Eric stopped. It wasn't something blowing in the wind. It was a person, but even from this distance, the hands looked small and close to the ground. There shouldn't be any children on the farm. Brian didn't have any, and Adam didn't, not anymore. He needed to find out who was in the barn and if they knew he'd been in the house. There couldn't be any witnesses. He could leave now like he was never here. The kid would never know who he was, but he had to make sure it was only the kid. If their parents were there, it would look suspicious if he left.

A head poked out from behind the rotting wood. The little girl giggled and ducked back behind the door. Small feet scurried across the dirt where the door didn't touch the ground. She was probably going to get her parents right now. Maybe it was a family looking at the house and Adam had left to give them time to see the place. But there weren't any other cars in the driveway. Maybe Mandy had brought them.

Eric crept closer to the barn and decided he was being too

quiet. He didn't want to seem creepy by sneaking up on people when he didn't own the property. The door creaked when he pushed it open wide and entered the barn, but nobody was in there. The tack room was vacant, now only housing dusty saddles and dry rotted bridles.

Small shoe prints running in all directions covered the barn's dirt floor. The girl had to be hiding in one of the stalls. Three stalls lined each side of the barn. Movement in the back of the barn drew his attention.

"Hello? Is anybody in here?"

The rustling continued. It sounded like it was coming from the back stall.

"I'm here about the house. I heard it was for sale. Are you the homeowner?"

Eric hoped it wasn't anybody he knew. They would see right through his prospective buyer guise. He approached the stall door.

"Are you in there?"

The bolt was open. The hair on his arms and the back of his neck stood on end. He slid the door on rusty rails and stepped inside. Something squeaked and ran across the top of his boot. Eric jumped back and the heel of his boot caught the edge of the stall. A sharp pain shot up his arms into his shoulders as he braced his fall. If he hadn't caught himself, only his ass would hurt. Now his arms were going to hurt all day too. He pushed his skinned wrists to his shirt. They burned, and he needed to clean them, but there was still movement in the stall. It moved again, and his breath caught in his throat. He searched for the closest escape, but the back door was shut and barred. The only way out was the way he came in.

He held his breath. Pinpricks flooded his body from a survival instinct he hadn't felt before. He'd been scared before, but never like this. Dust floated on stale air, touched by the scent of horse piss. Sweat poured down his face and his bladder threatened to release.

There was another squeak. He pushed himself back with his feet, and a big rat stepped out of the stall. He released his pent up breath, and stabbing pain ran down his throat into his lungs. He hadn't realized he had been holding his breath that long. The rat stood up on its hind legs and tried to make itself seem bigger than the small rabbit size it already was. They needed a barn cat out here. They probably had one before this monster evicted it. Eric felt foolish and began to laugh. He rolled on his back, picked up a rock and threw it at the rat. He missed, but the rock landed close enough to scare it off.

"Fucking rat," Eric said, and laid his head on the packed dirt.

"I'm not a rat," said the girl as her head came into view. She leaned over him so he could see her upside-down face.

"Holy shit," Eric yelled and rolled over.

"And you shouldn't use potty-words."

He jumped to his feet and said, "Where the hell did you come from?"

"Mommy says they're for people who don't know a lot of words, but Daddy says that's B.S. because he knows a lot of words," the girl continued.

Eric jumped to his feet. The girl had been in the barn the entire time, but he never heard her. She had to be the quietest kid he'd ever been around. That or the rat was making so much noise that he didn't hear her.

"Where are your parents?"

"They just left," she said, and pointed to the door.

"Just left? Did they go to the house?"

He hadn't been in the barn that long, and the back door was barred from the inside. He would have seen them come out, and they hadn't been in the house when he was there. Where were they?

"No," was her only response.

The girl wore a dark blue dress, but it didn't look clean. He looked down at his own clothes and knocked the dirt away from his pants, sending waves of burning pain across his wrists. She was probably dirty from playing in the barn, but her hair almost looked wet. It was hard to tell in the dark barn. Something about her looked familiar, but he couldn't place it. He'd probably seen her and her family in town somewhere. There was only one grocery store. It might have been there. He was wasting too much time. It didn't matter where this girl's parents were. The plans for the house would have to wait now, and he needed to get back to his truck before Adam and Mandy returned.

"Okay, well, I'm going to go now. Be careful playing out here. The rats are pretty big."

"I'm always careful."

"I'll let your parents know where you are if I see them, so they won't be worried about you," he said, and started toward the door.

The situation didn't feel right. Something was off about the girl. He didn't know what it was, but she was creepy. He didn't like the way she looked at him like he had done something to her. No recognition or light from her black eyes, only blank hatred. Pinpricks of fear slowly returned, and he didn't feel safe with his back to her. He turned around, and she was right behind him. A blue streak passed over her pupils and he tripped over his feet but managed to catch himself.

"Damn it. You're quiet."

"I've been practicing my sneaking skills."

"I'd say you've perfected them," he said, backing to the door. "What are you doing?"

The girl moved closer. "I can't let you burn down the house, silly."

How did she know what he was planning on doing? And what did she mean by let him? She was a child.

He stuttered as he tried to think of an excuse. "I ... I'm not going to burn down the house." He forced a laugh. "I was ... I was looking for one of the Blackwell brothers. We have some unfinished business."

"No, you weren't," the girl said. "You're lying."

"No, I'm not," Eric said.

He didn't let guys twice his size talk down to him, and he sure as hell wasn't going to let this little girl do it. Even if she did freak him out.

"Yes, you were," she said and stomped her feet. "I can smell the gas on you. You wanted to burn the house down, but I'm not going to let you."

The little brat was starting to annoy him. He'd admit, she had scared him at first, but that was when he didn't know she was there. Now, he could see what he was dealing with and no matter how dirty and homely she looked, he wasn't going to let her talk to him like he was the child. He stepped toward the girl, and she stood her ground.

"Why can't I burn the house down?"

"Because then they would all leave, and I can't let them leave. I need him here, with me. His sacrifice will calm the waters for now."

Obviously, the girl had a vivid imagination, but Eric didn't have any more time to listen to it.

"I'm not sure why you think a little girl like you can stop me, but when I get back to the house, I'm going to burn it to the ground and then come back and burn the barn down too, so you might want to be gone."

The girl stepped back and put her hands to her mouth. Eric couldn't read her face. He didn't know if she was upset or if she was about to scream, but he wanted to keep pushing her.

"What? Are you going to yell for help, now?"

A soft noise escaped the girl's lips. It was almost inaudible. A twinge of guilt pulled at Eric from the thought of scaring her. He just wanted the girl to leave him alone. He didn't want to make her cry. Then the girl started giggling.

"No, silly. There's nobody here to help you."

Help him? What did she mean, help him? He thought about closing her in the barn, so she couldn't follow him any further.

"I can't let you leave."

"Oh, really? What dare you going to do to make me stay?"

"I'm going to rip your face off and feed it to my pets in the lake," she said, and continued her soft giggles.

Eric was through dealing with the girl. He started to leave, and her eyes flashed a bright blue. Her laugh turned to a deep gargle like she was in the bottom of a deep cavern filling with water.

Eric ran through the barn door and swung it behind him as he passed. He looked over his shoulder and the door swung open fast on protesting hinges and slammed against the side of the barn. The girl ran after him with a pitchfork in hand. When he reached the driveway, one of the sharp tines pierced his leg above his ankle.

Eric rolled as he fell to the ground, and the pitchfork ripped through the tendon. He screamed, but the girl jumped on his stomach and forced the air from his lungs. He tried to cough, but the girl held him. Her legs squeezed his sides, and her cold, clammy hands wrapped around his mouth. Green and yellow dots crowded his vision.

The girl's fingernails tore into the skin at his hairline. His head burned as the girl peeled the skin from his face. Before his final breath, Eric heard the girl's bubbly laughter return.

Chapter Seventeen

The road that ran beside the lake on the Barlow's property was on top of a dam that kept the water from spilling over into farmland on the other side. Adam could see the ridge covering the stream that connected the two lakes, fighting its way from the thick forest and meandering between two tilled plots of land. Some of the water was probably irrigated to feed the fields, but the stream eventually dumped into the Barlow's lake from a crumbling concrete pipe running through the dam.

Adam let a truck full of rubbernecking field hands pass before he opened the door. When he left the house, he hadn't planned on getting in the water, but looking down the embankment, he was going to have to get a little wet if he wanted to see anything.

"We should have brought you some waders. Looks like I'm going to be the one having all the fun," he said, and took off his shoes.

He fought the waders over his thighs and slid them comfortably up the rest of the way. Hopefully, they would loosen up the more he moved around in them.

"No worries. I'm sure I'll have plenty of fun watching you."

He jumped off the tailgate and headed for the edge of the road. The rubber boots were heavier than the shoes he typically wore and caused him to walk heavy like a cowboy squaring up to show dominance.

"Are you at least coming to the edge of the water?"

"No. I think I'll be fine up here," she said.

She crossed her arms over her chest. She was nervous. Adam understood, and felt his own itchy nerves working through his body. The last thing he wanted to do was splash around in a dirty lake and find something, but that wasn't the reason he was going down there. The likelihood of finding their daughter was astronomical. When the divers searched for Grace Ann's body, they only looked in the Blackwell's lake. They didn't send anybody into the churning water of the pit because the water was too rough and they were concerned about the safety of their divers. Adam didn't blame them. When it got to the point the pit was the only place she could be, it had already been a few days and there was no chance of survival down there. They lost all hope. No one pushed the idea of where the water went when it left the pit. They all assumed it joined an underground river and met up with the Flint River on its way to the Gulf of Mexico. They couldn't cover that amount of water, and they believed that any debris or body would most likely never make it out of the underground system.

Adam took a deep breath and started down the embankment. The rubber boots attached to the waders were worn from years of gripping and sliding over river rock, and Adam nearly lost his footing twice before he even made it five feet off the dirt road. Both times Mandy laughed. It was nice hearing her laugh, even though it was sad and possibly forced. It had been a long time since Adam heard her happy. Not that he thought she wasn't happy with her life now, but he hadn't been around to see any of it. He turned back and smiled at her and threw his hand in the air as if to say, "I've got this." But he didn't.

He stepped in a gopher hole, and the sudden jar threw his equilibrium off. He over corrected and his flailing arms could not save him. He hit the ground and started to slide toward the water. Wildflower roots failed to stop his momentum as he grasped at anything to stop his descent. Rocks knocked loose joined the fall as they rolled across undisturbed moss. Adam bounced over the ground and tried to aim his feet at the trunk of a rapidly approaching tree. The rocks bounced in front of him and splashed into the water as he struck his target.

His boots threatened to slip off the edge of the weeping willow but managed to slow his progress enough that he didn't slide into the water. Adam dropped his head to the ground and looked back up the hill. Everything was upside down, but he saw Mandy's head pop over the side of the dam.

"You okay?" she asked, laughing.

"Yeah, I'm fine," he said. "You still glad we didn't bring those waders?"

She laughed. "Most definitely."

"Fine then. I guess I'll have all the fun down here without you."

Mandy backed away from the edge without responding. Adam grabbed the tree trunk and pulled himself up. The pipe was barely visible. Two more weeping willows bent toward the water flanked the pipe. Their thin branches stretched for the water but came up a few inches short. The wind blew, and they renewed their efforts. Kudzu climbed around the edges of the pipe and formed a dense carpet invading the surrounding area. It had been trimmed back in an effort to kill it, but there was no beating it once it occupied an area. The best anybody could hope for was to contain it. Adam shivered at the thought of what could be hiding underneath. The vines climbed the two willows and created a vine curtain. The only way around was through the water.

Adam stepped in and sank to mid-thigh. Flashbacks of the creature in his lake made him hesitate. Mud clouded the water around his leg. A fish jumped in the middle of the lake and he tried to jump back to shore, but the mud sucked his boot deeper. Fear caused Adam to freeze. He stood still and counted the different frogs he could hear yelling across the water to each other.

One ... two ... three ... wait, no, that was the first one again. Three ... four. Maybe four different frogs, or were they toads? He didn't know the difference, but he did know they were all amphibians and they had taken his mind off the monster that was not in the water.

As he continued to the pipe, the water rose above his waist, but didn't go any higher. The muddy bottom gave way to rocks, and he was able to move faster. The water got louder as he moved past the vine curtains and the water started to get shallower. He looked up through a hole in the reedy canopy and saw Mandy looking down at him. From this vantage point, he was able to see most of her body. She still had her arms crossed. He waved.

"Everything okay down there?"

"Nothing I can't handle."

"Not sure if I should be worried by that answer or not."

"Nope. It's all good," he yelled through cupped hands.

He slipped on a rock and caught himself before he went far enough under the water so it could cross the neoprene band across his chest and flood the waders. If that happened, he would be in a lot of trouble. They would be too heavy for him to walk back around the way he came.

"That's what it looks like from up here too," she replied.

He opened his mouth to say something, but a splash under the pipe caught his attention. He waded closer to the pipe. The water had been a clear trickle at first, but now it was flowing faster and turning darker. Something black bobbed on top of the water. Adam made his way to the pipe and reached out for whatever was floating in the water.

The loud siren chirp made him jump and snatch his hand back. Adam grabbed his chest and felt his heart pounding. The blood rushed through his body and beat in his ears. He looked up through the hole in the canopy again and saw another silhouette standing with Mandy. The sun blocked their faces, but he knew who it was.

"Evening, sheriff."

"You know what I'm doing here, Mr. Blackwell?"

"No, sir. Can't say that I do."

The sheriff hitched his pants. It was the only move a man

wearing a gun could make that said he was serious, but wasn't a threat, yet.

"Well, it's a mighty strange story. Though suppose a fella who writes like you wouldn't find it out the ordinary."

"So you've read my books. If you wanted an autograph, all you had to do was stop by the house. You didn't have to come all the way out here to find me."

John Brown gave the good humor equivalent to his pants hitch and chuckled. Adam couldn't see his eyes but was sure he wasn't in that good of a mood.

"Maybe I will. Course your writing's more my daughter's speed. More of a Louis L'Amour kinda guy myself."

Adam had to give him credit, he half expected him to pronounce Louis as Lewis. A rush of water poured out of the pipe and turned dirty grey.

"So, back to my story. I got home and was just about to sit down in my chair and have a beer, when I get a call that there was a couple of people nosing around somewhere they don't belong."

It was interesting he said he got the call at home. If somebody had bet that call had come in from dispatch, Adam would have taken the bet. He'd be willing to bet the call came from Vernon. There was a good chance Vernon didn't know it was Adam splashing around in his lake, otherwise he would have probably sent Eric down. The black object floated closer to Adam.

"I can see how that would sound strange, sheriff."

"Yeah, well, it gets stranger. I get here, and I find you two. It's strange because it wasn't long ago, I had a conversation with you about strange things happening on your land, then I find you here, wading around with no fishing pole. Though, I'm sure Vernon wouldn't be likely to be letting you on his land, no way."

The black thing was closer. Adam stretched out his arm and leaned toward it.

"Alright, Son. That's far enough. I need you back out here where I can see you," Sheriff Brown said. All the faux good nature drained from his voice.

Adam was too close to the thing to stop.

"I'm not going to say it again."

Adam pushed off his back foot and gave himself the extra two inches he needed. He grabbed it and stood up straight with his hands in the air. Sheriff Brown had his hand on the butt of his pistol.

"Sorry. Sorry, I was just trying to get this—," Adam looked at what he was holding and recognized it. "My hat. I was trying to get my hat. I don't have any weapons on me."

Adam looked to Mandy. She was saying something to Sheriff Brown, but he couldn't hear her. She was shifting her weight from one leg to the other.

"Why don't you go ahead and get out of that water, so we can talk?"

Mandy continued to talk.

"I'd like to, sheriff, but how am I supposed to do that when you don't trust that I don't have a weapon and I don't trust that you won't shoot me when I move?"

"Don't be a smartass, Adam." He heard what Mandy was saying that time.

"No need to worry, you're not in Chicago, Mr. Blackwell. And Mandy here tells me you don't have anything on you and I believe her, so come on up here. I'm tired of dealing with ya, and I still got that beer waiting on me at the house."

Black water poured from the drainage pipe. It didn't mix with the blue water of the lake. It cut through the top like a serpent going after its prey.

"Might want to get a move on. Looks like they closed the irrigation channels for some reason," Sheriff Brown yelled over the din of crashing water.

Adam turned to run and slipped. His boot lodged between two rocks and he couldn't move. The black water changed direction and headed for him like a snake sensing its next meal. He kicked the rocks with his other leg but couldn't free himself. The water crept within striking distance.

Adam pulled his leg and lost his balance. The boot tore loose, but he fell on his back and water rushed over the top of his waders. The heavyweight fought to hold him down as he pushed to his feet. Black water tendrils reached out for him. He lunged and caught the trunk of the weeping willow on the bank. The weight caused the thin grey branches to plunge into the water but provided no shield from the encroaching darkness.

Adam heaved one of his heavy legs on shore. The awkward angle caused water to run out of his waders. Most of it ran off his chest and splashed back into the lake, but some ran up his nose. He coughed up the water and looked behind him. The black stream slithered toward his face. He closed his eyes and expected the inevitable tug to pull him into the lake and drown him in front of the sheriff and Mandy. He wouldn't be able to escape with the waders holding him down.

The pull never happened. He opened his eyes and the black water swirled around his leg before finally mixing with the Barlow lake water and disappearing. Mandy and Sheriff Brown looked down from the cliff. Mandy almost looked concerned that he might drown. But even from this distance, Adam could see the wide smile of satisfaction on Sheriff Brown's face. His face would look the same if he'd known how much trouble Adam thought he'd been in.

The tree threatened to give up its roots and send Adam back into the water, but he managed to pull himself to shore.

He collapsed into the kudzu and coughed up the rest of the lake water, trying to choke him. It was a good bit cooler behind the vine curtain and made him shiver. He trampled through the kudzu and pushed the vines out of his way and tried to get to the warmth of the sun. Something moved off to his right. He didn't know what it was but didn't want to stick around too long to find out. Water squished around his ankle and between his toes as he barreled through the rest of the kudzu forest. Out of breath, he fell to the ground and spread his arms out like he was trying to make a snow angel in the timothy grass.

"Sure were acting like something was after you," Sheriff Brown called down.

"Nah, I call that falling with style," Adam replied.

"Whatever you call it, now's not the time to be taking a nap. Get on up here, cause I ain't coming down after ya."

The only thing Adam wanted to do was lie in the sun and dry out. He stood on rubber legs and looked up the daunting hill. There was no way he would make it back up the steep hill tonight. Probably wouldn't make it tomorrow either. The dam was on an incline, and he followed it back toward the highway. When the road came out of the woods, it was level with the pastures opening up on both sides. It would be a quarter mile hike, but it was the most promising choice at the moment.

"Hey, sheriff," Adam called. "I think we both know I'm not making it back up that hill. I'm going to head down there where it levels off. I'm not trying to run." Adam thought about adding, *so don't shoot*, but he was tired and didn't feel like dealing with the repercussions from Sheriff Brown or Mandy.

The walk didn't take as long as he thought it would, and he only fell two times, much to the delight of the good sheriff following him in his car from above. By the time Adam got to the side of the road, both cars were waiting on him. The questions began before he fully made it to the road.

"About them strange goins on. Do you know whose land this is?"

Adam bent over to catch his breath and thought about opening the tailgate so he could sit down, but he doubted he'd be able to jump up there.

"Don't have a clue," Adam said, looking at the ground. He could feel Mandy staring at him.

"This here is Vernon Barlow's land, and he don't take too kindly to strangers roaming around like they own the place."

"Vernon Barlow? You don't say," Adam said, and stood up straight.

"Yeah, figured a smart guy such as yourself would know something like that."

"I know, right? It has been a while since I've been home. And it's not really a place I have too many fond memories of. I thought I was turning down one of the many dirt roads around here."

"His name's on the road sign, but I suppose you'll tell me you missed it, so why don't you tell me why you were looking for a dirt road?"

"We were only trying to find—," Mandy started, but Adam cut her off. She didn't appreciate it. Her knitted brows and scowl telegraphed the sentiment. Adam shook his head in reply. Hopefully, she would understand.

"We were just going for a ride. We had a few things to discuss and didn't want to sit at the house."

"Going for a ride, you say? What was you looking for? Mandy was about to tell me before you rudely cut her off."

Adam sighed. Of course he heard everything.

"I did cut her off, didn't I?" Adam said to the sheriff and then to Mandy, "I apologize for that." He turned back to the sheriff and said, "What I think Mandy was referring to was my hat. We were driving down the road with the windows down and it flew right off."

Adam held the black ball cap up for Sheriff Brown to see.

"You went wading through a lake to fetch a hat?" the sheriff asked.

Adam could tell he didn't believe a word of what Adam was saying the way he shifted all his weight to his right foot and let his shoulders slump like all the hot air was being let out of him.

"What's that on the front?"

Adam held the hat out so Sheriff Brown could see it better.

"It's a bandit wearing a cowboy hat with a bandana around his face."

"Seems fitting."

"It's special to me. My father gave it to me a long time ago."

Now it was Mandy's turn to look at him incredulously, except she crossed her arms and looked pissed at the same time. It was a skill she perfected over time, and it looked like her new husband caused a bit of the refinement.

"Damned if I can make sense of what you're saying. And damned if I feel like trying to right now. So, let's act like I buy this half-assed story and we all go home. You stay off Vernon Barlow's land, and I'll tell him it was a couple kids fishing, and I ran 'em off."

"Sounds good to me. Thank you," Adam said, and held his hand out.

Sheriff John Brown looked at the outstretched hand and walked to his car.

By the time Adam and Mandy got in the truck, Sheriff Brown had left. But when they reached the end of the road, he was waiting for them at the stop sign. They pulled up behind him and after a few beats he turned right.

"I don't think that guy believed me."

Mandy finally broke her silence.

"Nobody would have believed that shit, Adam. It was obviously made up. He asks what you're doing, and you give him some sob story about a ball cap your father gave you?"

"Would it have made it better if it was a Stetson?"

"That doesn't matter. And I didn't appreciate you cutting me off like that. It felt like you were telling me to let the boys speak," she said.

"Oh, come on, Mandy. It wasn't like that at all. I didn't want you to tell him the real reason why we were there."

"Why? It doesn't sound any crazier than the excuse you gave him."

"I don't know," Adam said. "I think the lake is haunted."

Mandy sat quietly and stared out the window. That wasn't the reaction he had expected. He expected her to go off about letting his imagination get in the way of common sense. It was a tangent he'd heard many times over the years. Now, he didn't know if the same tired argument or the quiet was worse.

"I know it sounds crazy, but ever since I've been back, strange things have been happening around the house," he continued.

"Like the strange things John was talking about?"

"Didn't know you were on a first name basis with him."

"Oh, please. It's a small town. Everybody is on a first name basis with him."

"Except for me, it would seem."

"You're not from here anymore."

That stung. He didn't want to live here anymore and hoped he'd never have to return once he left, but to know they considered him an outsider hurt. It would have been one thing if the drunks on the barstools at Sharky's thought he was an outsider, but it hurt to think that even Mandy saw him as such.

"I'm not sure what strange things *John* was talking about. He just said he had reports about strange lights in the sky. They started before I came back. He wanted to know if I had seen anything."

"And you told him you hadn't?"

"Of course I did. I wasn't going to say, you know, sheriff, now that you mention it, there is something strange, and it don't look good."

"I'm serious."

"Who ya gonna call?" Adam said and laughed.

"That's not funny."

"It's a little funny."

"If you're seeing things. You really need to get some help. Talk to somebody. Losing somebody can be stressful. Are you getting enough sleep?"

"I'm not upset about Phil."

"I'm not talking about Phil. You told me the other day that you thought you saw her. Do you think Grace Ann is haunting the lake?"

His eyes were on the road, but he could feel her staring at him. She would never believe there was something large living in the lake, and there was no way he was going to tell her their daughter was haunting the entire Blackwell property. It would hurt her too much. She would think he was making it up, and it would hurt her more to think he was using their daughter as a ploy to get her to believe him. Telling her their daughter was a ghost wouldn't be the worst part. The worst part would be telling her he thought she was evil.

Adam already knew there was something going on with the lake and the whole property, at least, he thought he knew, but he needed to change the subject to something that had him worried. The ball cap.

He reached over and pulled it off the dash.

"What's the deal with the hat? Why did you keep it?"

That had been easier than he thought. She didn't want to hear what he had to say about the haunted lake and helped him change the subject.

"This looks like Brian's hat."

"How would it get into Vernon Barlow's lake?"

"It fell out of the water pipe. It came from my lake."

"How do you know?"

They turned into the driveway.

"Because Brian was wearing it when he said he was going fishing and shit—" Adam trailed off.

"What?" Mandy asked and followed his gaze as the truck came to a stop. "Who is she?"

Chapter Eighteen

Charlotte skipped down the steps and ran to the truck. Dried tear streaks ran down her puffy red face. She had been upset for a while. Adam got out of the truck, and she enveloped him in her shaking arms. He hugged her to him and looked at Mandy. Heavy convulsions rocked his body, and Adam pulled her away and held her at arm's length.

"What is wrong with you? Why are you so upset?"

"I re ... I read your book."

"A lot of people have read my book, but I've never gotten this kind of reaction." Adam cringed. He knew it was the wrong thing to say, but he couldn't help it sometimes. The look on Mandy's face confirmed his thoughts.

"No, you asshole. I read your first book," Charlotte said and pushed him away. She put the heel of her palms to her eyes.

Adam stood watching Charlotte. Nobody should have read that manuscript. Partly because it was his first attempt at writing and it was bad, he could have rewritten or edited it better, but he had other ideas and a publisher wanted his second book. The main reason he didn't want anybody to read it was because it scared him. It scared him because of how similarly the main protagonist, Charlie Random, lost his daughter. After Grace Ann died, Adam vowed to never publish or rewrite the story. He should have tossed the paper manuscript and deleted it off his computer hard drive, but he kept it. No matter how much he wanted to light the papers on fire and throw them from the top of his building in Chicago, he couldn't bring himself to do it. The idea of destroying a story in an absolute manner bothered him more than what the story was about.

But still, he didn't know how it could make her this upset. She was in a rental car, so at the very least, she had driven from Atlanta. He hoped she hadn't been this upset for the two-hour drive. Though her driving upset still wouldn't be worse than most of the drivers in Atlanta.

"You're right. You're right. I'm sorry. I shouldn't be making jokes when you're this upset."

Mandy cleared her throat and kicked at something on the ground. She kept her distance on the other side of the truck.

"Oh yeah, I'm sorry. Charlotte, this is Mandy."

"I wasn't trying to get an introduction, but nice to meet you," Mandy said and stuck out her hand. "I was trying to leave and give ya'll some space. I'm sorry."

"No. I'm sorry. I didn't mean to bust in here all emotional and crying."

Charlotte shook Mandy's hand.

"I was fine, but I've been sitting on the porch and I was thinking something bad happened, and then you guys pulled up and I was just so relieved and couldn't hold it in. I'm fine now."

"Well, I'm glad you're okay, but I should be going now. It was nice to meet you, Charlotte. Bye, Adam," Mandy said.

When Mandy pulled out of the driveway, Charlotte crumpled into his arms again and sobbed. The only thing he could think to do was hold her. After a few minutes of silence, she shuddered and pulled away from him.

"I thought you weren't coming back."

"Why? I told you I had a few loose ends to tie up and then I would be home."

Adam fell back against the truck.

"I don't know. You've up and left before, and I was afraid you might do it again," she said, and wiped her nose of her sleeve.

"That was under completely different circumstances. I didn't want to be here anymore. I want to be in Chicago," he said.

"You don't really like Chicago either."

"Tis true. I have often wondered why I didn't continue on up to Green Bay, then I remember they might have the better football team, but Chicago has you," he said, and pulled her to him.

"I'm glad you hold me higher than the Packers, if only a little," she said, and forced an anemic laugh.

Adam held up his hand and separated his thumb and index finger an inch and said, "a little," then made the gap smaller.

She laughed.

"I was cleaning, and I knocked your bookshelf off the wall. Your book fell out of the box. I know you didn't want anybody to read it, and I've never been curious before, but when I had it in my hands, it was hard not to read it. I'm sorry."

If he hadn't already felt like an asshole, he would now. It was true he didn't want it read, but had he been that protective over it? He hadn't ever caused a scene because of it, and she had never asked to read it before, though he wasn't sure if it was because she was respecting his wishes or if he had been adamant enough to cause fear of retribution. He had to admit, it was weird he kept it in a wooden box on the shelf with all his other books. It looked like a coffin. He had entombed the book but couldn't bring himself to bury it.

"There's nothing to be sorry about. I'm just—," *afraid, terrified,* "not happy with the book."

"But you said you thought it was prophetic in some way."

Drunk. He had to have been drunk to admit that.

"When Grace Ann died, I was in a real bad place and I couldn't write. I pulled the book out to see if I could salvage the story or at least give me some inspiration. It felt too close to home. Like I had finished living the story, and some jerk gave me the novelization of my heartache."

Tears rolled down Adam's face.

"I thought you were afraid the rest of it would come true. When Charlie jumped to bring his daughter back, I thought you might be thinking about that when you came back. I didn't want to lose you."

"So you came down here to save me?"

"It wasn't heroic, but there was definitely a lot of drama."

"Well, either way, I'm glad you're here. Let's go inside and get something to eat. Then we should probably take showers."

"I took one this morning. Are you saying I stink?"

"I fell in a lake and you've been hugging all over me, so yeah, it'd probably be a good idea."

A twinge of guilt hit him. He wasn't technically lying, he had fallen into the lake, but he was already wading in when he fell.

"Oh. A shower sounds like a good idea," she said and scrunched her nose. "We should probably conserve water too, don't you think?"

After their shower, they laid down in bed. Adam stared at the ceiling, and Charlotte faced the wall.

"How did you fall into a lake?" Charlotte asked.

Adam didn't know how to respond. There was no use in feigning sleep. The question would be there in the morning. She hadn't asked why he was riding around with his ex-wife. The problem wasn't that he was with Mandy. The problem was he couldn't tell Charlotte that he and Mandy were checking out the site where he thought the lake drained into another lake. And the reason he wanted to find it was because he didn't want the monster that probably killed his daughter and tried to kill him to get out. Now his daughter and some other entity were haunting him. There was no way he could tell her that after she flipped out over a book and hopped on a flight to Georgia to make sure he didn't kill himself while he was gone. He'd also held on to the crazy notion that he might find Grace Ann's body, or at least what was left of it. That had been a pipe dream, he kept telling himself.

"Adam, are you asleep?"

"Huh? What? Sorry. No, I was just dozing."

"How did you fall into a lake?" she repeated.

"It was more of a pond. Mandy took me to Grace Ann's head-stone. I hadn't seen it. It over looks a pond, and I got too close," he said.

Technically, now he was lying.

Chapter Nineteen

Mid-morning sun poured through the window. Heat spread across Adam's face. He stirred and ran his hand over the other side of the bed. It was cool, and he jumped awake. She had been gone for a while. He picked his jeans up off the floor and tripped his way to the dresser while trying to put them on.

"Charlotte?" he called down the hallway and knocked on the door to the bathroom.

No answer. She usually woke before Adam, but he thought she might sleep later because the day before had been emotional and travel filled. He stomped on the third step. The heavy thud of his foot echoed throughout the house, louder than the squeak of the step. Wherever she was, Adam wanted her to know he was up and moving around the house. He didn't want to walk up on her and terrify her because she didn't hear him. He walked into the dining and called out to an empty house.

The air was muggy and humid, as if it had been raining all night. He stepped into the damp grass and realized he had forgotten to grab his shoes. He decided to go back inside to get them when a figure in flowing white caught his eye. She stood beside the lake. It looked like she was staring into the pit. The white sheet flowing in the wind reminded him of the woman he thought he was going to hit when he ran off the road. Except this time, he knew she was real. She wasn't going to turn into a plastic wrapped traffic barrel.

He walked across the yard and stopped at the fence to make sure she wouldn't disappear. A cold chill ran down his spine and gooseflesh covered his arms as he slipped between the rusted strands of barbed wire.

Charlotte was worried about him and thought something might happen to him, but she was the one standing beside the water. He picked up the pace. The wind changed direction, and the white cloth changed with it. The sudden movement caused his throat to close for fear she was about to topple into the falls. The only sound he could make was a clicking noise when he tried to yell for her.

"Run," he finally managed to yell to himself. It woke his body from the momentary paralysis, and he scampered through the gopher hole infested pasture. Standing water and soggy clumps of grass made the pasture feel like it had received more rain than the yard surrounding the house.

He sloshed through waterlogged cow shit and slid through the grass on his heels. A rock patch stopped his uncontrolled motion and kept him from landing on his ass, but he was going to have a large bruise on the bottom of his foot.

Adam limp-ran. It threw his body motion off and felt like he was running with his left leg while limping on his right and trying not to hyperextend his knee.

"Charlotte," he called to her, but she didn't answer.

He tried to force himself to run faster but looked like a man running with only one shoe on. She had to be ignoring his calls. There was no way she couldn't hear him yelling for her now, even over the sound of the waterfall. He hobbled the last few steps and grabbed her shoulder and spun her around.

She didn't react. There was no moment of surprise in her eyes. She stared at him with a blank look that sent a shiver through his body. He took her by both shoulders and lightly shook her. Still no reaction.

"Charlotte," he called. His nose inches away from hers.

The shiver settled in his stomach and fractured into fear. He squeezed her arms tight and shook her hard. Her eyes rolled and only showed the white. After an agonizing amount of time, she tried to take a step back from his grip. When he didn't release her to fall to her death, she finally spoke.

"Oww. Stop it," she said. "You're hurting me."

Adam continued to shake her. She snatched her arm from his grip and slapped him across the face.

"I said, you're hurting me."

Adam let her other arm go and rubbed his red cheek.

"I'm sorry," he said. "You weren't responding, and I didn't know what to do. I was scared."

"So you thought the best thing to do was to shake me?"

"It seemed like a good idea at the time."

Adam stepped away and rubbed the back of his neck.

"Well, it wasn't. I'm going to have bruises on my arms now."

"Tell 'em you walked into a door."

"That's not funny. You're an asshole sometimes. You know that?" she said and pushed past him. But she didn't head toward the house. Instead, she walked toward the dock. Adam sighed and walked after her. She was right. He was an asshole. He'd spent so much of his life spitting out anything he thought was clever that he didn't always stop to think about how it sounded.

"Hey, Charlotte, wait up. You're right."

"Right about what?" she asked, turning to him.

"Right about ... uh..." he knew there were two things but had forgotten where he was going. "I am an asshole and shaking you probably wasn't the best thing to do. I was scared."

"Scared of what?" she challenged.

"That something was wrong with you. It looked like you were in a trance or something and then your eyes rolled back, and I panicked."

"Forgiven. I guess," she said, and presented her cheek. He kissed it and pulled her into a hug.

"It's weird though. I don't remember any of it. I think it was still dark when I woke up, but I don't remember anything until you tried to break my neck."

He blew air through his puffed cheeks and held her at arm's length.

"I told you I was sorry. I—" he started, but the Polaris sticking out from the other side of the shed distracted him.

"You what?"

"I need to check something," he said and shambled past her.

"What is it?" she asked, joining him beside the vehicle.

He didn't answer right away. He looked at the lake and back to the empty boat trailer. She started to ask again, and he cut her off.

"The boat trailer is backed to the water, and it's empty."

"Maybe Brian is fishing," she suggested.

"Do you see a boat on the damn lake?" he asked, motioning to the water. "Besides, he said he was going yesterday."

"Have you seen him since then?"

"No."

Adam looked back to the water. There was no way he'd gone fishing. He had plenty of other things to do besides trying to prove Adam wrong.

The hat.

Adam looked at the truck. What if the hat he'd found yesterday wasn't like Brian's hat, but was his hat? He tried but couldn't recall if his brother was wearing the hat the day before or not. Nothing was coming to him.

He walked to the edge and scanned the water. There was nothing there. Self-preservation kicked in and he realized he was standing closer to the water than the day the creature pulled him in. He looked down at the gently lapping water and took two steps back. A splash that sounded like a jumping fish caught his attention, and he looked up. Something was poking out of the water. It hadn't been there before, he was sure of it. It looked liked a metal triangle, but it was hard to tell because it was still close to the middle of the lake. A sinking feeling hit Adam, and he felt like he was going to vomit. He leaned over and put his hands on his knees. Where else could Brian be? His truck was still in the driveway. Somebody could have picked him up. But he wouldn't have left the Polaris out like this. And where was the damn boat?

"I'll be right back. I have to get something from my car," he said, and started back across the pasture.

Charlotte didn't reply. She continued to watch the water. He thought about asking her not to get too close to the water, but she looked like she had zoned out again.

Adam walked quickly through the short grass. The stone bruise on his foot was either feeling better or his feet were too cold from the wet grass to notice it anymore. He climbed through the barbed wire and walked to his car. The business card was still lying in the front seat where he had thrown it. His cellphone was in the house, but he needed to grab some socks and shoes too.

He sat down in Phil's recliner and pulled his socks on while the phone rang.

"Yell-ow. This here is Big D. If yer stuck, I gotta truck."

"This is Adam Blackwell. You towed my car a couple days ago."

"Blackwell you say?"

Adam thought he could hear the audible clicking as the tumblers fell in place in Darryl's head, then quickly realized it was undoubtedly the toothpick he kept wedged in the corner of his mouth being rolled from side to side as he searched for recognition. Adam was about to tell him who he was when Darryl gave a big laugh.

"Ah, yeah, the mud bogger. I remember ya now. What can I do for ya? You haven't been mud riding again, have ya?"

"No. Nothing like that. I had a question, though."

"What's that?"

"Have you ever pulled anything out of a lake with your tow truck."

There was a long pause and a big belly laugh roared through

the speaker. Adam pulled the phone from his ear and waited for the laughing to stop. For a second he thought about hanging up and seeing if there was anybody else he could call. Like the police.

"Damn, Adam. Please don't tell me you done upped the ante and drove your car into a lake," Darryl choked out.

Adam wasn't amused.

"No, not yet. There's something sticking out of the water and I wanted to know if you had a grappling hook or something you could hook up to it and pull it in," Adam said through clenched teeth.

The doorbell rang.

"Yeah, I suppose I could do that. It'll cost the same as a car tow, though."

Adam opened the door and held a finger up to tell Mandy it would be a minute.

"That's fine."

"Ight. Well, I gotta go get Hank Rodgers truck before Sheryl finds out whose driveway it broke down in. But I'm free after that."

"Okay, that sounds good. My address is One Blackwell Place."

"Look at you, Mr. Bigtime. Gotta road named after you and everything. Not just a road, but a place."

Adam was getting tired of the back and forth.

"Yeah, I'm fancy. Do you know where it is?"

"Yep. Dirt road a little down from Barlow Road. Guess all you Bigtimers is friends."

"Not really. Thanks. I'll see you in a little bit," Adam said, and hung up the phone before Darryl could get another word in. Mandy waited patiently on the porch.

"Sorry. Guess I could have invited you in instead of making you stand outside."

"No worries. I don't plan on staying long. We never got to talk yesterday, and I wanted to see if you had a minute, now?"

"Yeah, sure. What do you need?

"First, I wanted to apologize if I caused any problems between you and Charlotte. I hope she didn't get mad seeing us together."

"Nah, she's not the jealous type, plus—" Adam started, then paused. He'd gotten distracted by Darryl's nonsense on the phone and forgotten that he'd left Charlotte by the lake. "Oh, shit. I left Charlotte," he finished, and ran out the door with Mandy trailing behind.

Adam pulled up short of the fence. She wasn't where he'd left her. He climbed through and a barb cut through his shirt and pierced the soft flesh below his shoulder blade. The fabric didn't rip. It stretched as the barb ripped his skin. Pain caused him to pull up, and he tripped over the bottom strand of wire and landed on the ground. The shirt stuck to his skin with bloody glue. He forced the pain, and the inevitable tetanus shot in his future from his mind. He pushed himself up and stumbled the first few steps before he found his footing.

Charlotte still stood beside the water, but she had moved to the other side of the shed. She was facing the water where Grace Ann and Adam both had been pulled in. A stitch formed in Adam's side, and he slowed.

He cupped his hands around his mouth and yelled, "Charlotte. Charlotte, get away from the water."

She slowly turned to face him, and he thought she was going to listen and move away from the water. He wasn't sure how far the monster's reach was, but it had pulled him in, and he'd never seen what the tentacles were attached to, so it had to be huge. It hadn't crossed his mind until this point, but what if the arms could reach all the way to the house? Charlotte took a step toward him and turned back around and stuck her foot in the water.

"No. No, don't do that," he said and pushed past the pain in his side.

She pulled her foot out of the water and waited.

He arrived out of breath and doubled over.

"You ... you can't go near the water."

"Why not? There's nothing wrong with it. I was thinking about going for a little swim," Charlotte said, but it wasn't her voice. It was deep and raspy. Mandy caught up with Adam and didn't even look winded.

"I guess we're all here now, so we can begin."

Adam was confused, but Mandy must have assumed it was because she was at the house with Adam again, because she tried to apologize to Charlotte.

"Hey, Charlotte, I wanted to talk to you too. I wanted to say I was sorry about yesterday. I don't want you to get the wrong impression."

"I couldn't care less about you slutting around with him," Charlotte said.

Mandy's smile fell. That obviously wasn't the response she expected, especially since Adam had told she wasn't the jealous type. Mandy's hand went to her hip, and Adam stepped between the women.

"That's not her, Mandy. She wouldn't ever say anything like that."

Mandy turned her anger to Adam.

"If it's not her, then who the hell is it?"

"It's her, but it's not her voice."

"That doesn't make any sense. If it's her, then it's her voice."

"I told you. The lake is haunted."

"I'm not putting up with this. I don't have time to listen to her jealous insults or your crazy ghost stories. Don't worry about anything I had to say," Mandy said, and turned away.

Adam started to protest when Charlotte's cold hand fell on his shoulder. The smell of rotten fish floated on the hot air and Adam felt himself being pulled toward the water. Charlotte's grip tightened when he fought to remain standing. Gravel shifted under his shoes, and he heard the splash of water behind him. He dug his feet in and tried to twist free from her grip. In an attempt to catch her off guard, Adam spun to face Charlotte, but she was no longer behind him. He turned to call out to Mandy, and the hand clamped down on his shoulder again and pulled him off his feet.

The cold rush of water sent all his nerves into overload. He opened his eyes, and everything was inky black. Charlotte's hand clamped tighter and tried to pull him into the deeper water. He twisted away and kicked to the surface. Mandy was standing on the bank with her hand held out, but she was fifteen yards to Adam's right. He swam to a spot where he could stand and saw Mandy reaching out for Charlotte's hand.

"Mandy, don't," Adam yelled.

Her hand faltered as she looked at Adam like he'd lost his mind. She still didn't believe him. Charlotte sprang through the water again and screamed for help. It wasn't the same voice as before. This was the real Charlotte, and she was terrified. She screamed again.

"Mandy. You have to be careful. Something has a hold of her."

"Damn it, Adam. Drop it and help me out. I don't—"

A deep guttural sound shook the ground and Charlotte leaped from the water. Mandy didn't have time to react before Charlotte grabbed her and pulled her in.

Adam hollered, but his brain didn't register the words. He was a couple feet from the bank and slogged through the muddy bottom and climb out of the water. The water where he thought Mandy had gone in was deathly calm. He searched for any signs of either woman, but the water gave no hints of where to start. He looked across the water, but it was all eerily flat, like there hadn't been wind or any kind of disturbance at all. Adam didn't know what to do. Sweat poured down his face and stung his eyes. He couldn't go back into the water. He had escaped twice now and didn't believe the third time would be the charm for him. Or maybe it would be for whatever waited for him. Where would he start looking? The thought terrified him, but he had to try.

Before he had to make an impossible decision, Mandy and Charlotte both lunged through the water ten yards closer to the waterfall. He could hear the large gulps of air they both fought for. Both women swam for the shore. The creature grabbed them at the same time and pulled them back under the water. Adam ran to the spot and prepared to jump in after them when he saw the tentacles and black and blue creatures just below the surface of the water.

The women surfaced again.

The water current sped up and pushed them toward the

waterfall. The lake now acted like a free-flowing river. Water rushed with a fast current and poured over the falls. Blue-grey mist rolled from the edges of the pit and settled on the water surface. Adam tried to run ahead of them, but the water was too fast. They were coming up on a fallen tree that stuck out over the water. He yelled for the women to grab the tree.

He wasn't sure if they heard him, but he ran for it because it was his only hope of saving them.

Adam ran down the bank. A black flash flew out of the water and became entangled in his legs. He bounced off the grass and grabbed his skinned forearm. He looked up in time to see the two women grab on to the tree. He pushed himself up.

"Hold on. Don't let go."

Both women fought to keep their heads above water. Mandy was the closest to shore and tried to pull Charlotte to her. Adam reached the branch and held out his hand. Mandy jumped out of the water and swiped at his hand, but her wet grip slipped.

Adam lay down and reached out both arms. Mandy let go of the tree and pushed forward. She and Adam connected hand to forearm and pulled each other. Adam waved for Charlotte to let go and do the same. He could see the fear in her eyes when she let go of the tree and pushed for his left arm. She connected and both pulled toward shore.

The gravel beneath Adam crumbled. He slid back to the lake, leaving his chest inches from the water. If he didn't re-anchor, he would end up in the water too. But he had to let go of one of the women before he could do that. How could he choose? If he let go of Mandy, he could push himself back on the bank and grab her again, but he'd have to be fast. If he let go of Charlotte, he could push back while she held on to the tree again. Either way, one of them would have to float a few terrifying feet until they could catch the tree again. He slid further above the water. There was no more time to think.

"Charlotte. I'm going to let you go. Grab onto the tree," he yelled.

"No. No, you can't," she cried and pleaded.

He slid again.

"You have to trust me. If I don't, I'm going to end up in the water with you."

Charlotte didn't say anything. Adam released her arm, but she didn't let go of him.

"Damn it, Charlotte. Let me go, or we're all going to die."

Charlotte released his arm, and the water swept her away. She managed to grab the tree and pull her head above water. She was screaming at him, but he couldn't tell what she was saying. She looked like a kitten cornered by the neighborhood dog as soon as the homeowners put it outside. Fear and betrayal radiated from her and it broke his heart.

He dug his hand into the dirt and pushed back. The bank crumbled in his hand and his torso slipped into the water. The strength of the current startled him and he thrashed his free arm, searching for anything to keep from going all the way in.

The water pushed Adam's top-half downstream, threatening to sweep him and the women toward the waterfall. He pulled Mandy, and she hit the bank and let go of Adam. The water turned him sideways. Halfway in the water, he flailed his left arm and grabbed the tree before going headfirst into the lake. Adam released his pent up breath and shifted his weight so he could make it back to land completely and grab Charlotte.

"See. I told you I'd get—"

A loud crack cut him off. Adam and Charlotte locked eyes and the tree branch broke away. Adam lunged for her, but her shirt slipped through his fingers and she went under the water. He jumped to his feet, and her head broke the water line. She turned in time for them to see each other before she went over the falls.

Chapter Twenty

It was his fault. He didn't warn her to stay away from the water until she was already down there thinking about taking a dip. All the sheriff deputies swarming around the house and lake labeled her missing, but there was no way she survived that fall. The deputies knew she was gone too, but they had to keep up appearances for the friends and family. Adam was the only family she had left, and he'd let her down too. He recognized a few of the deputies from the search for Grace Ann. Charlotte was dead, and it was all his fault.

If he hadn't kept that damned book on the shelf like a weird memorial surrounded by the books that survived long enough to make it to print, she wouldn't have had the chance to read it and come down here on some crazed rescue mission. He'd made too much of the book. Made it more important than it was. All the prophetic garbage was more hyperbolic storytelling to give an undeserved reverence to a book that was never good enough to be published in the first place, but it made interviews more interesting when they asked if he had anything he'd never consider publishing. It always piqued the interest of the interviewer and set a mild frenzy through his modest fan base, begging for him to release something new or at least re-edit the book and release it.

Now, the book had an actual death attached to it. He'd never use Charlotte as a marketing tool. He was going to burn it when he got back to Chicago.

Adam sat on an upside-down five-gallon bucket in the middle of the pasture at what he assumed was a safe distance from the lake. Was there a *safe* distance? Two boats dropped divers into the water. He should have warned them to stay out of the water, but they would have thought he was crazy. Hopefully, the thing living in the lake would hide long enough for the divers to give up. No divers disappeared when they searched for Grace Ann, so there was a chance that none of these divers were in trouble. Maybe the entity only wanted his family or people who were important to him. One of the boat operators tied a yellow marker around the tip of the boat sticking out of the water. They had already tried to haul it in, but the small county boats weren't powerful enough to pull it through the water.

"Do ya hear me, Mr. Blackwell?"

The sheriff interrupted his train of thought. How long had he been trying to talk to him?

A slender hand lightly squeezed his shoulder. He reached for Mandy's hand, but drew it away before they touched.

He looked at the sheriff.

"Uh. No, sir, I didn't. I was lost in thought. I'm sorry."

The sheriff removed his hat and looked out over the water.

"I was asking, why didn't you call us when you realized Brian was missing? Hell, I just saw you yesterday evening."

Adam wiped a tear from his eye. He hadn't tried to process Brian's disappearance yet. The distance between the two numbed the loss, but it still hurt to know he'd never see his brother again. Charlotte's death overshadowed everything. It wasn't that he didn't care for his brother, but he had begged him to leave this place with him and Brian called bullshit and went fishing anyway. But the question wasn't why he was missing, it was why he hadn't told anybody, and Adam didn't have a clue. He was so caught up in Phil's notebooks, he barely remembered Brian telling him he was going anywhere. He had been selfish and fallen in with the crazy writings of a mad man. Adam didn't want to admit it to himself, but he hoped, and believed there had been a chance that he'd find Grace Ann yesterday, and he'd allowed it to cloud his judgment. Even when he'd found Brian's hat, he was more pissed at the sheriff for stopping his search. There was no excuse, so he did the only thing he could. He lied.

"I didn't know he was missing when I saw you yesterday."

"But you knew he'd gone fishing and hadn't come home?"

"Well, yeah, but—"

"You didn't think to check on him after you got done playing in Vernon's lake yesterday?" Sheriff Brown asked. He removed his hat, wiped the sweat from his brow and fixed it back firmly on his head. "What about you, Mandy? You didn't think to look for him?"

Adam could tell how nervous Mandy was by the way she transferred her weight between her feet and slid her shoes across the loose dirt behind him. She didn't know anything, but the sheriff would think she knew more if Adam didn't say something.

"Mandy didn't know Brian was gone. And no, I didn't think about looking for him. It's not out of the ordinary for him to come in from the fields and go to town and not come back until the next morning. When we got back from Vernon's, Charlotte had just arrived from Chicago."

"Bet that was an interesting conversation given your history with Mandy."

"No. Not really. Charlotte's not the jealous type. She knows about me and Mandy."

"So she wasn't upset?"

"No," Adam said. Mandy shifted her weight and pushed her knee into Adam's back. She knew he was lying about Charlotte, but what was he supposed to do? He couldn't tell Sheriff Brown that Charlotte was on the verge of hysterics when they'd gotten back, and it's a wonder she'd made the drive from Atlanta without killing herself or somebody else? It would only cause more questions that he couldn't answer.

"She couldn't make it down here for Phil's funeral because

she's a schoolteacher and couldn't get a sub before I had to leave. She came to be with me while I took care of Phil's estate and we were going back home. When I woke up this morning, she was down by the lake. Mandy pulled up, and we both came to check on her and they fell in. I was able to pull Mandy out of the water, but the branch..." Adam's voice cracked, and Mandy squeezed his should again, "the branch she was holding on to broke and she went over the falls. That's it, sheriff. Nothing else. No drama or ulterior motives. It was a horrible accident," Adam managed before overflowing emotion hit him again.

"Strange to be swept away by such moving water," Sheriff Brown said, and pointed at the calm water. He didn't wait for a response. Adam wasn't sure if it'd been a question or an accusation anyway, "And why did you come over this morning?"

"I left my phone in the truck and came by to pick it up."

Adam turned and looked up at Mandy. Who's lying now?

If she'd told Brown she came to apologize if she had upset Charlotte, then that would have made everything Adam told Sheriff Brown a lie and he'd have a lot more explaining to do. Mandy gave him a half-hearted smile. Adam returned the smile and looked around Mandy as a large flatbed tow truck barreled up the driveway with its horn blaring the first twelve notes of Dixie Land like it was Hazard County.

"Why the hell is he here?" Sheriff Brown asked.

Darryl climbed out of his truck, opened the gate to the pasture, and drove through.

"I called him earlier."

"Why?"

"I came outside and found Charlotte by the lake. We saw Brian's boat sticking out of the water, but we didn't know that's what it was at the time. I went back to my car to get Darryl's business card. I called him and Mandy showed up while I was on the phone with him."

"You failed to mention that you called him."

"I didn't think it was important. Does it matter?"

"It does if you were trying to cover up what happened to your brother and Charlotte by getting rid of the evidence."

"I didn't kill my brother," Adam yelled and jumped up from the bucket. Sheriff Brown stood his ground, hand rested on the butt of his pistol.

"Holy hell. What did I jus' drive up on?" Darryl clapped Adam on the back. "I knew it was important, but I didn't know you was going to have the cops from the tri-county area over here. Shit, I don't know that'd come had I known. Hey, Chief. How you doing?"

"I'm fine, Darryl, and it's sheriff."

"You all look the same when you're behind me with your blue lights on," Darryl said, and clapped Adam on the back again.

Darryl stopped abruptly and turned to face Mandy liked he just noticed she was standing there.

"And who is this lovely thing here? The name's Darryl, but the ladies like to call me Big D," Darryl said, and bit his lower lip.

"Darryl Grimes. Don't stand there and act like you haven't known me since you were in second grade. Your sister and I had to lock you out of her room and cover the windows so you wouldn't try to spy on us."

"Guess you still don't like to role play then?" Darryl said.

Before he had time to saying anything else, Adam stirred the conversation in another direction and sat back down.

"Sheriff, I know it was probably a bad idea, but at the time, I didn't think about it as disturbing a crime scene. I wanted to see what was in the lake. I didn't think it would be Brian's boat. But, since Darryl is already here, and you don't have anybody else to do it, why not let him haul it in?" Adam asked, and as an afterthought, added, "I'll still pay for the service."

Sheriff Brown looked from Adam to Darryl and turned toward the boats trolling across the water.

He sighed then said, "Okay, fine. You already came out here. I might as well let you get paid for it. But I'm telling you, Darryl, no funny business and leave Mandy and any other woman you come across out here alone."

Darryl clacked his boot heels together and saluted Sheriff Brown.

"And after you haul that boat in, I want you to collect and then get out of here. You understand me?"

"Sir, yes, sir," Darryl said and saluted again.

Brown shook his head and radioed for one of the boats to meet him at the bank.

Adam's knees popped and arthritic pain shifted in his back and he forced himself to stand. With heavy feet, he walked beside the bed of the truck while Darryl backed it closer to the water. In between the piercingly loud chimes of the trucks reverse warning, it sounded like the ground beneath Adam's feet was hollow. He stalled well short of the bank and buried his hands in his pockets. When the truck came to a stop, he jumped in the air and came down hard. The look from Mandy stilled him for a moment, then he shrugged and jumped again. He hoped the ground didn't give way underneath and deliver him to the den of the animal in the lake, but he couldn't resist the urge to test the hollowness of the ground like tonguing a sore spot in your mouth no matter how much it hurt.

Darryl stood beside the truck watching Adam jump up and down with his head turned to the side like an inquisitive dog. He then stuck his pinky finger in his ear and worked it back and forth while he released the brake on the winch. He pulled the steel cable to the bank and prepared to hand it to the deputy in the boat, but pulled it back at the last second, leaving the deputy gasping air.

"Well, hello there lit—" he started, but Sheriff Brown cleared his throat and cut him off. He turned in Brown's direction and slowly nodded his head.

"Yes, well, as I was saying. Hello there, madam. Would you be so kind as to place this here hook in a spot that is suitable to you upon that sunken boat?" Darryl said, trying to mimic what he believed was proper English, but there was no taking the country out of him.

The woman grabbed the hook and pushed the boat away from

shore. Darryl had a big grin on his face. He pulled his dirty hat from his head and ran his fingers through his hair, swishing it back only to have it fall down in his eyes again.

"I think she likes me."

Darryl shoved his hair back under his hat.

"Deputy Ramirez is a highly decorated officer from Crystal Valley, so I don't think she'd be too interested," Sheriff Brown said.

"Ramirez? She Mexican?" Darryl said, turning back to the boat. "Huh. Never would have guessed."

"She's married with two children, so there's that, too."

"Always something, I guess."

Sheriff Brown's radio crackled to life. "Okay, sheriff. She's ready when you are," Ramirez said.

"She don't sound Mexican, neither," Darryl said, walking to the cab of the truck.

Adam stiffened at the clunk of the winch brake being set and icy chills ran through his body as the motor engaged with a screeching whine. Adam didn't notice Darryl slip up behind him and Mandy.

"This here is the best hooker on the market. She can pull through anything. If you thought she got your car like it was nuthin' wait til you see her pull this boat."

Adam looked at Mandy and threw his hand in the air half-heartedly. His mouth moved, but no words came out, and then he waved her off like it wasn't anything important. It wasn't, but he also didn't want to explain how his car ended up in the median.

The winch reeled in the slack and lifted out of the water. It tightened, and the line twitched. Adam looked at Darryl for any indication that he was worried, but he only smiled like a fool. The line shuddered again, and the whine of the motor increased. Darryl's smile faltered. The whine hit another octave, and Darryl went to the truck.

"That thing's really stuck in there. Ain't it?"

Adam hoped it was only stuck and not something preparing for a tug of war. The line dropped under the water and popped in the air. Tires slid on crushed rock, and Darryl's face lost all color.

Adam grabbed Mandy's hand and stepped away from the truck. Darryl stopped the winch and ran to the cab of the truck and threw random stuff around the cab. Maybe they should get behind the shed? Darryl reemerged with a bright orange blanket. He ran to the back of the truck and threw it across the winch line and stuffed rocks into pockets on the side.

"She'll hold but can't be too careful just in case the line snaps. It'd damn near cut you in half if it hit you. Remind me to tell you the story about my Uncle Billy," Darryl said, and started the winch.

The battle began again, and Darryl stepped back from the truck as the sliding continued.

"If it don't break loose in a minute, I'm going to have'ta yank her out with the truck," Darryl yelled over the whine.

Sheriff Brown joined Adam and Mandy beside the shed. Everybody on the water stopped what they were doing and watched. Darryl shut the winch down again and climbed back into the truck. A cloud of black smoke shot from the exhaust pipes as he cranked the diesel engine. When he hit the gas, the back of the truck lurched and another cloud of smoked billowed through the air. The truck slid closer to the edge of the water, and Darryl gunned it again. The passenger side tires lifted off the ground momentarily and Adam thought it would tip. The engine roared, and the back end swerved in the dirt like a sidewinder across desert sand. Darryl yelled, but Adam couldn't tell what he was saying over the din of the fight. The truck paused and rocked back in place like it was catching its breath. Darryl punched the gas again, and the truck took a final lunge. Screeching metal against metal echoed across the land and caused everybody to wince in pain. Some dropped their gear to cover their ears.

Adam closed his eyes. The creature was about to pull the truck and Darryl into the lake. He held his breath and waited for the inevitable but never heard a splash. Instead, a loud blast of Dixie Land rang out, followed by the triumphant hoots and hollers from the over excited truck driver as the boat pulled free.

Darryl jumped out of the cab, threw his hands in the air

triumphantly, and took a bow. One of the deputies on the boat whistled and clapped for him. Adam doubted it was Ramirez, but Darryl's face flushed as he pointed to the boat.

"What a moron." Sheriff Brown said.

"Yeah, but he seems to be enjoying life. That's more than I can say," Adam said.

"Ignorance is bliss," Mandy offered.

"Yeah, and he's about as blissful as they come around here."

Adam held his breath as Darryl reengaged the winch motor. The line hesitated, followed by a snap that sounded like a healthy tree branch, and the line started to reel in.

"Holy hell. That thing was really stuck in there," Darryl said. "I don't think I've ever had that hard a time before."

The bow cut through the surface of the black water like a metallic dorsal fin. Small waves from its wake created blue foam when they crashed. A blanket of cold settled on Adam as he watched the approaching wreck. He already knew his brother was dead, but seeing the boat made everything real. Brian wanted to prove there wasn't anything wrong with the lake and Adam had let him go. He'd been too preoccupied with Phil's journals to try to stop him, and he never looked for him. Tears flooded his eyes again. Charlotte and Brian had both died because of him. If he'd been paying attention, they would both be alive.

Like you weren't paying attention when I died, a voice similar to Grace Ann said. Adam looked around, but nobody else seemed to have had heard the voice. Yes, it was your fault. If you had been watching me instead of the cliff, I would still be alive, too.

Adam was lightheaded and his vision blurred, though he wasn't sure if that was because of the tears or because he was dizzy. He was sure that if he didn't sit down, he was going to vomit.

He motioned for the bucket and Mandy brought it to him. He sat down hard and almost fell over backward before gaining his balance. Tears changed course and ran toward his eyes as he put his head between his knees. He stayed like that until the feeling passed, and Darryl caused a stir again.

"What the hell kinda fish is that?"

Was it one of those black fish? Or had the thing with the tentacles returned? No one besides Adam had seen either one. As far as he knew, nobody still living had seen one before. But if Darryl had one, everybody would see them.

Adam jumped to his feet and tried to run to the bank. At first, he veered to the left and was afraid he would go tumbling into the water if he didn't slow down and correct his course. He crossed his left foot over the right and tripped the rest of the way to stand by Darryl.

The boat rocked on the edge of the flatbed with the stern hanging over the eroded bank. Water poured out of a gaping hole in the steel hull and splashed back into the lake. A loud thump railed against the metal side and the fish jumped. Blue sequined scales traced lines down the fish's spine. The head looked like a barracuda, except the upper and lower front teeth were longer and stood out past the jaws. The teeth were no doubt dangerous, but the fish probably used them for holding prey, while the mouth full of small, serrated teeth ripped and pulled meat toward the throat. It whipped its body against the side of the boat with a dull metallic thud. Darryl and Adam both jumped back.

"I don't recall seeing anything like that before," Darryl said.

"Me either."

"Maybe it's a mutated catfish or something?"

"We don't exactly have nuclear waste or any other pollutants pouring in here. Maybe it's just a type of fish you haven't seen before?"

Darryl stood back and looked at Adam like he tried to kiss him.

"Naw, there ain't any fish I haven't seen before. At least not in these parts. Could've been one of those meteor things that fell from the sky."

Adam let out a loud sigh. It had been a bad idea to call Darryl, but at the time, he didn't know what else to do. Of course, if he hadn't, they wouldn't have been able to pull the boat out of the water with anything the Sheriff's Department had. Also, it's not like his meteor theory was that much crazier than anything Adam had already come up with. The fish snapped its powerful jaws and thrashed in the dwindling water supply.

"You might be right."

Darryl lowered his eyebrows and stared like he was in deep thought. Adam couldn't tell if he was mad or not, but Darryl was used to people treating him like a fool. It was obvious he and Sheriff Brown had history. Darryl continued to stare. Adam tried not to squirm so Darryl wouldn't know he was getting to him. If that's what he was doing. Darryl's eyebrows shot to the top of his forehead and a huge grin stretched across his face.

"Ah. You almost had me there. Trying to make me think this was some sorta alien fish. That's good," Darryl laughed and clapped Adam on the back. "If you're just going to throw ET here back, do you think I could have him? Might be good eatin'."

"It's all yours."

"Thank ya. I'm glad I got a cooler in the truck. This sombitch ain't fitting in no five-gallon bucket," Darryl said and went to the truck cab.

"What's he so happy about?" Sheriff Brown asked, looking into the bottom of the boat, "What the hell is that?"

"I don't know what it is, but I think Darryl is going to eat it."

"Looks like it might eat him if he tries."

A boat pulled up to the dock and Officer Ramirez stepped out before it came to a complete stop against the rotting wood. Adam would have ended up in the water if he'd tried to get out like that. She walked quickly across the dock and hopped over the bad boards like she already knew where everyone was and joined Adam and Sheriff Brown. Mandy walked up and looked into the boat. She squished her face up when she turned back around.

"It's weird, but we can't find anything," Officer Ramirez said.

"I don't think we're going to find Charlotte if she went over the falls. They can only rappel so far in that pit, and the water is too dangerous to get in. But, if Brian is out here, we should find him," Sheriff Brown said.

"I agree. But I meant it's weird because Simmons went in the water to see what the boat was stuck on. He couldn't find anything. We thought there might be a shelf that stuck out, so he went in the water to see if anything was under it, but there was nothing but open water. There wasn't anything to be stuck on."

The lightheaded feeling returned to Adam. It was the monster or ghost that pulled Adam and Grace Ann into the water. Adam couldn't tell them he knew what it was because they'd never believe him. Everybody would think he was stressed and lost his mind. Everybody except maybe Darryl, but he wasn't the type of guy you'd want to be the only person standing behind you when it came to logical reasoning. Adam wasn't crazy. Until a few minutes ago, he had been the only person that knew the fish existed, but he still didn't think it would help or change matters if he tried to warn them that there was a huge tentacled creature in the lake.

"Maybe Brian ran into a log and when Darryl pulled it loose, it fell to the bottom of the lake," Brown offered.

"Found it. Almost thought—oh now I see—" Darryl started, but Sheriff Brown stepped between him and Ramirez and stopped him.

"Now he sees what?" Ramirez asked.

"I'm sorry. Don't worry about him. He's ... well, he doesn't really have an excuse for the way he is. Nurture over nature with that one," Brown said.

"Okay, well it's getting dark and our lights aren't penetrating the water as is, so we might need to call it a day and start back in the morning."

"Looks like it's going to rain too," Brown said and looked at the sky. "I'll go ahead and call—"

"Hey, sheriff, what cha want me to do with this boat?" Darryl interrupted.

Everybody turned to see Darryl standing in the boat. He had the fish gripped in a strangle hold behind its gills. The jaws snapped shut as he brought it to his lips like he was going to kiss it.

"Darryl, get down from there before you end up losing your face," Sheriff Brown said, then turned to the others. "Excuse me while I go deal with this idiot."

Darryl dropped the fish into the cooler and kicked the lid closed.

"Hey Adam, don't worry about payment for pulling that boat. This fish'll cover the costs."

Adam threw his hand in the air to thank Darryl. Officer Ramirez started to walk away, and Adam stopped her.

"Officer Ramirez? I wanted to say thank you for all you're doing and to apologize for the truck driver."

"You're welcome, Mr. Blackwell. I'm sorry we haven't found your brother yet, but I hope we will tomorrow," she said and looked to the sky. "As long as the rain doesn't flood the area. And don't worry about the driver. I deal with bigger jerks every day. He's more like an overgrown child."

They both silently watched Sheriff Brown coax Darryl out of the boat.

"I was also curious if you'd been here before?" Adam's breath caught in his throat and he choked out. "There was another drowning a couple years ago. I didn't know if maybe you had been here then, too."

Adam felt Mandy's hand on his shoulder.

"No, sir, I wasn't. I joined the Crystal Valley dive team right after that. I'm sorry for your loss. This lake has seen its share of tragedies. It's funny you should ask, though."

"Why's that?"

"When I started, I replaced Officer Showalter. His last dive was at your lake."

Adam tensed. Showalter was the officer Phil had tracked down. He knew what was in the lake and it had scared him out of the water.

"Oh, I was unaware of that," Adam said, trying to be natural, but failing. Ramirez didn't react if she noticed.

"Yeah, he was a great cop, but he retired from the dive team and the police department."

"Was that a coincidence or did something else happen?"

Ramirez looked around like she was uncomfortable.

"I have known him since I joined the force fifteen years ago and he never told me anything. I got the impression he was seeing ghosts, and they finally got to him."

A cold flood filled Adam's body, and he tensed. He wasn't sure what kind of face he'd been making, but it obviously disturbed her because she continued,

"Oh. I don't mean actual ghosts. I'm sorry. You must think I'm crazy. Sometimes when you're diving, you think you see things in the shadows, especially in water as dark as your lake. We call the unexplained things we see ghosts. Most of the time it's probably fish, or vegetation, or maybe a change in water current."

Most of the cold left Adam's body, but he wouldn't call it relief. He tried to laugh it off and asked, "Did Officer Showalter happen to tell you about any of the ghosts he saw in my lake?"

Officer Ramirez hesitated before saying, "No, he didn't go into specifics, but when I took his place, he told me that one day we would be called back to this lake. Then he made me promise to not go into the water. I don't know what he thought he saw, but it messed him up. I feel bad for him."

"I noticed you haven't gone in the water," Adam said.

"Well, it was weird he was right about coming back, and I didn't want to press my luck by getting in the water. It's not that I think something is out there. I wouldn't let anybody else get in either if I did. I just didn't want his suggestion that there was to be in the back of my mind and start seeing things when I was down there. That wouldn't be good."

"I don't blame you, Officer Ramirez. Thank you again. I'll see you tomorrow."

Phil had spoken to Officer Showalter. Did Phil know Showalter saw something when he was in the lake that scared him so much that he decided to retire from not only diving, but from the entire department? Ramirez knew him. Maybe she would be willing to give Adam his number or give him Adam's number? If he could get away from Mandy, he could find out if Ramirez would be willing to get the two in touch. But what good would it do? Even if she did agree, what could Showalter tell him that he didn't already know? If he called him, the only thing he'd do is bring up bad memories for a man who was obviously trying to distance himself from them. He wanted answers, but he didn't want to risk upsetting a man who had been affected by what he'd seen to the point that he warned off other officers from future dives. How had he known something else would happen? When things that evil live in proximity to people, it is only a matter of time before somebody gets too close and something else happens again. Dixie Land announced the departure of Darryl Grimes and disturbed Adam from his reverie.

After Sheriff Brown, his deputies and the officers searching the lake and surrounding land left, Adam and Mandy sat on the front porch quietly staring at the water like it would give up its secrets if they watched it long enough.

"So what did you want to talk about earlier?" Adam asked, not taking his eyes off the water.

Mandy sighed.

"I didn't know her, but Charlotte didn't seem right yesterday. I wanted to make sure it wasn't over anything I caused by being with you when we got to the house."

"She was fine. What I mean is, she was fine with us being together. I don't recall ever seeing her jealous before. She was upset because she read my first book and thought something might happen to me if I stayed here too long."

"I'm not going to try and understand that, but I am sorry she's gone. I can tell you cared about her."

"And she's dead because of me. She shouldn't have been anywhere near that lake and if I hadn't put all of my weight on that log, I would have been able to save both of you."

"Guess I should thank you for saving my life," she said and put her hand on his forearm. "But there was no way you could have known that branch was going to break. It wasn't your fault."

"You didn't see the look in her eyes before she went over. I hope her last thoughts weren't that I didn't try hard enough, or that I was too rough with the log and that's why it broke."

Tears flooded Adam's eyes. The main thing he worried Charlotte thought before she died was that somehow Adam had chosen to save Mandy instead of her. She was dead, so it didn't matter, but a part of Adam had been questioning him ever since Charlotte went over the falls. Had he subconsciously chosen one over the other? Could he have reacted differently and saved both of them?

Everything happened so fast, and he didn't remember thinking about whom to help when. He reacted, and this is how it turned out. There was no way to know if the roles would be reversed if he'd gotten Charlotte out of the water first. He couldn't talk to Mandy about those feelings. He wasn't going to add to her potential survivor's guilt by telling her it could have been her. She was no doubt already thinking like that, and it would do no good to confirm it.

"She wouldn't blame you for what happened."

Too choked up to speak, Adam nodded.

Mandy stood and said, "I think I should be getting back home. Do you need anything before I go?"

"No," Adam said and cleared his throat, then, "Thank you for everything. I'll be fine. He's probably wondering where you are. You should go home. I'll be fine."

Mandy hesitated.

"Yeah, he probably is. I'm surprised I haven't gotten a phone call by now. I was only supposed to be gone for a little bit. If you need anything, please call me. I don't like the thought of you being out here alone after everything that happened today."

If she knew half of what was going on, she'd insist he leave right now and not return, but he wasn't sure if she would be telling him for his safety or mental wellbeing.

"I will. I promise."

"Good night. I'll check on you tomorrow," she said.

She got into the minivan and waved as she turned around in the driveway. When she turned and started down the road, he put his face in his hands and cried. The weight of pent up grief rolled out of him and dropped through the cracks between the boards on the porch. He thought about getting up and going to bed but decided he wouldn't be getting any sleep tonight and would rather sit on the porch and keep an eye on the lake.

Chapter Twenty-One

Something thumped against his head and fell in his lap. He wasn't sure how long he'd been watching the water, but the heaviness of his eyes told him it'd been a while. Another solid thump hit his head, and he looked up at the porch light. Maybe it had been a moth? It felt heavier than a moth. It could have been a horsefly. He hoped it was only a moth. A third attack hit him just above the left eyebrow. The suddenness of the projectile caused him to rock back in the chair.

He half stood but stopped when three red berries fell from his lap and rolled off the edge of the porch. A tiny laugh echoed through the porch and the bushes rattled like they were being stripped of their leaves.

"Gracie?" Adam whispered.

The laughter grew in volume and pitch. Adam covered his ears. A berry popped against the side of the house, followed by another and another. The laughing stopped, and Adam removed his hands from his ears. He walked to the edge of the porch but didn't see anybody in the hazy orange glow of the front yard under the old light pole. He thought about walking around the house but decided he would rather be under the light of the porch if Grace Ann returned. Grown man, and he was afraid of the dark again. Phil would love to see him now and prove nothing was out there by walking around the house with his hands in the air, inviting the fight.

He turned to sit back down, and the soft giggle returned. He waited, and the voice abruptly stopped. A berry hit his hand. Then his shoulder. His stomach. Soon, hundreds of tiny red berries pelted him. The berries stung and burned against his exposed skin. Red trails of berry juice ran down his arms and face as he ducked behind the rocking chair.

A volley of berries rained down on top of his head and suddenly stopped. He jumped to his feet and ran to the steps. He almost lost his footing as his feet rolled across the unripe mortar shots. He stopped to steady himself and kicked a clear spot to put his feet and shuffled without lifting his feet until he reached the steps.

Grace Ann stood at the bottom, waiting for him. They watched one another. Each daring the other to make the next move. Adam was the first to break.

"Why are you doing this?"

"Because I want to play, silly. Don't you want to play with me, Daddy?"

Adam held back the tears and coughed. How was he supposed to answer a question like that? There was nothing he wanted more in the world than to play with and hold his baby girl again, but not like this. This was unnatural and he couldn't come up with any sane reason how she could be here wanting to play with him.

"Let's play tag, Daddy. You're it," Grace Ann said, and disappeared from in front of the steps.

Adam clomped down the stairs after her. He didn't see which way she went. One second she was there, and the next, she had vanished.

"Run, run as fast as you can. You can't catch me because I'm Grace Ann," she sang in the distance.

Adam choked back tears and coughed through blurry-eyed pain. Grace Ann loved to watch that old worn out VHS tape they found at a yard sale. After watching *The Gingerbread Man* cartoon, she realized her name rhymed with can, and she made the song her own. She would sing it every time she wanted him to chase her around the house or in the yard. Many times, she would pop in his office while he was writing and distract him or throw something at him and run off singing the song.

When he reached the side of the house, he couldn't see anything, but a pitch-black yard and sky. He pulled his phone out of his pocket and turned on the flashlight. The beam didn't reach too far in front of him, but at least he would be able to stop himself from running into anything. A blue flash to his left caught his attention, and he changed course.

The grass on this side of the house was taller than the rest of the yard and slowed Adam's progress down. The light flashed again, but it was off to the right, then it dashed back to the left. Adam waded through the thigh high grass toward the light and adjusted his course as it lit up random places. It was like being a child trying to catch lightning bugs. When he lost track of where he thought she was, he stood still and waited for her to appear again.

In the distance, the outline of the fence posts separating his land from the Barlow's faded in and out of view. Grace Ann ran up and down the fence line. The strain of the day and now trudging through grass that pulled at his pants and held him back had an effect on him. He slowed down to catch his breath and heard Grace Ann call out.

"Come on, Daddy. Run, run as fast as you can. You can't catch me because I'm Grace Ann."

Bathed in blue light, Grace Ann waited for him to make his way to her. The dull glow didn't fade as he approached. She was letting him get closer. She wanted him to see her and think he was going to catch her. Was there a reason she wanted him this far from the house? Or was it the lake she wanted to distance him from? He stopped and turned back to the house.

"Daddy," she called, dragging out each syllable.

Adam looked at her and took a step toward the house.

"Daddy," she yelled, on the verge of a tantrum she wouldn't have thrown in life.

He stopped and looked from the house back to Grace Ann. He didn't want to leave her but couldn't get past the thought of why she would want him out here. Would she try to stop him if he went back now? He walked toward Grace Ann and stopped within a few feet of her and the fence line. She put her thumbs in her ears like antlers and wagged her hands back and forth. She stuck her black tongue out at Adam and started moving her hips from side to side.

"Run, run as fast as you can. You can't catch me because I'm Grace Ann," she said and ran off down the fence line.

Adam turned to go back to the house and a small hand wrapped around his ankle and pulled his foot out from under him. His cellphone flew from his hand as he braced for impact. The ground was hard and rocky under the canopy of grass. He rolled over to his back expecting to see her standing over him, but she wasn't there, and neither was her light or his cellphone flashlight. The stars shined brightly above, and it occurred to him that he hadn't taken the chance to look at the sky since he'd been back. Now, he was accustomed to not looking up at all because the only twinkling in the city was airplanes.

There was no time to admire the sky, so he rolled over and crawled around the ground, searching for his phone. It must have landed facedown, smothering the light. After searching for a few minutes in silence, a voice he didn't recognize startled him.

"If you're looking for your phone, it's over here."

Adam froze. Gooseflesh stood up and down his arms and legs. Grace Ann's soft laugh echoed around him.

"There's nothing to be scared of. It's just me," Grace Ann said. "Here's your phone."

He looked in the direction of her voice and a small foot slipped out of the grass and flipped his phone over so the light shined to the sky. The foot disappeared into the grass when he reached for the phone. A soft kick in the butt followed by giggling startled him. He rolled over and shined the light in the direction of the kick, but she wasn't there. He swept the light across the area and the light reflected off something on the other side of the fence.

Adam walked toward the fence and shined the flashlight at the dark adjoining pasture. The light reflected again off something metal. He stepped between the strands of barbed wire fence and the grass line. The chrome bumper of a large vehicle stood out in the dark. He tilted the light, and the tires came into view, then he moved the light higher and could see Eric Barlow's truck. No sounds came from the truck. Why had Eric parked his truck up here? Was he watching Adam? And if he was, where was he, and why would he be? There was no reason for Eric to be riding the fence lines because he didn't do any of the work.

It didn't make sense. The last time Eric came up the driveway. Why would he be sitting out here in the dark? Adam moved to the truck, not trying to be quiet in case Eric was in there asleep. He was already on edge and didn't want to scare Eric and scare himself in turn. At this point, he might scream and he couldn't let Eric hear that.

No heat or tick of a cooling engine came from the front tire well as he walked past. He shined the light at the window, but the truck was too high to see anything inside, so he knocked. If somebody said, "who's there," he probably would have turned and ran off, but nothing came from inside the cab.

Adam pushed the button on the handle with his thumb and pulled the door open and shined the light inside. Nobody was there. He turned around and shined his light at the surrounding pasture, but the dark swallowed the light after a few feet and he couldn't see anything. Where was Eric? Adam hadn't seen him slinking around the house, and he wouldn't have shown up while the cops were there. Adam put his foot on the sidestep, grabbed the paracord handle installed under the dash and hoisted himself into the cab.

Besides a few bags from Darlene's Kitchen, it was empty. The keys weren't in the ignition. Adam flipped down the visor to see if he had stashed them up there and caught a glimpse of his swollen face. The angle of the light made the bags under his eyes look darker than they were, or at least that's what he was going to tell himself. He stood up on the doorsill and shined his light in the back of the truck. It was empty. That would have been traumatizing to find Eric, and a date curled up asleep in the back of the truck. Adam laughed to himself. A date? Probably would have been his dog, if anything.

He sat back down and looked over the dash, not knowing what to do. The truck was here, but Eric was gone. Technically, it shouldn't matter to Adam because the truck was not sitting on his land. Not his problem, that is unless Eric parked here, so he could sneak on to Adam's land. What was he thinking? He was being paranoid. There was no reason for Eric to sneak on his land. Eric didn't have it in him to hold Adam up until he agreed to sell to Vernon, plus Eric was the type who only looked out for himself. He wasn't about to risk going to jail for somebody else, even if they were family.

Adam fell back in the seat with his hand on the wheel. He needed to go back to the house. Grace Ann had obviously left him out here. She had accomplished whatever she set out to do. Did she want him to find the truck? Maybe he had car trouble? The dome light was on, but the battery could have been too weak to crank the engine. Adam found the switch for the headlights and turned them on. The pasture lit up in front of him.

A large figure stood at the fence, watching. Adam turned the lights off. Who was that? They were too big to be Grace Ann or Eric. His hand shook as he reached for the lights again, and he couldn't keep his hand on the switch. It was only a trick of the light, or maybe Sheriff Brown had come back? Adam stilled his hand and flipped the switch.

When the lights illuminated the pasture again, Brian stood between the fence and the truck.

Chapter Twenty-Two

Two miles away, on the other side of the highway, Mandy lay in bed. She and Dan had gotten into an argument when she got home. He didn't accuse her of anything; in fact, he was fine with how long she'd been gone. He'd only become upset when he'd found out she'd fallen into the lake and almost drowned. She couldn't blame him. It wouldn't have taken long to call and tell him everything and that she'd be home after she spoke with the police. After the argument, he didn't say anything else to her. He stuck her dinner in the microwave, checked on their baby, Abby, and went to bed.

She stared at the wooden plaque that hung above the TV in their bedroom. It said, "Always Kiss Me Goodnight." She leaned over, kissed his shoulder, and fell back on her pillow. The ceiling needed painting. A long rust-colored slash ran across the stippling to the crown molding from when the roof leaked two months ago. At least he'd fixed the roof, but she was tired of looking up at the dirty watermark. She'd ask him about it in the morning if he was in a better mood. If not, maybe she would do it herself. She didn't have any summer projects lined up since school ended. There was a chest of drawers and a chifforobe waiting in the garage for her to paint and distress for Abby's room. There was time to do both the furniture and the ceiling. She could do it in a couple days and find something else to do before it was time to plan for the next school year. She wanted to go to the beach this year. They didn't make it last year because she was nearing the end of her pregnancy and didn't want to risk being away from home when the baby came. She was itching to get back, and Abby would love playing in the sand and water.

A metallic click broke her train of thought. She listened, but only found silence. The noise came again. It didn't sound like any of the noises she was accustomed to her house making. The thought of waking Dan crossed her mind, but he hated when she woke him because something didn't sound right. He'd survey the house only to find a new wreath or hanger bouncing on the door in the wind.

But this was different. It was the clank of metal on metal, like the doorknob being checked to see if it was locked. She quieted her thoughts, tried not to breathe too hard, and listened for the sound. It happened again, but this time it didn't sound like the front door, it sounded like the soft click of a window being pushed up against its lock. It wasn't the window beside the front door. The sound came from the kitchen on the opposite side of the house from the master bedroom.

Mandy sat up straight. If somebody was walking around the house checking locks, they were working their way to the backdoor. She couldn't remember checking the lock before she came to bed, but they often left that door unlocked. It opened beside the staircase that led to the second story where Abby's room was. She wasn't scaring herself with imaginary sounds, and she couldn't wait any longer.

"Dan. Dan. Wake up. Somebody's trying to get in the house."

Dan rolled over and covered his eyes as she turned on the lamp beside the bed.

"What? What are you talking about?"

"Somebody's trying to get in the house. I heard them trying the door and a couple of the windows."

Dan let his hand fall above his head.

"There's nothing out there, Mandy. You're probably still upset about earlier. Just lie down and try to go back to sleep. Everything will be better in the morning."

Mandy slammed her fists on the bed.

"Damn it. I'm not hearing things. If you're not going to check it out, I will. Is the back door locked?"

The loud creak of the backdoor hinges boomed through the quiet home. Dan shot up. He opened the drawer of his nightstand and grabbed his pistol. He racked the slide and crept to the door.

Before he walked out, he said, "Stay here. I'll be right back."

"Get Abby."

Mandy searched the room for anything to use as a weapon. She picked up shoes and hairbrushes and threw them on the bed. There wasn't anything heavy enough to knock somebody out, yet light enough for her to pick it up.

She stopped her search after a loud crash in the living room, followed by Dan yelling.

"Freeze. Don't move or I'll shoot. I'm not afraid to—oh my God. What the hell?"

Something flew against the wall, and the family picture shattered on the stairs. Mandy ran into the hall. The light was on in the foyer. Two shadows fought on the tile floor at the foot of the stairs. One of the shadows fell, and the other kicked them back to the floor.

Mandy ran down the hall and prepared to kick the intruder in the face. She arrived, foot drawn back and held up just before she kicked Dan in the mouth.

His face was bloody, and both eyes were beginning to swell. Red knots covered his chest and stomach from repeated blows. He groaned and protected his face as she stepped over him.

Mandy looked up and Charlotte stood on the second-floor landing. It couldn't be her. She was dead. Mandy saw her go over the falls. Nobody could have survived that, and she didn't look like she had either. Her face was ashen with black streaks like her mascara had run. Holes were torn in her jeans and half the buttons on her blouse were ripped off.

She looked down on Mandy with dull, lifeless eyes that had a slight blue hue. Mandy started up the stairs, and Charlotte hissed like a snake warning an unsuspecting hunter.

"Charlotte. Charlotte. Nobody wants to hurt you. Why don't you come down from there and we can talk," Mandy said and held her hands out to show she was unarmed.

Charlotte's head kicked to the side, and she hissed again.

"I think you need an ambulance. Come have a seat, and I'll call you some help."

"I don't need any help. I have been sent for you," Charlotte said.

Black water poured from her mouth.

She walked sideways to Abby's room. Mandy needed to do something to keep her away from that room.

"Sent by who? Come down here and we'll talk about it."

"Who sent me is none of your concern. I must take you back. A sacrifice must be made," Charlotte rasped. Her breathing sounded labored, like dirt and debris clotted her lungs.

She wanted Mandy to go with her, but she was still moving toward Abby's room. The only way to stop her was to go where she wanted.

"Okay. Fine. Let's go. I'll go wherever you want me to go. Just come down from there and leave my family alone."

"Lies."

Charlotte moved to the room, and Mandy jumped up three stairs. Both women froze and watched each other.

"I'm not lying. I'll do whatever you want me to do. I swear."

"Promises aren't guarantees. There is only one way to guarantee you'll come with me," Charlotte said, and jumped to Abby's door.

"No. Don't hurt my baby," Mandy screamed and ran up the stairs.

Charlotte locked herself in the room as Mandy reached the landing. Mandy ran to the door and pounded on it.

"Open the door, now. I'll do whatever you want."

A sudden cry of pain rang out and cut off as suddenly. Mandy kicked and beat the door. She stepped back and tried to ram it with her shoulder. The wood flexed and threw her to the floor. Pain flowed from her shoulder down her arm. She rocked up to her knees, and the lock clicked back.

Charlotte stepped out of the bedroom, cradling Abby in her ruined arms. She acted unstable, like she was going to fall over or drop the baby any second.

"No. Please, put my baby down. This doesn't have anything to do with her."

"But it does. Suffer little children, and forbid them not, to come unto me, for of such will my kingdom continue with the blood of their parentages."

Mandy didn't know what to say. She was stunned to silence. The only thing she could think to do was put her hands in the air and slowly get to her feet. Charlotte walked closer to the stairs. Mandy gasped when she saw Abby. The baby had been quiet since her cries were cut off. Her eyes were closed, and her lips were blue. It didn't look like she was breathing.

"Oh, God. What have you done to her?" Mandy screamed and moved toward Charlotte. The closer Mandy got, the more she could smell Charlotte. She reeked of death and stank like two-day-old road kill.

"Don't do it," Charlotte said, holding the baby over the rails. "I'll throw her over if you take one more step."

"But she can't breathe. She's turning blue."

"The child is fine. She is only in a state of tranquility until we reach our destination."

There was no reason for Mandy to trust Charlotte about Abby's state, but she did believe Charlotte would throw her over the railing. Mandy was in no position to negotiate.

"Okay. Let's go. I'll follow you," Mandy said. Her voice cracked, and her hands shook.

Charlotte headed back to the stairs. Her foot fished to find the first step. Mandy saw Dan pull himself up. He was waiting for a chance to charge up the steps. Dan slipped and knocked a plastic cup off the foyer table. When it hit the ground, Charlotte started to turn, but Mandy yelled, "Hey! Hey, be careful with my kid." Mandy took a deep breath to calm herself. "I'll go with you. I just don't want you to drop her."

"She's fine—"

Dan charged up the stairs and grabbed Charlotte's arm. They fought back and forth.

"Stupid man. You don't know what you're doing. Get off of me."

Dan punched her in face and hit her repeatedly in the arm. Black blood poured from her face, and dark black blotches formed on her arm. She stumbled, and Dan pulled Abby from her arms. He stood over her and kicked her in the face. Charlotte wailed. The baby slipped, and Dan had to readjust before he attacked again. When he brought his foot down, Charlotte caught it and flipped him back against the wall. The back of his head slammed against the railing, and the blow knocked him unconscious. He landed on the floor with the baby on top of him.

Charlotte rose to her feet.

"You stupid fucker. I will kill you. And after your wife's sacrifice, I will rip your baby apart and eat her piece by piece," Charlotte screeched with each word higher than the last.

She reached back and prepared to hit Dan with a glowing fist. Mandy grabbed the lamp off the hall table and swung it like a bat. The base connected with a sickening crunch against Charlotte's temple. Black blood and water sprayed from the wound.

Charlotte stumbled and flipped over the railing. Mandy rushed to the edge and saw her crumpled body in a heap on the floor. Black water spatter covered the floor and adjacent wall. A strangled cry erupted behind her and she picked up Abby. She looked fine, but they needed to get out of the house. She smacked Dan's face until he came to.

"Come on, honey. We have to go, now."

Dan struggled to stand and swayed on rubber legs.

"Where we going?" he asked, holding his head.

Mandy looked over the rail again, and Charlotte was gone.

"We have to go warn Adam, right now."

Chapter Twenty-Three

Adam choked back the sting of tears that threatened to overtake him. Brian had been missing for two days, and now he was standing in the middle of a field. Where had he been? His shirt ripped, exposing his maggot white belly. The torn fabric fluttered in the breeze and revealed a crusted, red area on his chest. Had he lain injured in the pasture since he went missing? Why didn't he call out to them? Adam wouldn't be able to forgive himself if Brian had been lying injured on the property this whole time. Adam flipped on the hi-beams, but Brian didn't flinch. He stared, unmoving.

Adam's chest tightened as he jumped down from the truck. The putrid smell of rotted wood and brackish water overwhelmed him. Adam willed himself to not throw up, but the longer he stood there, the more it looked like a losing battle. He stepped around the open door.

"Damn, brother. You look like shit," Adam said. "Smell like it too. Where have you been?"

Brian didn't respond.

"Uncle Bri doesn't look happy. You should probably do what he wants," Grace Ann said from the other side of the fence.

"Gracie, you just stay over there. Uncle Bri is just sick. He'll be okay."

The laugh started out as Grace Ann's, but the longer it went on, the raspier and more asthmatic it became.

"He can't hurt me because he's a messenger of the Badfish. And he ain't sick, he's dead. But not like me, cause he has his body. The Badfish took mine because you ignored it when it called for you."

Badfish? Her speech slurred the two words together, creating the one-word name. The Badfish must be the tentacled monster in the lake. It controlled everything that happened on the land and killed his family.

"It's all your fault I'm like this. He can go wherever he wants to, and I have to stay in the yard. It's not fair," she said, her laughing smile changing to a pout and a sneer.

The daughter he knew was not speaking to him now. No matter how pouty she acted, this was not the speech or vindictive actions of his child. Was the Badfish controlling her now? Had it been controlling her the entire time?

Brian lurched forward and Adam held his hand out in protest. Brian groaned, and dirty water ran out of his mouth.

"He can't talk. The Badfish's pets damaged him too much."

What did she mean damaged him too much? The Badfish must be the thing with tentacles, but how was it calling the shots?

Brian moved toward Adam again, and he jumped back. Adam looked in all directions, but dark field surrounded him. If Adam ran, he wouldn't know where he was going or where other dangerous fences waited to show him the boundaries.

"He wants you to come with him. You have to go to the lake."

"I'm not going anywhere near that damn lake," Adam shouted.

Brian didn't seem to like that reply because he screamed as loud and firm as his ruined vocal chords would allow and stomped toward Adam.

He didn't know what awaited him at the lake, but he knew he couldn't allow Brian to drag him there. Adam tried to jump back in the truck, and Brian slammed it shut. He turned to run, and

Brian's fist slammed into the back of his skull. Flashes of green and pink exploded in his vision as he fell to the ground. He tried to stand, but Brian was on him again and stomped on his leg. Adam screamed as bolts of fire shot up his leg.

He rolled over and pulled himself away. When he reached the back of the truck, Brian flipped him over and growled in his face. Streams of black saliva poured out of his mouth. Adam choked and spit it out of his mouth until Brian grabbed him by the throat. Adam tore at the field-strengthened hands. His sight faded, and he feared he was about to black out. He couldn't let that happen. If he blacked out, he would be dead, and end up like Brian.

Brian straddled his body, but Adam managed to twist to his side. Brian clenched his legs tighter and Adam couldn't move anymore. Adam punched up between his brother's arms and brought his elbow down and broke one of his hands free. A tiny stream of air made it to his burning lungs, and he punched up again.

His fist slammed into Brian's chest and black blood water rained down on Adam. It didn't seem to hurt Brian, but it did distract him enough, and Adam knocked his other hand loose. Waves of tainted air filled Adam's lungs. He swung at Brian again and hit him in the chest where his heart should be. Instead of the solid thump he expected, a sickening sound like a near empty ketchup bottle escaped and his fist sank into him. Brian screamed and lurched to his feet.

Adam drew his hand from his brother's chest and clenched a handful of his softened chest cavity. Rivers of water poured out from the wound as Brian stood. Adam, frozen by terror, watched as one of the black fish that Grace called the Badfish's pets, slithered out of the hole and clotted the leaking life force that kept Brian moving.

Brian grabbed Adam's ankles and pulled him. Adam kicked loose and moved under the truck, but Brian had a hold of him again and dragged him. Before Brian could pull him completely from under the truck, Adam reached up and grabbed the steel bumper.

Adam lifted in the air as Brian shook and pulled his legs. One of his hands pulled free and Adam could feel the other one about to go. The pressure on his arms relaxed as Brian pushed forward and prepared for another tug. Adam swung his free hand back to the bumper. He wrapped his hand around the metal lip and grabbed onto a small metallic box. It was a hide-a-key. At least Adam hoped that's what it was.

Brian snatched his legs again, and Adam let go of the bumper and brought the box with him. Brian ripped the box from Adam's hand and they both fell to the ground. The spare key jingled in the thin metal.

Adam rolled and jumped to his feet while Brian fought to gain his balance. He ran toward his brother and punched him where the fish clotted his wound. The pet and Brian hissed. Water seeped from the new wound and ran down Brian's chest.

Adam jumped into the truck and slammed the door. In the rearview mirror, Brian steadied himself, and the fish readjusted to stop the flow of water. Adam slid the box open, dumped the key in his hand and thrust it in the ignition.

The engine roared to life, and the driver's side door flew open. Brian grabbed Adam, but he managed to put the truck in gear and rolled forward. The rear tire caught Brian and pulled him underneath the truck.

Adam looked out the door, and Brian was still moving. He threw the truck in reverse and backed over his writhing brother.

Adam sat in the truck and watched Brian. At first, there was no movement, but then one of his arms moved. Adam didn't wait to see if he was going to get up. He put the truck in gear, lined Brian's head up with the front tire and floored it.

He didn't hear the truck run over his brother, but he felt it. He imagined it looked like running over a grape with a bike tire. The truck bounced through the pasture toward the barbed wire fence. Adam plowed through. Metal attacked metal as the barbs swung in against the intruding truck, but he didn't let off the gas until he stopped six inches from slamming into the side of Mandy's minivan.

Chapter Twenty-Four

Adam turned off the engine and slipped out of the cab. Mandy ran out of the house and down the steps.

"I killed Brian," he said and pointed in the direction he'd come from. "I ran him over with Eric's truck. I don't know where Eric is, but I didn't kill him."

Adam swayed on weak legs. His voice came out soft and anemic, and his body tingled all over.

"You didn't kill anybody. I don't know what's going on, but Charlotte attacked my family at our house," Mandy said.

The words floated in the air, just out of reach. Did she say Charlotte attacked her? His body stirred from its stupor and the tingling became sore and painful when he tried to move. It felt like red-hot iron pokers being driven into his joints. He looked over at the minivan and saw Dan sitting in the passenger seat holding a baby, then back to Mandy. It dawned on him that she'd never told him who she married. But why Dan? They were supposed to be friends. A migraine pulsed to life behind his eyes. The sudden flipping of emotions made him want to sit down, but the new anger made him want to walk over to the van and punch Dan.

"You fucking married, Dan? What the hell, Mandy? He was my best friend."

"Yes, he was, and you left him too. He was the only one I had to comfort me when I lost Grace Ann and again when I lost you. It just happened."

"Guess that's why he was pissed when I saw him the other day. Probably thought I was coming back after you."

"No, you jackass. You didn't just leave me. You left him too. He was hurt."

Mandy put her arms across her chest and leaned back. It was her I'm right and I can prove-it-pose. Adam had seen it many times. And like all the other times, he couldn't help himself and continued full steam ahead. He knew it was the wrong time to bring all this up, but he'd been holding everything in for too long, and was ready to release the steam.

"He's a big boy. He should be able to handle it. Hell, I just crushed my brother's head with a fucking truck tire. You don't see me—,"

"Shut up. We don't have time to have this conversation. Charlotte tried to bring my baby here. I stopped her, but when I turned around she was gone."

"You stopped her? Didn't turn out to be that big of a hero then, did he?" he said and winked in Dan's direction.

"Damn it, Adam. I'm being serious. I think she's coming back here. We need to leave, now."

"Oh, now you want to leave? Where are we going to go?"

Mandy stopped talking. He'd stumped her. Finally got to a question she couldn't answer. It was that, or he finally pissed her off. Her lips narrowed into a small 'o'. It was time for her to let off steam and she took a deep breath to unleash on him when a meek voice froze her where she stood.

"Mommy?" Grace Ann called. "Why are you and Daddy fighting?"

Tears ran down Mandy's face and she turned to see Grace Ann hiding behind a holly bush with only her head sticking out.

"I don't like it when you fight."

Mandy took a step toward her daughter and then a step back. She dropped to her knees and looked back at Adam.

"Who is that?" she asked.

"It's me, Mommy. Don't you recognize me?" Grace Ann said, and twirled in her saturated dress.

"I don't understand what's going on."

"I don't either. She's been showing up since I got back," Adam said.

"Why didn't you tell me?" Mandy choked out.

"Would you have believed me? I still don't believe it now, but Brian and Charlotte shouldn't be walking around either. I don't know what is going on."

Grace Ann giggled and stepped from behind the bush.

"I know what's going on, but I can't tell you. It's a secret," Grace Ann said.

Mandy cupped her hand around her mouth and cried as Grace Ann approached.

"I don't like it when you're sad, Mommy."

"I'm not sad, honey. I'm ... I'm not really sure what I am," Mandy said, and held out her arms to her daughter.

Grace Ann cautiously walked to Mandy. She looked past Mandy and smiled at Adam. Moments like this were the ones he missed the most. Adam tried to look away but couldn't help himself. The last two years of his life were mostly garbage, but seeing mother and daughter together, embracing, was too much for him to handle. He turned his head to hide his tears. As sweet as the moment was, it was fake. It was real for Mandy, but not for the thing controlling their daughter. Grace Ann hadn't been hiding out for two years. She was dead, and now something from the lake was controlling her to get what it wanted. But what did it want? He needed to intervene, but she sounded and acted like their daughter again. Maybe it controlled her sometimes, and other times it really was their daughter. If that were true, there could be a way to save her. She might still be dead, but she would be able to rest in peace. Adam cried. He hoped his little girl wasn't in pain and hadn't been hurting all this time.

Waves of emotion wracked through Mandy's body. She looked like she was convulsing and barely keeping it together. A cough behind a wall of glass rang out, and Grace Ann looked toward the minivan.

"Who is that?" Grace Ann asked.

"Who is who?"

Grace Ann lifted her head and stepped back from her mother. She pointed at the passenger side of the minivan where Dan sat holding Abby.

"Who is Uncle Dan holding?"

Mandy didn't look at Dan. She looked back at Adam, and he could see the fear in her eyes. Mandy reached for Grace Ann, but her hands faded through the little girl's shoulder. Mandy started to cry.

"Her name is Abby. She's your sister."

Grace Ann stepped away from Mandy. Black tears streaked her dirty face.

"Sister? You had another baby. You replaced me?" she whispered and looked at Adam. "How could you replace me?"

"She's not my kid. I didn't replace you," Adam said and winced.

Mandy gave him a look he'd never seen before. He'd reached a new level. Grace Ann looked at him, confused. A low guttural rumble started. At first, they couldn't tell where it was coming from and searched for something in the surrounding darkness, but as it grew in volume, they realized it was coming from Grace Ann and they both stepped away.

Fingers stretched out and closed into tiny fists over and over. Breathing came faster. Adam half expected steam to come from her nose, and with everything he'd seen lately, it wouldn't have surprised him.

Grace Ann opened her mouth wide and released a shrill, high-pitched scream. Mandy and Adam both stepped back. A blue light emanated from her eyes and fingertips as the pitch rose to a squeal. The light grew, and they had to cover their eyes. A loud sonic boom rocked them back and Adam opened his eyes soon enough to see Grace Ann disappear in a bolt of blue lightning and reappear beside the fence leading to the pasture. Everything was silent. Adam wasn't sure if she stopped screaming or the pitch was too high for him to hear.

A loud exhale echoed across the land and the scream started again. The light grew bright and dashed into the pasture. Another pulse of light and she stood at the top of the cliff overlooking the pit.

"Seriously? What the hell was that?" Mandy asked.

Adam stuck his hands in his pockets and kicked at the dirt in front of him.

"I don't know. She was looking at me like it was my fault. It just came out."

"She's sitting up there all alone. We have to go explain it to her."

"I don't think that's a good idea."

"Why? Cause it's not your baby? She's your daughter."

Adam stopped sulking like a berated child and walked to Mandy.

"It's not a good idea because I don't think that's our daughter. There's something in the lake and it's controlling her."

"Do you realize how crazy that sounds?"

"No crazier than our daughter who has been dead for two years being back and upset about her mother's new baby."

Mandy stood and started moving toward the lake.

Adam walked to the minivan, and Dan rolled down the window.

"I suggest you leave with the baby if you see anything weirder than what you just saw happen."

Dan didn't reply. He stared at him, wide-eyed and slack jawed. The baby broke the silence and Adam walked away when Dan looked down and started bouncing her in his lap.

There was no breeze. The air felt dense and weighed in his lungs as he followed Mandy. He caught up with her at the gate. Grace Ann danced and twirled and illuminated on the edge of the cliff. Adam wrestled the gate open, and both parents went to their child.

The closer they got to the cliff, the more electric the air

became. Adam felt his hair standing on end like he'd been rubbing a balloon on his head. When he looked at Mandy, her hair was doing the same thing.

"I don't think this is a good idea. I feel like we are being led here for some reason."

"Why would you think that?"

"I don't know. You haven't been around lately. There have been a lot of weird things happening and I can't figure them out."

"Maybe she just needs peace, so she can move on."

Adam didn't reply. He didn't think she was looking for peace. She was a captive of the thing living in the lake. Maybe she would gain peace if she was freed from its captivity, but that wasn't the motivation behind what she was doing. The creature in the lake was using her, but he wasn't sure what it wanted with him or Mandy. It obviously wasn't feeding; otherwise, it wouldn't have sent Charlotte and Brian back after them. After they failed to get them to come out here, it sent Grace Ann to trick them into chasing her. She probably wasn't even upset about the baby. It was the best way to act upset so they would chase her. They were walking into a trap. Lost in thought, he fell behind and when he looked up to yell for Mandy to stop, she was almost at the top of the cliff. He didn't have time to stop her, and yelling wouldn't have done any good. He ran up the last part of the hill.

When he arrived at the top, he was winded and bent over to catch his breath. He put his hands on his knees and cursed himself for not staying in better shape. A flash of blue lightning pierced the air and enveloped him in a shroud of ozone. Mandy was on bended knee coaxing Grace Ann from the edge of the cliff.

Adam approached the two people who meant the most in the world to him, and the light grew brighter. When it dimmed, he didn't see the dirty waterlogged waif who had been troubling him since he returned to Georgia. He saw his daughter as she was the day she died. It was a gut punch, and Adam was overrun with emotion.

"Grace? Gracie?"

"Daddy, I'm scared," she said.

She twisted her fingers in the waist of her dress and crossed her right foot behind her left like she used to do when she was scared but couldn't tell him what she was afraid of.

"Hey, baby. There's nothing to be scared of. Mommy and Daddy are here. We won't let anything happen to you."

"But you already did. It's your fault that I can't come home."

Adam fought back the tears. He tried to speak, but the words stuck in his throat and he coughed.

"It was an accident. It wasn't Daddy or Grandpa's fault," Mandy said.

Grace Ann glared at her mother.

"It's his fault I'm here, and he knows it."

"That's not true," Mandy said and stood. "It was a horrible acci—"

"No. It was my fault. I should have been watching her. I left her with Phil, because I was distracted, but he was working, and I should have stayed with her. The thing in the lake pulled her in."

Mandy looked at Adam but didn't say anything. What did he expect her to say? She'd never seen the thing he was talking about.

"It was your fault, but it doesn't have to be forever."

Adam cleared his throat and walked to the edge of the cliff beside his daughter. He looked down at the pitch-black pit and didn't see anything. A cacophony of water crashed below. It wasn't possible, but he thought he could hear the fish snapping at each other while they waited for their next meal. Pets. The Badfish's pets is what Grace Ann called them. Loose gravel crumbled under his shoes and fell into the water below, and he stepped back from the edge before he ended up sliding in too.

"What do you mean?"

"You were supposed to be the next sacrifice so the Badfish could rest again, but you stayed away from the water because you were afraid. Even when he called you, you ignored him, so he took me instead."

Mandy walked closer.

"That doesn't make sense," she said.

"Nobody asked you. The Badfish told me he sent Charlotte to get you but found out you had another child to speak for now."

"Who's the Badfish?" Mandy asked.

"I don't know. He scares me, so I hide when I can and I don't talk unless he makes me," she said to Mandy and then, to Adam, "You can fix everything and make it the way it was supposed to be, but you have to hurry."

"How do I do that?"

Grace Ann stepped to the edge and pointed.

"You have to jump. If you jump, I can come back. The Badfish will let me come back if you jump."

Adam looked over the edge again. If he jumped, he would die, but his daughter would get another chance at life. Every good parent would give their life without a second thought to save their child's life. They didn't always have time to think about it, but given the chance, they would make the same choice. Adam was tired of dwelling on the past. This could be his chance to set everything right. It wasn't Phil's fault that Grace Ann died. Instead of taking responsibility, he blamed everything on his father. It was too late to right that wrong, but there was still a chance with Grace Ann. He cradled Grace Ann's hand in his. She wiped the tears from his face with her free hand and rubbed it on his shirt.

But how could he trust the Badfish would honor the deal if he jumped? He would never know, unless he came back as a ghost or one of those things like Brian. The Badfish allowed him and his brother to live after their mother jumped. Maybe he could bring Grace Ann back from the dead? He wouldn't get a second chance to be her Daddy, but Mandy would have another chance to be her Mommy.

"Adam, don't think about it. That's crazy. You can't come back once you're dead. It doesn't work that way. Whatever this thing is, it's lying to you."

Adam shook his head and took a step back.

"Don't listen to her, Daddy. I want to live," Grace Ann cried.

The lump that burned in his throat fell and shattered his

heart. He didn't do anything for her the first time, but if he jumped, he would be making up for it. He didn't want to die, but the past two years without Grace Ann hadn't been living anyway. It hadn't been fair to Charlotte. He cared for her, but she never had all of him. The broken man who showed up in her life stayed broken no matter how hard she tried to fix him. There wasn't anything worth living for anymore. Even if it didn't work, he'd no longer be in pain.

"You always said you would die for me, so why are you surprised I'm asking you do it. Jump. Mommy would do it if she didn't already have another baby."

"I don't know if this will work, but I have to try, Mandy," Adam cried.

Adam toed the edge of the cliff. He stared into the black water and hoped his life wouldn't flash before his eyes when he jumped. Reliving Grace Ann's death, if only for a moment, was too much to bear.

"That's the stupidest thing I've heard you say. I can't believe you're going to listen to her. That's not our daughter."

"I am his daughter, you bitch. When he jumps, I'm going to take your baby and throw her over the cliff, too," Grace Ann yelled.

Her face twisted in anger. Black lines under her skin pushed to the surface and dirty water poured from her eyes. The sticky, clammy look returned to her skin. Mandy stepped forward.

"You're not our daughter," she yelled, and slapped her.

All sound went silent. Even the crash of the water in the pit stopped. Adam stepped back from the edge and the ground began to quake. Slabs of earth fell away into the water below and Adam jumped back to keep from going over. Three large, black tentacles flew over the cliff, creating a blue hazy in their wake.

Two landed with a heavy thud five feet apart, and the third one hovered ten feet off the ground between them. The tips of the tentacles glowed bright blue. Bolts of lightning shot out from the tips of each tentacle and converged in the center. A loud howl rang through the air and the tangle of electricity stretched out.

Two legs formed at the bottom tentacles and an ancient skeletal head appeared below the tip of the third. Bolts shot up and connected with the head and created a hunched body.

When the entity from the Badfish fully formed, Grace Ann shrank out of sight. A cough of sparks shot through the air, and the entity that owned the voice he'd heard introduced itself to Adam. Mandy screamed. She didn't run away but continued to scream until a bolt electricity hit the ground in front of her feet.

"That's enough of that," the Badfish said. Its gravelly voice sounded like it had smoked two packs a day for the last fifty years.

"Run, Mandy. Get away from here," Adam yelled.

"I only need you, but if she tries to run, I will strike her down."

Adam took a step back, and a tentacle shot up from the dark and grabbed him. He twisted and the buttons on his shirt popped off. Another tentacle came over the cliff. They grabbed him and stretched his arms like he was hanging from an invisible cross. The Badfish laughed. Another tentacle pulled back Adam's shirt to expose Grace Ann's name tattooed over his heart.

"Isn't that sweet? Do you have her name over your heart because it was your fault she's dead?"

Adam didn't answer. He pulled his arm and tried to free himself.

"You seem to be missing a few names. Let me help you out."

A bolt of lightning hit Adam in the chest. He screamed, and the light moved below his daughter's name and carved a B. The red-hot pain burned through his entire body. His vision faded black like he was going to pass out, but the pain renewed and stirred him from the darkness as the Badfish carved the letters R – I – A – N into his skin. The bolt moved down, and Adam slacked in the tentacles grasp. He tried to find a distant star in the sky to focus on as the Badfish carved C – H – A – R – L – O – T –T – E into his skin.

Laughter rose above the pain and smell of burnt flesh.

"I have one more name. It's the shortest but will bring you the most grief knowing it was your fault and you would have prevented all of these deaths if you hadn't left," the entity said and carved. P – H – I – L into Adam's chest.

Adam's legs buckled, and he hung from the tentacles.

"What do you want from us?" Mandy screamed and diverted the Badfish's attention away from Adam.

"Suffer little children, and forbid them not, to come unto me, for of such will my kingdom continue with the blood of their parentages."

Adam tried to stand on his feet, but they buckled again.

"Blasphemy," Mandy yelled, and the Badfish laughed.

"I have been here far too long to be held accountable for blasphemy. The world blasphemes me every time I'm ignored. Once I have my sacrifice, I will leave you and rest. But the sacrifice must be one of parental love."

Mandy picked up a rock and threw it at the Badfish. It flew through the center of the electrically charged body and fell into the water below.

The tentacles released Adam, and he dropped to the ground. He had to make the sacrifice to make the Badfish go away. That thing would never let Grace Ann live again, even if it had the power. He stumbled to his feet and moved to the edge of the cliff. The Badfish didn't interfere. He looked over the side and Mandy screamed. He turned and expected the Badfish to have attacked her, but instead, he found Charlotte stomping through the tall grass. She reached the cliff, and a tentacle swatted at her.

"Go, my child. There is nothing here for you to do anymore. I will handle this."

Charlotte didn't leave. She moved closer to Adam and the edge of the cliff. Her eyes looked as dead and hazy as Brian's.

"You're the reason I'm dead," she said, and ran at Adam.

He was too weak to defend against the blows as Charlotte repeatedly punched him in the head. He felt himself falling again, but he needed to get away from Charlotte and jump on his own to make everything stop.

Mandy grabbed Charlotte by the hair and swung her from him. She spun in a circle with her arms stretched wide like she was trying to catch her balance. Adam ran at her and drove his shoulder into her sternum. Charlotte lost her balance and tripped over the tentacle behind her. She fell to the ground and bounced over the side of the cliff into the water below. Adam and Mandy fell to their knees and covered their ears as the Badfish screamed in writhing pain.

"No. She's no mother and is unworthy," the Badfish cried.

Lightning bolts shot in all directions. The tentacles began to shake, and the Badfish collapsed in on itself and a horizontal beam of blue light spread across all the Blackwell land.

The ground quaked and Adam and Mandy fought to keep their balance.

"Come on. We have to get out of here."

Adam looked over the edge of the cliff. The water was rising. Large chunks of dirt fell from the top of the cliff and splashed into the water. They ran down the hill toward the house. The pit was full, and the water flooded its banks. When they got to the bottom of the cliff, they splashed through ankle deep water. The water gained on them while they ran through the pasture. Rain and hail beat down, stinging their exposed skin. They reached the gate and jumped on the cross rails and threw themselves over.

Adam's foot got caught, and he landed on his back with a splash. The ice-cold water sent shocks through his body. He attempted to roll over but fell back into the puddle. Mandy ran back to Adam and pulled him to his feet. He coughed and leaned to the side and tried to regain the breath knocked from his lungs. The water continued to rise and forced Adam to his feet.

Water swirled around their thighs and slowed their progress. Mandy reached the house first and ran up the stairs to the porch. Adam climbed up the stairs behind her and looked back at the lake. The entire pasture was under water. He turned to the house and back to the rising water. Would they be okay in the house? The house sat on an incline from the lake, but the water was rising too fast and had already flooded its banks with more water than it held. Where was all the water coming from?

"We need to leave before the water gets any higher," he said.

"We should be fine if we go to the second floor, shouldn't we?" Mandy asked.

"Normally, I would agree, but nothing about any of this is normal. Looks like Dan decided not to stick around. Looks like a theme for you."

"He has our baby, you asshole. What else was he supposed to do? The longer he stayed here, the bigger chance she would get hurt."

She was right. Dan faced an impossible decision too. Try to save his wife and risk losing the baby and her anyway or leave and insure their child would live.

Mandy moved toward the house and back to the steps. She was conflicted. He wasn't sure what to do either. After a last second hesitation, Mandy jumped off the porch and waded through the water to Eric's truck. Adam followed her off the porch and the current from the rising water threatened to sweep him away. The water wasn't to the cab of the truck yet, but if he didn't hurry, it would flood the interior and the engine. He ran in slow motion to the passenger's side of the truck and Mandy helped pull him in. He flipped around and slid across the bench seat. His hand trembled as fought to get the key in the ignition.

The engine roared to life and Adam fought the urge to floor it. The truck turned in a wide circle, and they headed up the hill to the Barlow's pasture where he found it. The tires spun in the wet grass. He gave it more gas, and the tires gripped, and the truck pulled them up the hill. Adam crossed the broken fence line onto the Barlow's land. He stopped the truck and got out. Most of his father's land was under water. A low groan followed by a splintering crash ripped the house from its foundation and the black water took it away.

Adam grabbed the paracord handle to get back in the truck when a flash of white linen caught his eye and he went back to the fence line. A woman in a long flowing dress walked on the rising water, carrying something across her arms. Adam recognized the woman, but it took a moment for the realization to hit him that it was his mother. She approached with a sad smile and tear streaked porcelain face and laid the bundle at Adam's feet. Helen didn't say anything and faded from sight as she walked back across the water.

Adam pulled back the sheet and Grace Ann lay motionless. She looked like she was sleeping. He didn't want to wake her and carefully picked her up. He walked back to the truck and Grace Ann's color started to fade. Her rosy pink skin turned pale and was ashen by the time he reached the back of the truck. Mandy lowered the tailgate and Adam gently laid the sheet containing Grace Ann's bones in the back of the truck.

Chapter Twenty-Five

Adam straightened his tie. It'd been a while since he'd worn a tie. It was navy blue and matched Grace Ann's favorite dress. He propped a foot on the bottom step of the funeral home and contemplated going inside. The last time he was here for Grace Ann, there was no body, only a cheaply framed photo.

He and Mandy thought about having the ceremony somewhere else, but Stephen Barlow had been accommodating. It surprised Adam because of the family history, but the death of a child always made people stop to think about the important things in life. They inevitably thought what it would be like if they were to lose their own children. But in the end, it didn't matter why they were being empathetic to an enemy. As long as it made them hold their children closer and if possible, love them more. Maybe one day the hatred and bitter feelings between the families could be lost to time or forgotten. He wasn't able to sell the land to Vernon. The lake flooded all the Blackwell property. The new bank of the lake was the barbed wire fence line that ran around the perimeter of the land. Vernon had no interest in buying a large black lake with no surrounding land. Also, Eric was still missing, and it didn't look good when Adam and Mandy showed up at the

Sheriff's Office in his truck. Perhaps Stephen had been helpful in hopes that they could shed some light on what had happened to his son.

Adam walked into the funeral home and found Mandy, Dan and Abby waiting for him. After the ceremony, they would lay Grace Ann to rest under the Japanese red leaf maple with the view Mandy had picked out for her two years ago. Adam always expected for his daughter to remain missing and never believed he would find any closure in knowing where she was. To him, she was dead, and that's all that mattered. When he approached the small pearl white coffin, he realized he was wrong. Knowing where she'd be, and that she was at rest, was the best feeling he'd had in a long time. What the future held for him was still in the air. For now, he would bury his daughter and return to Chicago, but only to clean out the apartment he and Charlotte shared. Beyond that, he would get in his car and drive until he felt like stopping.

Acknowledgments

Every author gets asked where they get their ideas, whether it's from fans, interviewers or their worried mothers after they've read a story about a serial killer. The truth is, we get them from everywhere. Small conversations had or overheard and observations of perceived strange occurrences have inspired many stories. The trick is you don't have to see things the way they actually are to be inspired by them.

This book doesn't happen without Greenlee. Or I should say it's a far different book without her in my life. Without her, it's a typical ghost story. She gives the story heart and is my heart and the reason for any choices I make. For those who know her story, I beg that you not try to draw too many connecting lines. You probably won't find them and will end up wandering down the wrong dark path if you look too hard.
I'd like to thank my family and friends for their continued support since the last acknowledgements page.

This novel was my MFA thesis project and the following writers/professors helped me immensely along the way: Bobbi Miller, Cindy Skaggs, Shana Chartier, Melissa Hart, Rachel Carter, Jennifer Brissett, Diana Francis, Gabino Iglesias, and Angie Smibert. Thank you all.

There is one writer who I did not put in the above list, but she was not forgotten. No, I wanted to give her her own paragraph. A special thank you to my thesis advisor, Patricia Lillie. Her guidance and advice throughout the entire process was invaluable to this book and me as a writer.

I can't speak about my MFA experience without thanking everybody in our MFA Whinery group. I'm not sure if we kept each other sane or each of us went a little crazier during the process, but I do know that we helped each other along the way. Much love.

Thank you to Eva Mout. She is one of my favorite artists, and I was lucky enough to have her create the amazing cover art.

Thank you to A.A. Medina for the graphic design work on the covers.

And finally, I would like to thank the readers who have taken the time to read this story. Extra thanks to those who read my first book and came back.

About the Author

Zach Lamb is a fictionist who creates thriller, horror, and dark fiction stories. He is the author of The Suicide Killer and Mourning Glory. Zach has an MFA in creative writing from Southern New Hampshire University. He lives with his wife and kids in the non-fictional town of Ellerslie, Georgia, named after the fictional character Captain Ellerslie from the Waverly Novels.

www.ingramcontent.com/pod-product-compliance
Lightning Source LLC
Chambersburg PA
CBHW020153310726
48970CB00006B/2127